Through The Rift

Paul B Kohler

Global Endeavor Publishing

Also by Paul B Kohler

THROUGH THE RIFT

PAUL B KOHLER

Portions of this collection have been previously published as noted below:
Absolute Dark: Previously published in 'Tales from the Canyons of the Damned' (2021)
Jacked: Previously published independently (2020)
Gateway: Previously published independently (2018)
Not Your Typical Lunar Day: Previously published in Gravity City Digital Magazine (2021)
Rememorations: Previously published in 'The Immortality Chronicles' (2015), and independently (2015)

Cover and Interior design by Paul B Kohler

ISBN-13: 978-1-940740-26-3 (tpb)
ISBN-10: 1-940740-26-6 (tpb)

www.PaulKohler.net

Give feedback on the book at:
info@paulkohler.net
Facebook: facebook.com/Paul.B.Kohler.Author

Printed in the United States of America

First Edition

Contents

For Cheryl

Miles and Nina are sent to Lunar Base 63 for a simple two-week mission. But when strange inconsistencies emerge, suspicion takes hold. Their assignments as an aerospace engineer and botanist never quite aligned—now, the station's true purpose begins to unravel. Stranded among humanity's brightest minds, they must uncover why they were really brought here ... before it's too late.

Façade

As with many of my stories, *Façade* began in a dream. One vivid scene stood out—Miles experiencing a flashback—and that moment stayed with me after I woke. It was the spark that set everything in motion. The rest of what you're about to read was built around that single, moment. The first draft came together in one long sitting, driven by the urgency of the idea. Since then, it's been revised several times—layered with detail, refined for rhythm—always with the goal of keeping it within the bounds of a true short story, while doing justice to the characters and their world. *Façade is the first of four NEW short stories included in this collection.* | 4,852 words

Façade

M iles MacArthur snapped awake to the sharp chime of the station-wide broadcast. His pulse was already hammering before he even processed the words from the crisp, detached voice of the base's AI.

"Attention all residents of Lunar Base 63. This is a station-wide broadcast. Please report to your designated muster stations by 1500 hours for a mandatory evacuation readiness drill. Locate your environmental suits in your hab units but leave them secured in your quarters. Attendance is required."

The message repeated as a soft glow illuminated the display screen on the far wall of their small flat. A map of the station appeared with their current location marked in green, while a blinking orange icon labeled "Observation Arena—Muster Station" indicated their destination. In the lower right corner, "8 minutes and 29 seconds" showed their estimated commute time.

Miles glanced at the clock—just shy of 1430 hours. He groaned and ran a hand down his face. "Great. Mandatory drill. Just what I needed today."

Across the room, Nina Petaluma, half-dressed in an azure tunic and compression leggings, glanced at the screen while securing her hair in a loose bun that immediately began to unravel. "A muster station? Feels very 'cruise ship on Earth' to me. Are we worried about sinking on the moon or something?"

Miles smirked despite himself. "If we're about to go down with the ship, I'd say we've got bigger problems."

Nina grinned, and Miles felt that now-familiar flutter in his chest. Three weeks of training in close quarters, and he still hadn't built up an immunity to her smile.

"Maybe they'll at least serve margaritas," she said, leaning against the wall.

He let out a small chuckle, but unease pressed at the back of his mind. They were only supposed to be here for two weeks. Why waste time on a full-scale evacuation drill?

Nina seemed to share his thought. She folded her arms. "We're not even here long enough to need a damn evacuation plan. Why bother?"

Miles exhaled slowly. "Probably just protocol."

"Or it has something to do with your confidential mission." Her eyes narrowed.

Miles scoffed. "You're really hung up on that."

"Well, excuse me for being curious." She grabbed another hair tie from the small desk and twisted it tighter. "I got shipped to the damn moon with a guy I barely know, forced into a fake marriage, and told I shouldn't ask questions. So yeah, Miles, I'd say I have a right to be hung up on it."

Her sarcasm cut through the air, the weight of their forced partnership hanging between them. But there was something else there too—an electric undercurrent that made the small room feel even smaller.

Miles sighed, rubbing his temple. She had a point.

"Alright," he said, giving in. "Seeing as we're on the *damn moon* now, I guess I can tell you."

Nina raised an eyebrow, waiting. Her lips parted slightly in anticipation, and Miles found himself momentarily distracted before continuing.

"My job is to analyze the station's layout and operations—how everything functions at full capacity. I report my findings to Driscoll back on Earth."

She frowned. "That's it?"

"That's it." Miles hoped his answer was direct enough to end her questions. He was finding it increasingly difficult to maintain professional distance with Nina, especially in moments like this when her intent gaze seemed to see right through him.

Nina squinted at him and tilted her head slightly. "And why would a fully operational base need an aerospace engineer to check its efficiency? This place has been up and running for, what?"

Miles opened his mouth, then closed it, acutely aware of how close she was standing.

Damn. She had a point. Again.

Driscoll's orders to share only the bare necessities had seemed logical on Earth, but now, standing inside a fully functioning lunar station, the explanation felt ... thin.

"I don't know," he admitted. "It's what I was assigned."

Nina smirked, victorious. "Oh, so you just follow orders without question?"

Miles scoffed. "You're one to talk. What's your mission, then?"

She turned away, pretending to straighten her bunk. "Classified."

"Come on," Miles said, stepping closer. "You just got on my case about secrecy. Spill it."

Nina was about to answer when the walls suddenly seemed to close in on him. The air pressed against his chest like an invisible weight.

His throat tightened.

The station was too quiet. Too enclosed.

His breath caught. He staggered back onto the edge of the bed, hands gripping the mattress.

No. Not now.

His vision tunneled, sweat beading on his forehead. The air in his lungs wasn't enough.

"Miles?" Nina's voice cut through the rising tide of panic.

He tried to answer, but his mouth refused to cooperate.

Nina was suddenly beside him, kneeling by the bed. "Dammit, breathe. Like we practiced."

She took his hands in hers, her touch warm and grounding. Her fingers interlaced with his, and despite the panic, he registered the sensation of her skin against his.

Miles squeezed his eyes shut, trying to focus. Trying to count. *Breathe in. One.*

Breathe out. Two.

His hands trembled in hers. It wasn't working. Miles opened his eyes and looked directly into Nina's as she kneeled beside him, her hand now on his thigh. As he continued to breathe slowly, his racing pulse began to steady.

Nina jumped up and hurried to the shuttered portal window. "Maybe a view will help."

She tapped the control panel, fingers flying over the screen. "Let's get you some perspective."

She pressed the manual override.

Nothing happened.

A soft chime from the station's AI made them both freeze.

"Exterior viewing portals are not operational at the current station status."

Nina frowned. "What?"

Miles tilted his head in her direction as his breathing stabilized. "What do you mean, 'what'?"

She tapped the panel again. Nothing. The shutters remained closed.

Another chime. "Exterior viewing portals are not operational at the current station status."

Nina turned to him, unease flickering in her expression. "Since when do station drills lock down the windows?"

Miles' chest tightened for an entirely new reason.

Nina pressed the panel a final time. Nothing. The shutters remained sealed.

"They don't want us looking outside," she muttered.

With his heart rate settling and vision clearing, Miles stood and began pacing their small quarters. Something wasn't right.

Nina turned to him, arms crossed. "Still think I'm paranoid?"

Miles exhaled, the last remnants of his panic fading into something darker.

"No," he admitted. "Not anymore."

The fifteen-minute warning chime echoed through the hab unit.

Nina grabbed her jacket. "Well, let's go see what this is really about."

Miles turned toward Nina, his shoulders tense. Together, they stepped toward the hab door.

Miles and Nina stepped out of their hab unit and made their way through the maze of residential corridors toward the pedestrian level. The curved hallways—designed to maximize lunar construction efficiency—were lined with recessed lighting that pulsed subtly to guide residents in the designated travel direction.

The station's AI voice followed them through strategically placed speakers: "Reminder to all residents of Lunar Base 63. Today's gathering at 1500 hours is mandatory. Participation is required by colony charter section 4.3. Non-compliance will result in resource allocation penalties."

Miles glanced at Nina as they walked. Her jaw was set, eyes forward, clearly still on edge.

They emerged into the promenade, and Miles faltered. Despite having studied the station schematics for months, seeing the vast, domed space in person still took his breath away. The artificial lighting system mimicked Earth's daylight cycle, projecting a convincing late afternoon glow across the circular plaza. Hundreds of people moved between storefronts arranged in concentric rings around the central arena—a cross-section of humanity transplanted to the lunar surface.

Technicians in station jumpsuits with department color-coding along the sleeves mingled with civilians in Earth fashion. The ambient hum of conversation echoed off the curved ceiling thirty meters above, punctuated by the occasional chime of a shop's entry sensor.

"Oh," Nina sighed, pausing. "Look at that. I wish I could buy it for tonight."

Miles followed her gaze to a boutique where a shimmering blue gown hung suspended in a zero-G display field, rotating slowly to catch the light from every angle. The fabric looked like liquid starlight, embedded with tiny filaments that must contain programmable light-reactive elements.

"But you just changed," Miles said, glancing at Nina's current outfit—practical leggings and a fitted tunic that complemented her athletic frame. He caught himself before adding how stunning she looked, just as she was.

"I know, but that shade of blue would bring out my eyes." Nina tapped her wrist terminal, and her credit balance flashed briefly—nowhere near enough for a luxury item such as that.

Miles allowed himself to gaze into Nina's eyes—precisely three seconds by his internal count—before shifting his gaze away. He hadn't been completely honest with her earlier about his assignment, and he certainly couldn't trust himself to reveal his growing feelings for her. During their pre-mission "marriage" preparation on Earth, they'd spent weeks together establishing their cover. Each day, he'd found himself enjoying her company more—her sharp mind, her irreverent humor, her surprisingly extensive knowledge of twentieth-century cinema.

But acting on emotions did not fit in with the mission parameters. Driscoll had made that painfully clear.

"Hey, there's a directory terminal," Miles said, grateful for the distraction. "Let's find the quickest route."

He pressed his palm against the interactive holo-display, and a three-dimensional projection of Lunar Base 63 materialized above the terminal. Their location blinked green, while a pulsing orange pathway highlighted the most efficient route to the gathering arena.

Miles rotated the hologram with a gesture, studying the layout. "Don't you find it strange there are so many commercial establishments? Look—grocery markets, laundry services, hardware suppliers, electronics outlets—even a dedicated entertainment sector."

"What about it?" Nina asked, clearly not following his train of thought.

"It's just ... excessive for common lodgings," Miles said, choosing his words carefully. "These are long-term amenities. For people who *live here*."

"So it's a short mission, then?" Nina pressed, her eyes narrowing.

Miles ignored the question, focusing instead on another anomaly in the station schematic. "Look at this—three levels down there's a massive hydroponics garden, and below that, an industrial-scale waste reclamation center. The energy requirements alone would be ..."

"Let me see," Nina said, taking the deflection in stride. She stepped closer, her shoulder leaning against his as she manipulated the hologram. "Would you look at that. I wonder how large the garden actually is. Do you think we could visit after the drill?"

Her enthusiasm for the hydroponics level reminded Miles of their first meeting at Driscoll's office nearly a month ago—how her background in botany had made her the perfect candidate for this mission, though neither of them had known the true stakes.

***

"And you're absolutely positive this is imperative?" Miles asked, already knowing the answer.

Fletcher Driscoll, his operational supervisor, leaned forward across the polished graphene desk. "In order for your mission to have complete success, you will need to be present in one of the twenty-four Dyad sectors. And for that to happen, you need a spouse." His expression remained impassive. "Unless you're already married and somehow managed to hide that from your global verification audit, you'll need a partner. Soon."

Miles exhaled and sank back in his chair. "Fine. But I want it noted for the record that I'm not happy about this."

"Noted." Fletcher tapped the communication panel inlaid on the surface of his desk. "You can send her in now."

"Wait, what?" Miles straightened. "I thought you called me in to talk me into it, not to be part of the—"

"The sooner you two meet, the better. You'll need to sell this all the way." Fletcher's tone left no room for debate. "Completely."

"But does she kn—" Miles tried to protest, but Fletcher simply raised his hand as the door slid open with a soft pneumatic hiss.

"Ah, hello. Nina Petaluma, in the flesh?" Fletcher stood and crossed the room, extending his hand.

Nina smiled—a genuine smile that reached her eyes. "Yes, it's nice to finally meet you in person after so many vid calls."

"Likewise." Fletcher gestured toward Miles. "If you would?"

As Miles rose to his feet, he felt the weight of a thousand moons on his shoulders. He hadn't expected Fletcher to be so hands-off, so cold. A knot formed in the pit of his stomach.

Fletcher settled back into his chair. "You two don't know each other yet, but that'll change quickly. Nina, I'm sure you've been given a rundown on the mission parameters, so I'll leave it at that." He turned to Miles. "Do you have any questions for our bride-to-be?"

Miles stared at Fletcher for a moment, then turned to look at Nina properly for the first time. Her auburn hair fell just above her shoulders, framing a face with alert, intelligent eyes. "N-no, I'm good." Inwardly, his mind was doing backflips as he struggled to maintain his professional composure.

Fletcher smiled thinly. "Excellent. Now, you'll need to be married by 1000 hours tomorrow."

"What?" Miles felt panic rising. "Why the rush?"

"We're submitting your paperwork immediately after the ceremony. If it's late, you'll be disqualified."

"So, I have to actually marry her?" Miles glanced back at Nina. "Can't we just both agree to a status change and—"

"Sorry, no. The marriage contract is airtight. The admissions director will require proof of marriage before you arrive." Fletcher's expression hardened. "And we can't delay the launch, so you'll need to go through with it."

"Wait, this is real? You're not joking?" Miles felt his face contorting with concern.

"The marriage will be annulled as soon as the mission is successful," Fletcher said flatly, placing his hands on the desk. "But our partners won't know that until after you land, so you're going to need to do this for show."

"I—I understand, I think," Nina said, her voice steady despite the circumstances.

"Great. That will be all for now." Fletcher rose abruptly. "I need to get to a meeting, but I'm sure you two would like to get acquainted. Please, use my suite for as long as you need. Just be sure to lock up when you leave."

Before either could protest, Fletcher strode out the door, leaving an awkward silence in his wake.

Miles looked at Nina and managed a smile. He was nearly speechless at her composure—and yes, her beauty. She wore a light blue blouse that complemented her complexion and black slacks. Her hair looked as smooth as silk. "So, that Fletcher has quite a disappearing act," he said, his face flushing with unease.

Nina turned toward him and smiled, her expression surprisingly warm given the circumstances. "So, what do you do for a living?"

"For a living?" The mundane question caught him off guard. "Uh, well, my degrees are in engineering. I'm an architect, sort of. What about you?"

"I graduated from the university in Gebar City." She tilted her head slightly. "What *sort of* architecture?"

"I'm really more of a structural engineer. I design and oversee construction of space stations, ships, and all that sort of thing."

"Oh, that sounds fascinating." Her eyes lit up. "I'm a botanist."

"Really? Do you have a specific field, or just general botany?" Miles backpedaled. "I promise I'm not trying to sound judgmental."

"No, it's alright." She smiled. "My research focused on plant ecology."

"That must be exciting work."

"One would think, but I've not actually worked in the field since graduation." A shadow briefly crossed her face. "That's part of why I took this project."

Miles felt himself relaxing slightly. "Tell me, Nina, how did Fletcher manage to wrangle both of us into this situation?"

Nina laughed—a genuine sound that eased the tension in the room. "He said he received my application from a mutual acquaintance. I have no idea how he found you, though."

"The only thing I can think of is that he might have tracked my academics."

"So, your classmates gave you up," she teased.

"Very funny. No, they had security measures in place to protect student information. I'm actually surprised he found me at all."

"Well, whatever it was ..." Her gaze met his. "I'm glad they did."

Miles felt his heart flutter as Nina smiled at him. "So, you're really on board to go through with this?"

***

"Miles? Are you with me?" Nina tugged at his arm, pulling him from his memories. "You've hardly said ten words since the promenade. We're here."

Miles blinked himself back to the present and saw the entrance to the observation arena just over Nina's shoulder. He straightened his posture and extended his arm to her with a practiced smile. "My dear," he said as he opened the door.

Nina gave him one final, reluctant look before crossing the threshold.

The arena was packed. Though the domed room was the size of a gymnasium, it felt stuffy and confined. Seats were so tightly arranged that the audience spilled into the aisles, with people already standing at the back. The combination of stale recycled air and perspiration made it smell like a locker room. Miles felt instantly surrounded, his claustrophobia threatening to resurface at the worst possible moment. Nina's hand touched the middle of his back, a silent acknowledgment that she sensed his discomfort. Looking around, Miles estimated there had to be hundreds of people—far more than he'd ever imagined would fit into a single lunar module.

"There, on the far side," Nina said, pointing to a few open seats. They weren't together, but they were at least in the same row. "You lead and I'll keep up."

Miles didn't hesitate. Without a word, he guided Nina across the floor, weaving through legs and knees. After catching a few appraising glances from the audience, he felt the nerves in his stomach twist. He made it to the row and held out his arm for Nina to step in first. Once she had, he sat two seats away, on the other side of another couple.

The sound of the crowd buzzed around them, and Miles read Nina's lips say "Sorry"—apologizing for their delayed trip through the shopping district. Had they gone directly to the arena, they'd certainly have been able to sit together.

"Say, would you two like to be together?" asked the man beside him.

"If you wouldn't mind," Miles said, standing back into the aisle for the couple to shuffle over. "That's really quite thoughtful of you."

"Hey, don't mention it. We're all neighbors for at least a few weeks, right?" the man said as Miles stepped past him.

Miles nodded nervously. "Yeah, sounds about right." He sat next to Nina and instinctively placed his hand on her knee. She brushed it off, then looked embarrassed.

Miles leaned close and whispered, "Come now, dear. We have to maintain at least a modest pretense of marriage."

Nina smiled and placed his hand back on her knee, squeezed it, and replied, "Enjoy this while you can, fella."

Though the lights were dim, Miles could see she was clearly glowing. It made him feel like the primary catalyst in a cold fusion reaction. For a solitary moment, Miles wondered if there could be more between them than just a covert operative and his "arm candy," as Nina had cynically put it earlier.

"So, this is all pretty exciting, yeah?" the man sitting next to Nina said, his grin wide.

Miles wondered how much of their conversation he'd heard. Still, he smiled and answered in kind, "Yes, it is. I'm Miles, and this is my lovely wife, Nina."

Nina smiled diplomatically, a hint of color touching her cheeks—playing her part perfectly. She maintained her grip on Miles' hand while extending her other to shake firmly with the man. 'It's a pleasure to meet you both,' she said with measured warmth, her eyes betraying a quick, calculating assessment.

"Nice to meet you too," the man replied, his smile widening. He gestured to his partner, and they introduced themselves as Austin and Rachel, two space enthusiasts who had decided to take their first Lunar trip aboard the Moon Express launch vessel.

"How about you two? Either of you been off Earth before?" Austin asked.

"This is my first trip, but Miles has been up many times as part of his job," Nina boasted.

"Well now, you can't just stop there," Austin pressed. "What kind of job takes you into space regularly?"

Miles felt the familiar pressure building in his chest. The faces of the people around him seemed to blur, their features becoming indistinct as his mouth and throat went dry. The room appeared to contract, and Miles felt enveloped in a tunnel of white noise that rose and fell with his heartbeat.

"H-hey, is he alright?" Rachel asked from over Austin's shoulder. "He looks a little queasy."

Nina placed her hand on Miles' thigh and rubbed his leg ever so slightly. "Oh, he'll be fine. Miles has a mild case of claustro-phobia, and ..."

"Well, ain't that something?" Austin interrupted. "A guy who's claustrophobic but part of his job is riding rockets into outer space." He paused to wipe sweat from his brow. "I'd imagine this trip is going to be hell on you, being locked in nothing more than an enclosed cave the whole time."

Miles gripped Nina's hand, looked her in the eyes, and nodded a silent 'thank you.' He took a deep breath and shifted his gaze to Austin. "The claustrophobia comes and goes, and is more often triggered by crowds than enclosed spaces. Don't get me wrong, too long in the rockets, as you put it, has proven difficult. But I manage."

"Well? What's this job you do that keeps you up here and not down on Earth?" Austin pressed.

"I'm an aerospace engineer," Miles answered, wondering about the third degree.

"Isn't that neat, Rachel? Miles here is one of those space architects we've heard so much about."

Miles wanted to correct Austin's misclassification, but decided against it. "Something like that. I help with the design of orbiting space stations."

"Now, that is really something," Austin exclaimed. "Tell us, what sort of work have you been doing recently?"

Miles smiled and glanced around the arena, wondering when the director would appear. He returned his gaze to Austin. "My team just finished the build-out of Alpha 41 a few weeks ago."

Austin's eyes widened as if Miles had revealed the secret of life itself. "Well, I'll be. Rachel and I stayed on Alpha 23 not more than a month ago. We really love experiencing weightless living, if you know what I mean."

Miles caught Austin's implication and winked his understanding.

"The only thing about the Alpha trip was the tightness of all the spaces. You're probably thanking your lucky stars that you're not spending a few weeks in one of those tin cans, am I right?"

Before Miles could respond, the lights in the arena dimmed, and the metallic dome above them began to slide open, revealing a secondary glass dome that separated everyone from the airless lunar surface.

"Oh, it's starting, dear," Austin said to Rachel, completely forgetting about his conversation with Miles.

Miles peered through the glass dome, watching as the lunar landscape slowly came into view. His heart sank as he realized what he was actually seeing. Earth, visible far beyond the horizon, was different. Different from just days ago when he and Nina had left it. The planet that used to resemble a majestic blue marble—his home that once sparkled in the night sky—now glowed only a dull orange, its atmosphere visibly depleting.

But by what?

As he stared longer, Miles could see it wasn't simply discolored—the atmosphere was actively dissipating. Wisps of what had once been Earth's protective shield seemed to be streaming away from the planet like smoke from a dying flame. Tendrils of atmospheric gases trailed into space, creating an ethereal halo that was beautiful and horrifying in equal measure.

Miles sighed heavily, feeling helpless. He glanced around at everyone else in the arena, witnessing their horrified expressions as they looked upon Earth in its altered state.

The room grew eerily silent, aside from occasional gasps and whimpers. As he tried to comprehend what had happened, he felt Nina slide closer and lean into him. Instinctively, he wrapped his arm around her and held her tight, feeling her body shudder.

"My God, Miles. What have we gotten ourselves into?" Nina whispered.

Miles looked around again, taking in the entire observation arena, the people, the unexpected stillness that hung over the

room. The excessive commercial establishments, the industrial-scale hydroponics garden, the waste reclamation center—it
all suddenly made terrible sense. This wasn't a temporary base
or a way station. It was designed for permanence. For survival.

"Miles?" Nina repeated.

Miles sighed, the weight of his partial knowledge pressing
down on him. "Look, this has been on my mind since the day we
left. The whole time we were on the transport, the entire time
in our hab unit. I felt like I needed to tell you something, but I
couldn't tell a lie." He paused. "But I just couldn't say anything.
I'm sorry."

Nina looked up at him and wiped her eyes with her sleeve.
"Apology accepted, but what are you talking about?"

Miles held his tongue—he couldn't tell Nina everything. Not
yet. Not here, not with everyone around. He had to wait until
they were alone. But it was killing him inside.

"I-I don't know what happened here," Miles whispered to
Nina. "That's the absolute truth."

"Should we talk to someone? We can't just sit here," she said,
louder than Miles would have liked.

"No, I don't think so," he replied. "We're not in a position
to do anything right now." Miles glanced around, wondering
when the director would finally make an appearance. "And besides, what can we do from up here? We have to wait ..."

As if on cue, the lunar base director, followed by none other
than Fletcher Driscoll, stepped up to the solitary podium with
Driscoll standing behind and just to the side of him. He tapped
the microphone. "H-hello? Can everyone hear me?"

The room fell silent as all faces turned toward him. He cleared
his throat and rubbed the back of his neck, looking around with
visible unease.

"My fellow Lunar guests, I regret to inform you that we
are witnessing something unimaginable." The director paused,
exhaling slowly. "Earth is experiencing what our scientists are

calling Atmospheric Cascade Failure due to an unknown form of energy from outer space."

He cleared his throat again and continued, "This energy came at us rapidly and has compromised our planet's atmosphere, making continued habitation impossible."

Miles felt the air escape his lungs as he absorbed the director's words. This was far worse than what he had feared since leaving Earth—that something catastrophic was happening back home. In the final weeks of mission training, he had sensed a shift in attitudes, but he never imagined it was this severe.

The claustrophobia that had plagued him his entire life suddenly took on a cruel irony. The vast open skies of Earth—the one place where his lungs could fully expand, where his anxiety would retreat—was gone. Now everyone would know what it felt like to have the walls closing in, to have nowhere to escape to. The entire human race now shared his condition, trapped in artificial environments, counting breaths, maintaining control.

The director continued, detailing their current situation—the resource limitations, the threats to Earth's survival, and their increasingly narrow options. The audience listened in stunned silence before erupting into questions.

"When can we go back home?" someone called out.

"Unknown at this time," Driscoll said, stepping in to field some of the questions out of the director's purview. "We're provisioned for an indefinite stay here on the ninety-seven moon colonies, as well as the forty-two orbiting 'Alpha' space stations."

"How long have you known about this?" another voice demanded from the back of the arena.

Driscoll swallowed hard. "We first detected the atmospheric anomaly eighteen months ago. We knew the outcome was inevitable and saved as many people as we could."

Hysterical cries echoed throughout.

Miles glanced at Nina and saw the fear in her eyes slowly transform into anger as she pulled away from him.

"Tell me the truth, Miles. Did you know about this? Was this your secret mission?" Nina demanded.

"I swear to you, Nina, I had no idea this was going to happen. I was told to come up here and observe the environment with the resort at full capacity. That's it." Miles took her hand in his. "Nina, I had no plans for any of this to happen—especially for falling for you."

Tears welled in Nina's eyes again, and as she was about to speak, Driscoll continued.

"We will need to determine how to manage these circumstances," Driscoll stated, addressing the director with a tone of firm determination. "We're going to have to figure out how to restart Earth."

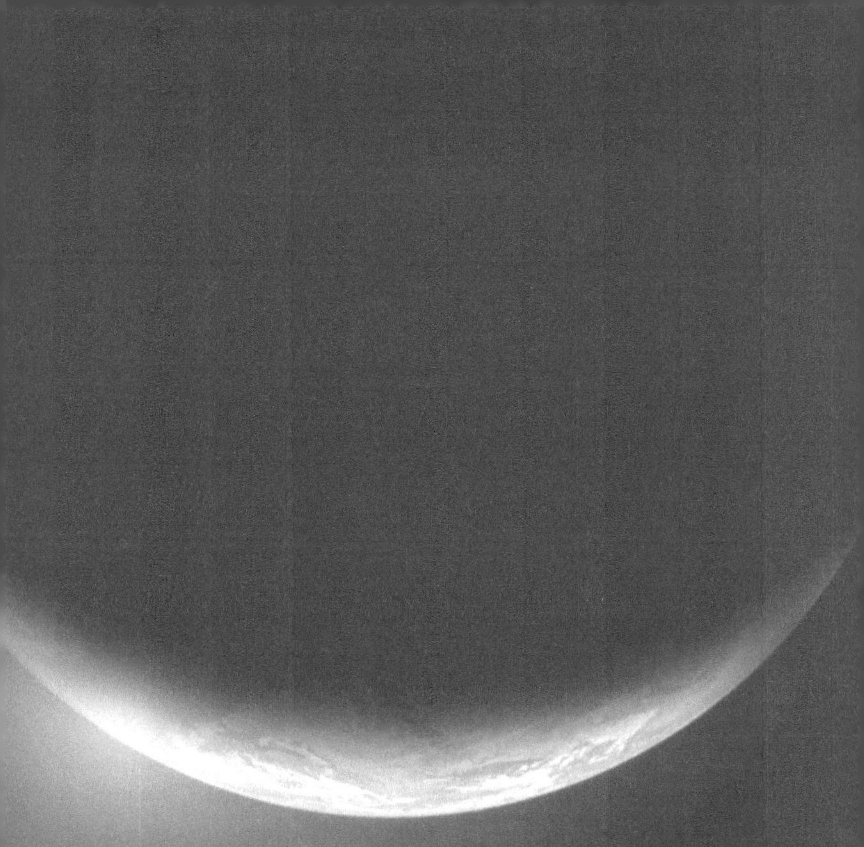

ABSOLUTE DARK

On Vobos-3, Scott and his daughter face a deadly planetary disturbance that threatens their colony's survival. Venturing into the unknown, Scott is haunted by memories of his wife, Hannah, and the painful past that brought them to this distant world. As two timelines intertwine—the perilous present and the tragic past—Scott must unravel the mystery connecting them before it's too late. A gripping, emotional sci-fi thriller of loss, survival, and redemption.

Absolute Dark

Absolute Dark first appeared in *Tales from the Canyons of the Damned, No. 39* in mid-2021, where it was met with enthusiastic reviews. From the outset, this story had a clear purpose: to blend cerebral horror with a strong dose of science fiction, crafted specifically to fit within the CotD universe. The writing process was as thrilling as the concept itself—intense, immersive, and incredibly fun. In fact, the world of Scott and Hannah still lingers in my mind. I often catch flashes of what might come next for them. Absolute dark is the first of three short stories in this collection that are quite literally ... On The Moon! More on that later. | 7,655 words

Absolute Dark

1

They say when you die in a dream, you die in actual life. Kind of like if you were to jump off a skyscraper and plummet to your death, you'd never reach pavement. And if you did, it'd be lights out.

Who are *they* to know this? If they personally experienced death in a dream, in theory, they would have also experienced it in actual life. Therefore, how would anyone know that they were dreaming about dying if they were no longer living to share the experience?

Or, did they experience someone else's death in their own dream, therefore extrapolating the cause of death while dreaming about someone else?

More dream research is needed to determine if one's own mortality is in jeopardy within the depths of their own sleep patterns.

2

When we lived on Earth, free time was usually spent outside, in nature; either hiking or on family picnics. Here on Vobos-3 life is much different.

I was between shifts working on the terraforming rig and was spending time with my daughter. Actually, I was hanging out in our hab, alone, and my daughter was up in her bunk—surfing Skynet, no doubt. And I know what most would say, but it's true, they actually do allow families on deep space missions, especially when terraforming new planets is the objective. Otherwise, the workers would go insane—much like my wife, Hannah, did more than two years ago. But I digress.

Like I said, I was on a bit of downtime and catching up on the news from home—news from Earth. I was relaxing on the gravity couch; an incredible device the scientists back home created to replicate the Earth's gravity here on Vobos. The gravity here is substantially less than that of Earth, and it's quite overwhelming because of its general lack of planetary motion.

Anyway, I was lying there in our hab ... and let me tell you, these units are like no other. They're not just tin cans scattered about the alien world. No, not at all. They tried to mimic our earthly surroundings as much as possible. You know, creature comforts from home.

For example, our hab has a living room, a kitchen, and a small dining area, all clustered on the main level. Up the steep ship ladder, there are two bedrooms and a bathroom. I know it sounds luxurious, but there's nothing grandiose about it. The spaces are really quite ... economical in their use of floor space.

So, there I was, lying on the grav couch, kiddo was upstairs trying to distance herself from her old man. I was drifting in and out of a catnap while the news was droning on in the background. I occasionally looked out the quadruple pane window at the arid landscape. And although the atmosphere outside was breathable, it wasn't quite up to human standards, yet. To limit our exposure to the environment, we were typically scheduled to work rather short shifts. No more than three hours at a time. It was three hours on and two hours off, to be precise. That cycle repeated three times per day, with 14 hours in between cycles. That was our 29-hour Vobian day.

It had been like that for the last 814 Vobian days, the equivalent of nearly three Earth years. But this day was turning out to be quite different.

Anyway, I was lying there, and I was staring outside, and in the distance the weather was ... stark. No more than usual, to be honest, but there was something about the atmosphere that was peculiar. And when I say all of us wayfarers longed to see a blue sky, I'm not exaggerating one bit. The mustard yellow skies on this planet reminded me so much of baby vomit, it's not even funny. But today, that baby vomit sky was mixed with a nice eddy of milk chocolate swirls. Not only that, the activity was high. I mean, the atmosphere seemed like it was moving faster than commonly possible with our limited gravitational pull.

3

I dropped my feet to the floor and stood up a little too quickly. With our reduced gravity, I nearly vaulted myself to the ceiling. But my eyes never left the impending doom. The darkened cloud mixture was moving at a rapid pace now, and it was heading right toward us.

"Hey, kiddo, you see that out the front window?" I knew she wouldn't hear me right away; she probably had her earphones in. "Marie!"

I leaned my forehead against the glass and watched as several of the other colonists began to take notice of the cloud formation. Strangely, it was as if they were all frozen in their tracks, gawking at a disastrous train wreck rapidly approaching.

"What, dad?" Marie's rebellious tone echoed throughout our unit.

"Look out front. Do it now. Do you see it?"

I didn't wait for an answer.

Seeing as I was in between shifts, I still had my environmental suit on, just having unzipped the top portion. I quickly rezipped it and donned my helmet. I stepped into the vestibule and waited for Marie to catch up. "Are you coming?"

"Holy Hell, dad. What is it?" She nearly tumbled down the steps, but the lack of full gravity saved her from taking a header into the support beam.

"No idea, kiddo. Let's go take a look."

A moment later, Marie was standing by my side, also having jumped into her own enviro-suit. We moved out through the vestibule and into the gloom.

If you've ever stepped from the comfort of your own home and into a virtual tropical storm, you'd understand what it was like. The whirlwind, not two meters from our hab, nearly sucked us up. The other colonists from the surrounding units were all huddled together, trying to maintain some sort of mass grounding. Like that was going to work.

Marie and I joined the nearest cluster and stared up in disbelief. The ever-darkening clouds were lowering the ceiling height in the area. I felt as if I could reach up and touch the clouds. An obvious exaggeration, but the oddity of the situation was surreal.

Then, suddenly, it was like a tornado. A funnel dropped from the cloud and touched the ground. The cyclone began kicking up Vobian dust and debris about 30 meters away from where we were standing. The majority of the colonists around us were wearing their terraforming gear. Still, others like Marie, only had their light-duty enviro-suits on. No helmet, just a slightly thicker jumpsuit than one would typically wear inside their hab. With the debris flying around, my immediate concern was for everyone's safety.

"Marie, go grab your helmet and get the PVD. Do it quick." Thankfully, Marie did not need to be told twice as she ran back to our hab and disappeared through the port door. I returned my gaze toward the cyclone as it continued to bounce across the surface. It never really stayed down, touching the ground for any concernable amount of time. It just skipped along at a moderate pace.

"Jesus," I gasped. I spun around to see if Marie had returned yet, but only found that more of the colonists had left the comforts of their own units and joined the mass assembling outside. "This is not going to be good."

A few moments later, I felt the tug on my sleeve; Marie had returned. She did as I had asked and had donned her own helmet as she handed me the PVD.

PVD is short for Personal Video Device for all you Earthers. Each family grouping in the colonnade received one upon landing. It was part of our welcome kit. I guess they wanted us to document what life was like early on. We were the history makers, reluctant or otherwise. And well, this was something that was going to go down in history, I'm sure.

I took the PVD from Marie and flipped it on. As I started recording, the cyclone moved much closer. I had to zoom out to catch its entirety in one frame. It was moving so quickly that I could barely focus. In that horrifying moment, I noticed something that I was nearly certain none of the other colonists could see with their naked eye. This was no regular weather cyclone.

It was machine-like.

In the briefest of moments, I could see mechanical jaws open and consume a colonist before bouncing back up into the cloud. I gasped.

"Marie, get back to the hab. Do it now. Don't come out until it's gone."

"What is it, dad?" she asked, taking a few steps back. "You're scaring me."

"I don't know, but just get inside. And close the blast shutters once you're in."

Thankfully, she didn't dillydally. She ran with great urgency—more than I'd witnessed from her in a long time—and into our hab. I watched her every step just to make sure she followed my instructions. Being a single parent of a 15-year-old girl, you just never know what you're going to get.

By the time I refocused my sight on the monstrosity, it was nearly upon us. Thankfully, the mass of colonists had begun to disperse. I still had the PVD on, trying to focus as best I could, but the cyclone was moving at a frenzied pace. It just kept popping up into the air and then dropping down like it was dotting the ground. And with each poke, we lost another colonist. Hysteria spread quickly as the other colonists began to recognize what was actually happening: The cyclone was murdering our own population. I kept at it, though, trying to capture what was happening on the PVD.

As I watched in horror, I tried to second guess which direction it was going so I could get even closer. It looked like it was heading away from me and to the right, so I followed a few steps behind, continuing to adjust the zoom. Just as I got it dialed in, the cyclone dipped down, and just like before, a mechanical jaw opened and swallowed up Cliff, my shift supervisor, who I'd just had a meeting with, not two hours earlier. He was no more than five meters from me. And this time, before the jaw retracted into the swirling cyclone, I noticed something else.

There appeared to be some kind of eye on the front edge, just above the metallic mandible. It was quite humanlike as it articulated inside its socket. It was looking for its next victim. As soon as it locked its sight on someone else, the device retracted, and the cyclone moved toward the next casualty. And again, just like before, it dropped out of the cloud and consumed Veronica, Barney's wife, and lead civil engineer.

I'd decided then that I had enough footage of the disaster and began to put some distance between it and myself. I still left the PVD on, but I backstepped as best I could. Obviously, I did not want to stumble and fall. And that's when I saw it. The articulating eye stared right at me.

Jesus, I'm going to be next.

At that point, I turned and fully ran in the opposite direction. I was not going to let it get me. For the briefest moment, I was thankful for the reduced gravity of Vobos. The strain on my joints was far less than running on Earth. I was able to sprint much faster than I ever had before. I flipped the PVD to front mode to record my own face.

"Marie. If I don't make it back, know that I love you. I know since mom died, it's been tough with just you and I. Trust me, we both loved you more than anything in the world." I could barely keep it together as I recorded what may very well have been my last words to her.

I had no idea if I would need them or not, but I wanted to say something. There I was, running for my life from who-knows-what, this mechanical monster on this alien world. It was chasing me, and I could feel it getting closer. As I ran, I noticed the horrifying faces on the colonists that I whizzed by. They knew it was coming, coming for me. And they knew that there wasn't a damn thing that was going to save me. I felt utterly helpless in that moment.

I held the PVD out in front of me, and on the screen, I could see myself still being recorded. In the very short distance behind me, the spinning cloud was closing in. As if in slow motion, the mechanical jaw dropped out of the cyclone and came right for my head.

But, before it could consume me, I thrust the PVD toward the nearest colonist and yelled, "Take this! Get it to Mar—"

Darkness.

4

"Marie."

Silence.

"Marie, I know you can hear me."

The low hum of the ion engines droned on, but otherwise, nothing but silence.

"Marie! Come sit down this instant," Hannah said as she nervously adjusted her own seat harness. "I can't believe you talked us into this, Scott." Hannah turned her attention to her husband.

Scott was intently studying the specifications of the terraforming reactor that he'd be building on Vobos-3. "Hmm?"

"Are you even listening to me?" Hannah waved her hand in front of his face, drawing his attention toward her.

"Oh, Hannah," Scott moaned. "I don't think you can lay this on me. It was your idea from the start. Besides, it's for the greater good. You know as well as I that without this outpost, Earth stands no chance against the Dominion. We made this decision as a family, including the heavy hand of your mother. If your dad had his way, we'd obviously be home right now, barbequing up some exotic meat he'd trapped in the wild."

Hannah's eyes narrowed as Marie finally floated into the seat next to her. "Thank you, sweetheart. Would you please fasten your safety harness? Commander Brooks will no doubt be by to check in on us."

Marie fumbled with the six-point harness as she fought to hold herself from floating away again. Zero-g's had its challenges. She giggled.

"Remember how I showed you, kiddo," Scott said as he demonstrated for what must've been the 10th time on their journey. "First, you hold the center buckle over your chest. Next, you take the middle strap on your right-hand side and fasten it in. Then, counterclockwise around your belly, fasten each and every one until you've made a full circle. The first two straps will hold you in place while you finish everything off."

Marie nearly rose to the ceiling before Hannah grabbed her leg and pulled her back down to the cushion of the seat. Once down, she followed her father's instructions and, one by one, attached each of the harness straps to the center clutch. Upon finishing, Marie looked up and smiled.

"Great job, kiddo." Scott winked and gave her a thumbs up.

"And there's that, too," Hannah continued. "All you want to do is be her best friend. Can't you be her father once in a while?"

"Jesus, Hannah. She's twelve years old. You don't have to overreact at every single thing that happens." Scott returned to his technical manual, barely able to focus on what was in front of him.

After some time, he closed the book and looked around the cabin. Across the aisle, Todd McBride, Scott's superior and lifelong friend, sat next to his wife, Darla. They were both fast asleep. In front of them and to the left sat another couple that Scott remembered seeing on the manifest but didn't know them personally. They were also asleep.

Once he was sure they would not be overheard, he spoke. "Hey, hon, you remember what the doctor said?" Scott chose his words carefully.

"I do. Your point?"

"Oh, Hannah. Even he agreed that it was probably a good thing for you, mentally, to get off Earth. A change of scenery was going to do you better than the medication that you've been taking. Isn't that worth something?"

Scott glanced over at Marie; she too was dozing off. Scott remembered that, as they approached the jump gate, the oxygen level in the cabin was going to thin slightly and, in turn, would cause drowsiness. He felt the pull of sleep inside his head.

Hannah sighed heavily. "I ... I know. It's just so—" She paused and rubbed her temples gently. "It's just so fast. It seems like we just talked about going on this six-month mission, yesterday."

"You know it wasn't yesterday, Hannah. It was nearly a year ago when we signed up for this."

"But did we have to sell everything? I mean, couldn't we have put things in storage for when we return? We are returning, right?"

It was Scott's turn to sigh. "Yes, dear. We're going to return. But what if we like this ... this new life? What if being colonists on a new world is really what we're good at? It seems like nonsense to continue paying some kind of storage credit indefinitely, while we, I don't know, skip around the universe until we find where we really want to call home. It's just better this way.

"Is *that* what this is all about? Really?" Scott asked, fighting the urge to fall asleep. "Is it that all our possessions—"

Just then, the forward gangway hatch opened and in stepped Commander Brooks. Once inside, he closed the hatch just as abruptly. Scott paused their conversation for a moment as he analyzed Brooks' demeanor.

Commander Jason Brooks was a hard-nosed military man that Scott had dealings with in the past. He was not a man to cross, and he spoke truthfully. He was no-nonsense, and that was needed for this mission.

"Folks, we're approaching the jump gate. It's probably best that you all get some shut-eye. I know this is your first time going through, and it's not as pleasant of an experience as one might think. There's nothing to see out the port windows, and the entire experience leaves you quite queasy. Experience dictates that the exposure is far less invading when you're asleep. But again, the choice is yours how you want to experience it."

The commander spoke the words as he walked through the passenger cabin, glancing at each of the passengers—the future colonists of Vobos-3.

"How long will we be in the jump gate, commander?" Scott asked as Brooks walked by.

"From the point of entry here in this sector to the moment we come out in the Malfinio Expanse, it'll be about 90 minutes."

"That's it?" Hannah asked. "I thought our journey was going to take months."

"Cumulatively, yes. It is a four-month itinerary. Once we're out of the jump gate, we still have a few month's cruising time left." The commander appeared agitated at Hannah's questioning. "All of this should have been explained before we left. Did nobody talk to you?"

Hannah guffawed. "Oh, yes. I remember now. I'm sorry, commander. I'm just a little *off*, I guess. We'll be sure to get some shut-eye, as you suggest."

Commander Brooks nodded and continued his path through the cabin and out through the rear hatchway. As soon as the hasps were engaged, Scott spoke up.

"Hannah, have you already stopped taking your medication?"

Hannah ignored Scott's question. She eased her seat back, closed her eyes, and very nonchalantly brushed her chest against Scott's resting arm. "We must get some sleep, Scott. Commander's orders."

Scott chuckled and rested his hand on Hannah's thigh. "You really are too much sometimes, dear. Maybe that's why I love you so."

Hannah placed her hand on top of Scott's then leaned into him as they both drifted off to sleep.

The passenger cabins lights dimmed until all that was left was pure darkness.

5

Darkness.

I could say no more words before I was entirely consumed by the monstrosity's mammoth jaws. I did a quick check of my facilities and was surprised to find that I was in no pain. It appeared that none of my limbs were broken, or severed, for that matter.

As I tried to balance myself in my new alien surroundings, I was thrown hard against a metal surface. "So much for no broken bones," I mumbled as I heard a gruesome snap in my ribcage. And then came the pain. Without even a moment to catch my breath, I began tumbling in all directions, unsure which way was up. I tried to stabilize myself by thrusting my arms out to my sides until I made contact with what felt like curved walls. I tried to grasp a hold of something, but my hands came up empty. With no way of seeing, it felt as if I were encased in a large clothes dryer from back on Earth. Then it hit me. Or, was it that I hit the side with my helmet?

My helmet!

I reached up and turned the mounted headlight on. It flickered at first but then shone brightly. I found that I was in a circular steel shaft. Along one edge, there were metal bars, almost like rungs of a ladder. I wasn't sure how, but I somehow avoided grasping any one of them as I was spinning out of control. I was sure, however, that one of them was the culprit for my newly sustained injury, and I was shocked that I hadn't end up impaled on one of them. Not exactly being a God-fearing man, I moved on without gratitude and started climbing in what I thought was the up direction.

As I ascended, it was nearly impossible to keep myself from losing my grip, both figuratively and literally. The fresh pain in my chest did me no favors, either. The more I was jostled around, the more I was sure at least two or three of my ribs were broken.

After several dozen steps, I noticed that the rungs were coated in some kind of wetness. Upon closer inspection, it appeared to be blood, probably human. I stopped for a moment and looked back down. I could see flashes of daylight as the mechanical jaw again started up its motion, opening, and closing. It was hunting for its next victim. I looked ahead of me, or above me as it was, to see if I could find another person—it's previous victim—but nobody was in sight.

"Think." *What can I do?*

I was still wearing my terraforming suit when it hit me. "Wait, do I still have it?"

I fumbled through my pockets, and sure enough, I found a handful of detonators that I had been using earlier in the day.

"Jackpot."

By then, I had noticed the daylight from below had stopped its intermittent flashing. I was still being jostled around, but it appeared that either something was blocking the light from reaching me or the monstrosity had stopped feeding.

"Hello!" I yelled.

My voice merely echoed around me. The curved steel seemed to somehow deaden my tone. I tried again.

"Is anybody there!"

All I could hear was the whirring sound of the monstrosity, and a little bit of my own heartbeat pounding inside my chest.

Then, I heard it. It was faint at first, but as the seconds ticked by, I was sure what it was.

"S-Scott? Is that you?"

"Holy shit!" She's still alive.

6

"Scott, is that you?" The voice was screaming now, and Scott could barely make out where it was coming from.

"Hannah, where are you? I can't find you." Scott continued climbing the metal stairway in near darkness. Having been assigned to the subterranean excavation division, being this high up in the reactor core was somewhat out of his comfort level. He didn't know what anything really was or where each of the blind corridors or stairways led to.

"I'm here. But be careful, the monsters are everywhere!"

What was she talking about? Scott wondered. He knew it was a bad idea to completely take her off her medication, but that argument was in the past.

As he reached the top of the stairway, he was faced with two decisions. First, step outside the conical structure and into the alien atmosphere. That wasn't an option. Second, he could walk across a narrow platform into the peak of the reactor core. "Jesus Christ. I'm not a fan of that option, either."

But Hannah's latest scream drove him forward without hesitation. He stepped out onto the steel gangway, his hands gripping tightly to the side rails as he inched himself out into the open air of the reactor. After several steps, he finally caught sight of Hannah. She was standing near the end of the platform, her back toward him.

"My God, Hannah! Get back from there! There's no railing in front of you, you could fall." Scott increased his pace but did not want to startle Hannah.

"I-I can't. I can't ... make it stop! Scott, they're everywhere. Can't you see?"

"Slow down, Hannah," Scott begged. "What are you talking about? It's just you and I here."

Hannah's eyes enlarged far bigger than Scott had ever witnessed, and darted all around, not stopping to focus on any one thing.

"They're everywhere!" She hissed and then let out another gut-wrenching scream.

"Hush, hush baby," he said, hoping to soothe her. He tried to remember what the doctor back on Earth had told them about how to cope with her hallucinations if they were to come back. But in this situation, Scott only drew a blank. His mind was utterly overloaded by his surroundings. He stepped forward. "Honey, it's going to be okay. I won't let them get—"

"Don't patronize me!" she yelled. "You're just like everyone else. Why is it I'm the only one that can see these ... these aliens? These alien monsters! They're everywhere." Hannah leaned out over the edge of the platform and looked straight down. From their height, Scott assumed that they were close to three-hundred meters above the floor surface below.

Having inched that much closer to Hannah, he could see the sweat covering her skin. And her hand, moist as it was, was barely holding on to the steel handrail. He knew that she could let go at any moment.

Scott took another cautious step forward, now only about two meters from Hannah. "Baby, I believe you. I can see them everywhere too. Just step back, and we can talk about how to make them go away." Scott prayed that his tactic would not backfire. Of course, he couldn't see the alien monsters that she'd been rambling on about for the better part of a month. He'd just chalked it up as playful banter because every time Hannah brought it up, she would giggle and laugh it off. He prayed to God that he could've seen the signs sooner.

"Y-you do? You see them? Do you see ..." Hannah paused and turned to face Scott. She gazed passed him and onto the platform beyond. "Do, do you see that one right there, Scott? Tell me you see it."

Scott turned, looked, but there was nothing there. He took a deep breath and began to nod his head.

"Oh, that's not that scary. I see it, and it's—"

"You sonofabitch. You don't see it! All you can do is patronize me. You think that my medication levels are way off, I can read right through you, you bastard."

Before Scott could stop her, Hannah turned and stepped right up to the edge of the platform and was about to step off.

"Wait! Don't do it," Scott pleaded as he lunged for Hanna's arm.

Hannah fully stepped off the platform and began falling, but before her momentum took over, Scott grabbed her wrist as he fell to the platform surface.

The look on Hannah's face was of profound confusion. Then as the seconds ticked by, her eyes grew wide with terror. Full, unbridled terror.

"S-Scott! Get me up! Help me!"

Scott felt Hanna's sweat between his hand and her wrist, and he was beginning to lose his grip. "Baby, give me your other hand. Reach up, grab my—"

Before Hannah could react, her damp wrist slipped from Scott's hand, and she plummeted to her death.

"Scooooottt!"

7

"Scott? That you?" Came a distant voice from below.

"Oh, Hannah!" I yelled.

"Uh, no, sir. You bump your head or somethin'? It's me, Mags."

My God, it got Maggie!

Maggie was an early colonist that refused to return to Earth after her last tour. She said that she loved the place and wouldn't return because this was her new home. And now Maggie was going to die.

"What the hell is going on?" she bellowed. I couldn't see her, but I could hear the fear in her voice.

"Hell if I know, Mags. Are you protected?"

I knew before the question was asked that she'd been decommissioned weeks ago, and that meant she was no longer wearing a company-sponsored environmental suit. But I hoped anyway.

"Um, no. I-I'm just wearing first clothes. Can you believe it?"

Jesus, first clothes were garments given to new colonists upon arrival to wear around our hab units until more suitable attire could be manufactured or provided. They were quite minimalistic and were not made to last for much longer than a few months. But some of us, including myself, and Maggie apparently, still wore them from time to time.

"Quick, climb up to me," I said. "I know it's difficult to see but feel around and you'll find a ladder along one of the sidewalls."

After a few moments, I started to hear the clanking of feet climbing the rungs. The sound echoed flatly through the tube. She was on her way, and as she came closer, my mind raced for a solution. I was holding on to the ladder rung with one hand, and in my other, I was holding one of the blasting caps. All the while, the metal tube we were in continued to shift and spin.

I had a flash. If I could just ignite one of the blasting caps, perhaps it could sever the tube from whatever this monstrosity was.

"Maggie! Are you close?"

"Yeah, I can see your light now. I'm almost there."

"Mags, no. Stay there and hold on to the ladder. I'm going to try something."

I removed the protective cover from the blasting cap and chucked it as far as I could above me. I heard it clank against the sidewall and waited.

And waited.

The 10-second timer seemed to take forever, and I wished I would've changed it to five before throwing it.

And I waited.

Four, three, two ... One.

Nothing.

Suddenly, something was pulling on my leg. I looked down, and there was Maggie.

"Jesus, you scared the crap out of me."

"You tried a blasting cap, didn't you?" she asked.

"Yeah, but something happened. I threw it up there, but it didn't go off."

Maggie was old-school. She had more knowledge about terraforming better than anyone I knew. I could only imagine what was going through her head at that very moment. She was probably devising a way for everything to happen just the way it should. She had an engineer's mind for sure.

"Maybe when you threw it, it bounced and switched off. Maybe if you set it and get away?"

"Not enough time. These new caps have a ten-second timer, and that's not near enough time to climb back down."

Just then, from far above, we heard the scream of what most likely was a previous victim.

"What the hell are we going to do, Mags?"

Maggie didn't say anything, but I felt her move up next to me. "Sorry, my friend. I know it's close quarters in here."

She continued to slide her body past and then above me. "I'm just trying to get by."

"Maggie, no. You don't know what it's going to do to you. That scream didn't sound good."

"Quick, hand me another one of your blasting caps."

I fished out another cap and handed it to her. "Maggie? What are you going to do?"

"I'm not sure what the hell this thing is, but I know I'm not going down without a fight. You have a daughter, Scott. I am alone. I'm an old woman living on an alien world, and I have nothing to lose. I'm going to take this blasting cap and shove it up its ass."

"Jesus, no, Maggie. We can figure this out."

From above, another scream.

"Not this time, Scott. Work your way back to the jaw and wait for the explosion. If everything goes right, I'll have severed this part of the monster and hopefully killed whatever is doing this."

Before I could protest, Maggie had already scampered out of sight. She was now in full darkness, and I wish I would've given her my helmet for at least sighting purposes.

As I climbed my way back down toward the metallic mandible, what appeared to be a trapdoor closed right below me. It was as if they knew what was going to happen. I looked up but could only see darkness. If I went back up, I'd risk injury from the explosion. I had to sit.

And wait.

8

"Thank you for waiting, Mr. Phillips. Commander McBride is just finishing up a telecall back to Earth. He should be done any moment," McBride's personal assistant Gary said as he tapped away at his communication display.

Scott remained seated at one of the dozen or so gravity chairs scattered around the cavernous administrative unit. Admin was one of the first to be established on Vobos-3, nearly 12 years previous. In comparison, it's quite similar to the colonists' habitation units but at a much grander scale.

Inside the main level resides all engineering disciplines, as well as reactor implementation. There was little doubt that the admin unit would be repurposed as a command center for the impending war against the Dominion. With all the digital displays already plastered upon nearly every surface, it would have been very ideal.

Various solar systems and orbital trajectories were laid out on half of the panels, while the others were detailing specifications of ongoing Vobos-3 projects. And although Scott had been in the admin unit numerous times, never was it for official business-like today. Besides Gary and himself, the room was empty, which Scott felt peculiar.

Then, without notice, a tall digital panel just to the right of where Scott sat slid horizontally and disappeared into a wall cavity. Behind it was another room that Scott never knew existed. He sat up and tried to peer in, but before he could catch a glimpse of anything, Commander Todd McBride walked through, and the door closed promptly.

"Hey, Scott. Glad you could make it. How are, um, have you been holding up?" McBride walked up to Scott and shook his outstretched hand. Scott and McBride went way back, all the way back to their college days. Despite the passing years, Scott still looked up to McBride as a superior, even a role model of sorts.

"I suppose I'm doing well, considering. Marie is your typical teenage girl. Her rebellious streak is just starting to form, and that's of concern." Both Scott and McBride chuckled.

"So, Scott. Have you considered my offer? I know it's only been a few weeks since … the ordeal, but our window is closing."

Scott began to pace around, attempting to analyze the nearest digital display. He did, in fact, make a decision, and it was one that he wasn't proud of. One of the last conversations that he had on Earth was with Hannah's parents, and he remembered the moment vividly. They'd made him promise to protect Hannah while off Earth. And he was damn scared to face them after what had happened.

"Scott?" McBride prodded.

"Yeah, about that. I think Marie and I are fine to stay on Vobos for another tour, if that's all right with you."

McBride stepped up next to Scott, staring at the same display and exhaled. "Scott, if that's what you want, I'll support it. But most everyone here, as well as those back on Earth think it's probably better for you and Marie to return. To head home. If you two don't leave within the next few days, you'll miss the window through the jump gate. You'll be fixed here for at least another eight months. Nothing can change that timeline."

Scott was well aware of the jump window as he'd gone through this process of decision-making numerous times before Hannah died.

"I think I'm okay with that," Scott said, turning to face McBride. "I just feel that I'm not through here, and if you could cut me a little slack, I'll be back up to speed in no time."

McBride's eyes widened, and a slight grin crept across his face. "On a selfish note, I'm happy to hear that, Scott. We have a long history, and I feel that I can guide you through whatever it is that you're dealing with. Quite honestly, it's Marie that I'm concerned ab—"

"Well, she's fine." Scott cut him short.

"Sure, she might be fine now, but what about when she starts really missing her mom, or distant family for that matter? At least back on Earth—"

"I get it, Todd. But we've talked about it, and our decision is set. We're staying. Talk to me again in eight months, and we'll see if our mood has changed."

McBride slapped Scott on his shoulder then pulled him in for a hug. "I'm here for you, man. Not just as your station commander but, you know, for whatever you need."

Scott returned the embrace and contemplated telling McBride how his dreams, or nightmares rather, have kept him up most nights since it happened. But he didn't want to give his friend any more reason to force him home. He'd just have to live with the screams in his mind.

Scott broke from the hug before it got awkward. "Thanks."

"Don't mention it. Really, we're understaffed as it is, and having you around for at least another cycle certainly relieves the pressure from back home. How about you take the next couple of weeks and just ease your way back into things. I won't expect anything monumental from you until you tell me you're ready. Deal?"

"Sounds good, Todd."

9

After waiting a bit, I decided to be somewhat proactive about the situation. I'd noticed the cyclone monstrosity had started slowing its gyration. Seeing as I was not being knocked around like a ragdoll anymore, I switched my focus to the trapdoor below. Unless I could get it open, the odds of me surviving the ordeal were not significant.

I took an inventory of what I had in my environmental suit's pockets: I still had three more blasting caps, a sparging wrench, and half a dozen wire leads. I examined the trapdoor, but it was void of any fasteners. It was a smooth sheet-metal like substance that spanned from one side to the other of the cylindrical tube.

My first effort was to try and kick through. I gripped the lowest ladder rung and lifted myself up as far as my arms would allow. Then, I dropped as fast and hard as possible onto the trapdoor. I felt a small budge but not enough to make a difference. I tried this a few more times with the same result. Then I got the idea to possibly drive my wrench into the edge where the trapdoor met the sidewall. Amazingly enough, I was able to get the wrench's tip down into the crack a few centimeters, until I heard the next scream.

I froze and stared up. Obviously, it came from Maggie. *My God. It's too late.*

Abruptly, her screams stopped and were replaced with actual words. But they were spoken so far away I could barely make out what she was saying.

"Garble, garble *hold* garble *something* garble," and then it broke off. It was dead silent for the next thirty-seconds and then another horrendous scream.

"AHHHH!"

In mid-scream, the monstrosity began to move quite differently than it had up until then. The twisting and shaking that my aching body became accustomed to were replaced by a low rumble that practically vibrated the molars out of my mouth. Just as I thought the vibrations had reached their peak, they got worse. Far worse. I dropped my tools and placed my hands over my ears because the sound was so loud. Then, the vibrations just stopped.

Hesitantly, I pulled my hands from my ears and waited for a second or two before dropping my hands to my side.

That was one of those moments that I wished I wouldn't've reacted so quickly. The explosion that came was so earsplittingly loud, I could feel my ears begin to bleed. Literally. And then, just as suddenly, the entire monstrosity began revolting and spinning and shaking in all directions. Unfortunately, I could not grasp hold of anything to stabilize myself. I just had to ride it out.

At one point, the upward force drove me down onto the trapdoor so hard that I felt it begin to buckle. As I laid there, pinned to the metal plate, my darkness was interrupted when far above, shards of light began to creep into the metallic cylinder. At first, the light was faint, but it was there. Then, moment by moment, I could see the seams of the cylinder begin to split. It started from way up high and worked its way down toward where I was. After a while, I felt the pressure relieve a bit, and I was able to right myself and stand up. Just as I did so, the splitting metal tore all the way around and launched me out into the sky.

"Sonofabitch!"

It only took a moment for me to realize why I was feeling so much pressure on that trapdoor. It was because of the force caused by the monstrosity jutting up into the sky. I was now falling to the Vobian surface, nearly 500 meters below, if I had to guess.

As I plummeted, I could feel my heart beating, pounding ever harder. The wetness leaking from my ears spread across my face as the wind whipped by.

"Oh, Hannah. Baby, I'm coming to you," I declared, suddenly realizing the eerie similarities between her death and my own impending doom.

As I tried to maintain focus, my vision began to cloud over. I was going to lose consciousness, thankfully, before impacting onto the surface of Vobos-3.

"I love you, Marie. I wish—I wish I were a better father."

I repeated these words over and over, willing them into her mind. It was the only thing I could do to maintain any sense of awareness.

As I fell toward the rapidly approaching surface, I sensed more and more of my vision escape me. It was minor at first, but then it became so enveloping, all I could see was black.

At the moment just before impact, I was surrounded by absolute dark, and only silence could be heard.

10

At the moment of impact, I opened my eyes and stared up at the ceiling. I expected to see the mixture of baby vomit clouds but instead found Marie's face hovering over me.

"Dad? Dad, are you all right?" Marie said as she shook me.

"Wha, what happened?"

"You fell off the grav couch, again."

"Again?" I sat up and patted my chest out of instinct. The anticipated rib pain was nonexistent. "Again?"

Marie rolled her eyes. "I thought you'd gone back to work, and I came down to fix a snack. I found you thrashing around on the floor. Dad, you really scared me. Are you all right?"

I stood, rushed to the window, and stared out. "I, I must've been just having a bad dream or something." I rubbed the sleep from my eyes and turned toward Marie. "Has there been any weather changes today?"

Marie stepped up to the window and peered out. "Like what? It's been like this for, I don't know, since we got here all those years ago. It's just so ... drab."

"Tell me about it, kiddo." I chuckled. "Do you think we've overstayed our welcome? You think it's time for us to go home? Go back to Earth?"

I watched her and waited for a reaction. At first, there was nothing. But then it appeared that blood drained from her face. She backed up and sat down on the edge of the gravity couch.

"Dad, are you being serious right now?" Her eyes wide.

I sat down next to her, and she leaned her head on my shoulder. "I don't know, kiddo, but I think we might have gotten just about all we can from this place. With everything that we've gone through here, it might be time for us to move on."

We sat in silence for several minutes, neither one of us knowing quite what to say. As we sat there, my mind replayed various snippets of my dream. What did it mean? What did any of it mean?

Finally, I took a deep breath and asked, "Are you ready to hear about it?"

She didn't answer right away, but I could feel her tears begin to fall on my arm.

Her head nodded almost imperceptibly. "Yes. I think so."

I wrapped my arms around her and held her tight. "I was with your mom when she died. Here's what happened."

When recovering addict Ava Blake awakens with more than just a mild case of amnesia, she's unsure if the procedure performed on her was against her will, or - even worse - her own idea. They say that with time, her memories will return. But will they be her own, or will they be something completely unexpected?

Jacked

Originally written as a standalone novella in late 2020, *Jacked* is the longest piece in this collection. It was meant to launch a nine-volume series of near-future science fiction and suspense stories. While the broader project didn't receive the reception I had hoped for, the world—and especially its protagonist, Ava Blake—still holds a special place in my imagination. Ava is a force of nature: bold, brilliant, and relentless. Given the chance, she could absolutely take the future world by storm. Whether or not her story continues will depend on one thing—demand. But make no mistake: there's plenty more waiting just beneath the surface. | 24,414 words

Jacked

1

I am in complete darkness. As far as I can tell, I sense nothing. I know I exist, but I cannot feel any part of my body. I think about my hands, my fingers, my toes, but it's as if they've been removed. I know they should be there, but they seem absent from my presence.

Am I awake? Am I unconscious?

My mental senses are intact, otherwise, how would I even ask myself the question?

Movement. The first sensation—in I don't know how long—that I feel. I am lying face down, and I'm floating. I cannot see, but I hear feet shuffle below me.

The movement is small and transitory, and the moment I stop, I feel hands on me, from the back of my head all the way down to my calves. It feels like I am being covered with a blanket.

But I'm not cold. I have no temperature awareness whatsoever.

A voice: "Standard procedure, doctor?"

A short pause.

Another voice, female, I think: "Yes, but be sure to note her past addictions. You've read the file?"

My addictions? But how did they know?

Hey, what's going on? I yell, but my outcry is only in my head. I cannot move my lips. I can feel them, along with my tongue, safely parked inside my dry mouth. But I can utter no words.

"Yes, I skimmed the important parts before I gave her the general anesthesia."

Common sense tells me that I am in some kind of hospital. But for what?

HEY! Can you hear me? I scream, but it's still just to myself.

"No shortcuts, Kevin. Read the whole file. You're going to love this one," said the female voice. The doctor's voice?

"Patient, Ava Jacqueline Blake. Age twenty-seven. Marital status: Single." Kevin pauses, and there is a sound of shuffling papers next to my right ear. "Doctor, is there anything in particular that you want me to see, or are all the *generals* relevant?"

Well, he got my name and age right. But what happened? Did I OD or something? And if so, is that any reason to be in the OR?

I try to look around and am finally able to open my eyes. I look forward and see a reflection of myself. A mirror lies on the floor directly below. My face rests in some kind of cradle—like what massage therapists have on their beds. I can see, but my eyes are near fully dilated which causes a strange haze around everything. I cannot tilt my head, but my eyes are able to rotate somewhat. I see the reflection of Kevin. He sits in a chair next to me. He's intently reading a yellow, Manila folder.

"Jesus. Presence of ketamine, heroin, philoxicodine? They found all these narcotics in her system, and we're still going forward?" Kevin asks.

"I thought you'd get a kick out of that one," says the doctor just out of my peripheral vision. "Now, are we ready to proceed? Scalpel."

NO! I scream at the top of my proverbial lungs. *I'm awake! Can't you see?*

"Scalpel," Keven says as he puts down my medical file and reaches out of my sight. I hear him fidget with something that sounds like cellophane before handing the instrument to the doctor. "Who's the client, anyway?"

The doctor takes the scalpel and again moves from my sight. "Trident, of course."

Suddenly, I am fully aware that the doctor is about to cut me open, and I feel my heartrate escalate.

I'M AWAKE, DAMNIT! The voice in my head is severe. And all I can enunciate is "Thplpl," which is something.

"Did you say something, Kevin?" asks the doctor.

Finally! They hear me. What kind of crack-pot setup is this place? Don't they check on the patient before it's slice and dice time?

"No, doctor. I was just wondering about Ava here, and why was this procedure even approved, considering her history?"

"Well, you know how Denninger is. Whatever Roger wants, Roger gets."

HEY! "Rplthp."

The gurgle escapes my lips just as I feel the initial incision at the base of my skull. Thankfully, the doctor stops instantly. Then, the image of her masked face comes into view, reflected in the mirror.

"Jesus, Kevin! She's awake!" the doctor yells. "Put her back under, and prepare her memory blocker while you're at it. This is the second time this month that you've not been focused during a procedure."

I let out an enormous sigh of relief, but then it hits me. *Memory blocker?*

As I toss that notion around in my head, my vision begins to blur. I hear Kevin mumble something, but before I can grasp his words, I am overcome with darkness.

2

I gazed out into the vast, night sky filled with thousands of pinpoint lights, glimmers of hope in the surrounding darkness. Some of them, stars twinkling in the distant ether, while others floated just out of physical approximation, an ever-present reminder of the Overwatch.

I stood next to the tattooed man, Mr. Hendrick's bodyguard I assumed. He greeted me when I arrived and ushered me through the luxurious penthouse apartment and out onto the roof deck. He didn't strike me as of the butler type, as he was dressed far more modern. His suit was silk and all black. His shirt and tie matched the ebony hue. If it weren't for the tribal tattoos that bled out from beneath his collar and crept up his cheek, he'd been a strong candidate for model of the year.

We stood next to one another for several awkward moments in complete silence. It was as if he was waiting for me to come forward with information that I had no idea I possessed. To avoid making eye contact, I took in my surroundings.

The area directly outside the sliding glass door was covered by an immense dimly lit overhang. Large, potted palm trees sat to each side. To the left, taking up nearly the entire wall, was a full height marble sculpture with sheets of water cascading over it. To the right, a walk-up bar, adorned with several half-filled crystal bottles and shelves of empty goblets and tumblers. Beyond the covered portico sat an intimate furniture arrangement beneath the stars.

The stars. They shone far brighter than I thought possible considering our downtown location.

I hesitated briefly then stepped past the tattooed man. I smiled, praying that he wouldn't notice my nervousness. Before I could think twice about it, the extraordinary view sucked me in. I walked by the furniture setting and stepped up to the glass guardrail separating me and the luxurious rooftop deck, and the fifty stories of darkness below. I took in the expanse, wondering just how I made it to where I was at that moment.

"Miss."

Agreeing to be a part of this bizarre "assignment" was not only a surprise to myself, but—

"Miss," the voice came again. It was the tattooed man invading my thoughts. "If there's nothing else, Mr. Hendrick will be with you shortly."

I turned to face him. "No, I'm quite okay. This place is ... incredible. The view, I can almost see ..." My gaze drifted back over the glass guardrail in search of my own meager flat.

"Yes, it's quite breathtaking." He smiled for the first time since he'd greeted me downstairs, and as he did so, a silent alarm went off in my head. I caught a glint of something from my past. The tattooed man's toothy simper reminded me of ... something, or someone. Someone that I would much rather forget. It was the sparkle of his gold encrusted tooth that caught me off guard.

"Um, yeah, breathtaking. That's the word I was looking for." I raked my eyes back out across the night sky, hoping that it was just case of a mistaken identity. A moment later, I heard the sliding door close, isolating me from the impending doom.

As I stood there, doubt seeped into my soul, triggered by the sight of his smile. My feet ached from wearing the stupid stilettos, that they said complemented my dress, but didn't help matters much. Like the dress needed anything else to sell my cover. With my tits practically pouring over the top and the hem high enough that you could practically see my pubes, the shoes were just plain overkill.

I pushed the self-doubt aside and did a quick check of my clutch. In it, I had just a few items. First, I had my lipstick with its accompanying compact mirror. I had an inhaler, which really wasn't an inhaler but something far more lifesaving. Still, it had my prescription information on the label to avoid suspicion. And at the very bottom, I had a tube of mascara, which, if anyone looked at closely enough, they'd discover it was a completely different shade than what I was currently wearing. Thankfully, men are not as bright as they lead us to believe. Besides my lipstick and mirror, the other items were part of my mission.

Thinking of it as *my mission* was unbelievable. Just weeks before, I was in quite a different lifestyle with completely different priorities. Inside the fake mascara tube resided the most critical aspect of my assignment. Once I had Hendrick where I wanted him, a cringeworthy thought on its own, all I needed to do was inject him with the contents of the hidden vial. It sounded far more complicated than it did when they first explained it. *How the hell am I going to get him unconscious long enough to inject him with this? Won't he feel the prick?*

Breathe. I needed to breathe.

I looked out at the city lights. The view was calming and after only a few moments I could feel my pulse return to normal. I realized my hands were still holding the contents of my clutch. As I began to stuff everything back in, a husky voice startled me, and I involuntarily squealed.

"Ha, ha. I'm sorry to laugh, I didn't mean to alarm you," he said.

I spun around, expecting to find the face behind the name. Until then, my controller knew Horatio Hendrick by name only. He has somehow, as I've been told, been able to avoid having his picture taken. As I looked in his direction, I found a handsomely dressed man standing at the bar, his back to me. I quickly shoved everything back into my clutch and moved to the sofa. "That's quite all right. I ... I was just in deep thought."

"Good thoughts, I hope. Can I make you a drink?"

"A drink? Um, sure." In my rush training, we never talked about alcohol consumption. I knew that to decline could possibly jeopardize my objective. But what should I ask for? I've never really been a big drinker. No, that wasn't my vice. "How about something exotic?"

"Something exotic coming right up." He pulled two highball glasses from the shelf and filled them with ice before pouring various bottles into a shaker. I watched him for a few moments, studying his movements as something seemed ... familiar.

"Not again," I whispered to myself.

"Come again?" Hendrick asked.

"Sorry. I was just commenting on your penthouse. It's quite beautiful."

He continued to add shots to the shaker. "Thank you. I've not seen you before. Are you new?"

With my hair up—a style that I've never tried—I could feel my neck begin to perspire. And with the coolness of the evening, I instantly began to shiver. "Me? No. Not that new. I, I've been with the agency for at least five months." What else was I supposed to say?

"I have to imagine that even at just five months, that must feel like an eternity in your line of work."

My line of work? What the hell was that supposed to mean? Oh yeah, I'm playing a hooker in today's episode of Jackie's Life.

I looked at Hendrick just as he poured the tangerine tinted liquid over the ice. I could feel my pulse rise again. Nervously, I popped my lipstick out to do a quick touch up before he came over. I leaned down and dabbed Ruby Red #6 along my bottom lip and then pursed them together to distribute, all the while studying my reflection in the compact mirror. Before I finished, he'd placed my drink on the glass coffee table in front of me. As I slid the lipstick back into my clutch, I looked up and saw his face for the first time.

"It's you! What are—" he stammered.

"Antoine?" I gasped. "You're Horatio Hendrick?"

He took a step back. "What, what are you doing here?"

"I, um. I ... I was—" Words were apparently lost to me.

"You know what, save it. It doesn't matter. I should've known how you would turn out. It's really quite too bad."

I was completely stunned at the quick turn of events. I was frozen in place and utterly speechless. I finally sputtered out some words. "Too bad? How is this too bad?" I asked, trying to recover even the smallest semblance of pride.

"I really would've liked to have you, again, but now that you've seen me," Hendrick's voice trailed off, and his hand disappeared inside his sport coat.

I knew he was going for a gun; Antoine always had a gun on him. Thankfully, my hand was still resting, frozen, inside my own clutch. I grasped my inhaler and pulled it out, yanking the lid off in one swift motion.

"Have me again? You really are a bastard." Beneath the inhaler lid resided what my controller promised me as the most compact and efficient neutralizer in the industry. Having never even heard of one until recently, I didn't know how to compare that to anything else. I pointed it at Hendrick and watched his eyes widen.

"You think that is any kind of comparison to this?" Hendrick said as he pulled out his SIG Sauer.

"Don't do it, Antoine. Or should I call you Horatio?"

He grinned and jacked a round into the chamber. "It doesn't matter, my sweet peach. You won't be alive long enough to know the difference."

As he leveled the pistol at my chest, I triggered the neutralizer. A split second later, a bright flash emitted from its tip, landing in Hendrick's abdomen. A look of surprise overcame him as he dropped to his knees. He tried to clutch his chest but only spilled his own drink all over himself. He then crumpled forward. As he did, his outstretched hand hit the tile surface and discharged his pistol.

The report, despite being fifty floors above the city, echoed louder than I imagined.

I released the neutralizer button and stared at it in amazement. It wasn't smoking nor did it look any different than it did before. It looked like a broken inhaler.

I jumped to my feet and nearly fell over. *These damn stilettos are going to be the life of me.* I rushed to Hendrick's side, pulled out my mascara, and revealed the small, glass vial hidden inside. I removed the tip and jabbed it into Hendrick's neck. Within seconds, the serum emptied into his body. I knew time was short as I was sure Hendrick's bodyguard heard the gun fire.

I stood up, still reeling from the last time I'd seen Antoine. I kicked him several times for good measure. And that's when I saw it. A pool of blood began to seep from beneath his chest. The broken glass from his drink must have impaled him.

"Son of a bitch." He wasn't supposed to die. I was just supposed to inject him with the tracer serum and nothing more. "My God, my life is over."

In a panic, I stumbled back, knocking my own drink to the floor. The sweet, woody scent instantly hit my nose.

"What am I going to do?"

I looked around, hoping to find an exit stairwell from the rooftop, but nothing was in sight. The only door I saw was the one that I came in through. But, not far from there, I remembered the small niche behind one of the potted palm trees. I rushed over and ducked into the shadows. I knew that the tattooed man was just moments from bursting through the door. And no sooner did I press myself into the corner, he and another man rushed out. They hurried to Hendrick's body and just out of my sight.

I had to move quickly. I sprang from my hiding corner and darted in through the sliding glass door. Before I passed through the penthouse apartment, I slid the door shut and threw the lock. On the wall next to the patio door, I noticed a crudely drawn pink flamingo that I'd failed to notice before. *How could I have missed that?* I wondered. I dismissed the oddity and moved on.

Praying that there were no more guards in the apartment, I made my way to the entry door and out into the elevator vestibule. I looked for the call button but found just a blank wall. *Shit, did I miss it inside the apartment?*

"How the hell am I going to get out of here?"

"Request noted. Lift arrival in ninety-five seconds," said a friendly female voice.

I spun around to see where the voice came from, but I was alone.

The voice continued. "Eighty-five seconds ... seventy-five seconds ..."

I waited and thought about my options.

Being fifty floors up, I knew that my exit wasn't going to be instantaneous. I shot my eyes around and noticed the exit stairwell not three meters from where I stood. I tapped my foot, wishing and praying for the elevator to move faster.

"Sixty seconds until lift arrival," the cheerful voice announced.

"In a minute, I'll be almost certainly de—"

"Hey!" one of Hendrick's men came barreling out of the penthouse, holding a pistol. I had to move.

I kicked off my stilettos, thankfully, and burst through the stairwell door at full speed. I nearly fell over the guardrail before I caught my momentum. I began taking the steps down two at a time. I glanced back up as I rounded the second landing and saw the guard's head pop out. He squeezed off a shot but missed far left. I increased my pace and started taking the steps three at a time. As I rounded the fourth landing, I noticed that he was no longer following me. *Why did he stop?* I wondered. No matter; I kept running.

After two more flights, I slowed my pace slightly to reduce the noise I was making. I listened intently. There were no footsteps chasing after me. Then came his voice. "You can run, Jack, but you can't hide. You see, we have all the building's entrances covered. You are never going to get out alive. And that's a fact, Jack."

Isn't he a clever linguist, I mused as I increased my pace.

Replaying his words, I knew he was probably right. I had to think. I had to improvise and ... I had to get out of sight. Just then, I noticed that the doorway for level forty-two was slightly ajar. I slowed my momentum as I arrived at the landing and was thankful for being barefoot so that my footfalls would not be heard. I slinked up to the door and peeked in. Nobody in sight. It appeared to be just another elevator vestibule. I stepped back onto the landing and listened for an advancing bodyguard. In the distance above, I heard footsteps, casually it seemed, climbing the stairs after me. How far up were they? Two, three flights, maybe?

"I'm coming for you, dearie. Don't go too far."

I glanced back at the door and decided that it was my best option. I pulled the handle and stepped inside. I closed the door silently so that my chaser would not hear it. As I was certain the click was inaudible, I turned to explore my new path. As I did so, I felt the pinch in my neck and then an instant warming sensation.

I'd been neutralized.

As I turned in the direction of the pain, I saw a stout man, bald, sporting a grey goatee. As my consciousness began to slip, I felt his arms close around me.

I drifted into darkness.

3

"Let go of me!" I scream as I try to break free from his grasp. But I can't. Not because he's stronger than me, but because he's simply not there. *Was it a dream?* More like a nightmare.

Still, I can't move. My wrists are bound, restrained somehow. With a pounding headache, and feeling quite dizzy, I drop my head back, landing on an unseen pillow. I can feel the inertia of the room spinning. *Or is that in my mind?*

As the moments pass, the memory quickly fades. It's replaced with more darkness.

Somewhere, I hear voices. Faintly at first, as if they are spoken from a great distance. The sounds turn into moans as they get louder. I try to look around, to find the source of the now moaning cry. But I can't. My eyes are fused shut.

A loud crash ricochets all around as the moans morph into screams. I again try to see. Instinctively, I lean forward enough so that the tip of my finger can scrape away the encrusted sleep from my eyelids.

The darkness subsides, but only slightly. The room's lights are out, except for a solitary florescent fixture over another bed in the far corner. It's clear where the excitement is coming from.

There's a man in the bed, and he's thrashing from side to side. Although my vision is blurry, I recognize what appears to be two doctors or nurses on either side of his bed. They are attempting to attach the same type of restraints to his wrists that are on mine. The orderlies converse in an urgent tone, but I can't make out what they are saying. I hear a few key words though, but they make virtually no sense.

"... tranquilize ... corrupt ... rejected procedure ... purge ..."

"Where am I?" I utter, my words barely audible.

The threshing man lurches forward, knocking another rolling cart to the ground, and various medical equipment scatters across the floor. The sound is nearly earsplitting.

I look back at my restraints. I'm able to situate myself so that I can almost sit up fully, supporting myself on my elbows. As I do so, I'm able to see the rest of the room.

To my left is another bed with a man fast asleep. How he can sleep through the commotion is beyond me. But, unlike the thrashing man and myself, the sleeping man does not appear to be restrained. He's just lying on his side with his bedsheets nearly covering his face. I can just make out a scruffily beard and dark hair beneath a head bandage.

My eyes dart back to the thrashing man, and I see a similar head wrap on him. Unable to touch my own head completely, I'm unaware if I am in a similar condition, but I sense that I am. That would partially explain my head pain and whirling sensation. I close my eyes and try to remember what happened. Was it all a dream? Or was it a real memory from my past? And that's when it hits me fully.

Who am I?

"Hey! Who—who am I?" My voice still too faint to be heard.

Fear sets in, and I start to thrash about myself. Here I am, not knowing my identity or my location, and I'm strapped to a hospital bed, in a room full of other patients. Of course, I'm going to freak out.

Just as my flailing about picks up pace, I hear a new voice.

"Stop!" the yelling whisper comes from yet another hospital bed straight across from me and just to the right. I'm not sure how I missed it on my initial scan of the room.

"If you know what's good for you, you'll stop that flogging about right now."

That part of the room is particularly dark, and I can just make out the silhouette of another person, a woman, sitting straight up in her bed. She is just out of the cast of light.

"W—what? I—" I begin, but I can't form anything coherent to say. My head is still spinning, and I'm having trouble staying focused.

Then, the woman leans forward into the faint beam of light. Her head is also bandaged, but I can see platinum blonde locks dropping out from the sides of her head wrap. Her eyes are dark and intense. She stares at me as if I were the crazy one.

"Unless you want to get purged yourself, you'd better shut your piehole!" she bellows.

As I stare at her in disbelief, her gaze widens to the point that I can clearly make out the whites of her eyes. It's the silent exclamation point that drives her command home. Then she leans back into the shadows.

4

I sit in my hospital bed in total disbelief. Should I worry about what the orderlies are doing to thrasher man or should I be more concerned with the state of my own being? Maybe they're connected somehow.

After a few moments, the thrashing begins to subside. It appears that whatever they gave him—most likely a tranquilizer as they stated earlier—is working. From what I can see, his eyes are closed tightly, and his head lobs back and forth.

One of the orderlies steps away and starts picking up the scattered equipment. As he does so, he happens to glance up at me. I just sit there like a deer in headlights. He holds my gaze for a few seconds then continues with his task. I glance back at the other woman, and she's now laying on her side with the bed sheet up and over her head. Much like the guy to my left. The sight makes me wonder if I should also avoid eye contact.

What the hell is going on?

After a few more minutes, all the dumped medical supplies are picked up, and the formerly thrashing patient is nearly comatose. The lead orderly, maybe she's the ... doctor? Yeah, her voice sounds familiar somehow. She speaks.

"If you've got everything, swipe out and take 273 to suppression. I'll fill out the report and meet you in the lab."

He nods, pulls a key fob from his waist, and slides it along the wall surface next to the door. A mechanical click sounds, and the door pops open a few inches. Within moments, he pulls the gurney away from the wall and out of the room. The doctor follows, closing the door behind her. Another audible click.

The woman across the room instantly springs from her bed and begins crawling all about the floor. She looks like a deranged lunatic, scavenging for dropped crumbs.

"What are you looking for?" I ask hesitantly.

She ignores me as she disappears beneath my bed then pops out on the opposite side. Only to slip under the next bed.

"Hey? W—what's going on?" I can barely get the words out because of the pain. I lean back onto my pillow and squeeze my eyes shut. The spinning continues.

After a while, she finishes her sweep of the rooms floor and suddenly stands up next to me. "I was just checking for anything useful, in case they missed something." Her eyes shoot around the room wildly.

"Something ... something useful? For what?"

"You know. In case they come back for me. I don't want my marbles scrambled," she exclaims, her eyes intense.

I take several deep breaths to get my next words out. "What are you talking about. I—I don't know ... what's going on, or even who I am. Marbles scrambled?"

The woman sits next to me and draws her face up close to my own. "This place is not at all what they say." She shoots a quick glance at the sleeping man in the bed next to us. "They say they're performing these operations based on good faith, but I've seen far too many patients get messed up. Like the one they just wheeled out. He's a lost cause, and they're probably purging his memory as we speak."

Between my headache and the twirling space in my head, I can barely keep up with what she's saying. Still, I press on.

"What is this place? I don't remember anything. My name, or how I got here. Who are you?"

"You see, that's just how they want it. They want us ambivalent to their ways. Plausible deniability. That way they don't have to answer to anyone. You'll see. You better start thinking about your own escape, that's all I'm saying."

And just as quickly as she came to my bedside, she's gone. She bounces up and darts back to her own bed.

"Wait. Do you have a name?" I ask, hoping for something.

"You'd better get some shuteye, girly. They'll be back before you know it, and you'll need all your energy."

Before I can press her for anything else, she slips beneath her sheets and rolls over. I can hear her deep breathing within moments.

Despite the silence in the room, I try to force myself to stay awake, to figure out what the hell is going on. But with each breath I take, the drowsier I get. Before long, I can do nothing to keep myself from the demanding pull on my eyelids.

5

The sensation of being followed overwhelmed me as I stepped off the crowded sidewalk and into the dingy lobby. I looked back to the street as the door clicked shut. There was no one there, just the busy afternoon traffic. I felt my heart pound inside my chest.

I swear I saw him. A man with no hair.

I shrugged, an effort to convince myself that it didn't matter.

When I turned away, I saw him. The silhouette of the bald man with a goatee leaning against a building across the street.

Shit.

"In or out," a voice behind me boomed.

I spun around; my fists clenched. My eyes landed on a rail-thin man sitting behind the counter, his desktop covered with adult paraphernalia. "What?" I gasped, far louder than I intended.

"Easy, there. You comin' in or not?"

"In." I start to move past him and toward the stairway.

"Slow down, toots. You know how this works." He held his hand out.

I stopped, took two steps back, and pulled out a single bill—a fifty, I think—and threw it in his general direction. As swift as a cat, he caught it midair, and I'm halfway up the stairs before he returns to his porn collection.

The corridor walls were faded, the floor stained. All I could think about was H. The junk that was in unit 242. My pulse quickened at the mere thought of it.

My walk was visceral, a well-worn path. Down the hall and to the left, I could practically feel my eyes dilate from anticipation. I moved quickly, ignoring the putrid smell.

I glanced to the left, 222. To my right, 224. Further ahead was unit 232. Across the hall, I expected to find 234, but there was no room number. Instead, an image of a pink flamingo jumping over a moon was in its place.

Dismissing the oddity, I looked ahead and found room 242. I rapped on the door. Before anyone answered, I pulled another fifty from my pocket—my last—in preparation. I waited.

Moments passed, then the door swung open. A large, burly man stood, blocking the entrance.

"Antoine," I said and held the bill out. He accepted it and silently stepped aside.

I walked by and headed straight for the bedroom. That's where he'd be, and where I'd find my dragon.

I stopped at the door, my shaky hand resting on the handle, but I waited. My pulse quickened. I breathed in deeply, accepting my fate for what it was. I wrenched the door handle and stepped inside.

Antoine sat at a small desk. Next to him was a twin bed. He wore a dingy, white T-shirt. His fingers were smoke-stained. His hair was pulled back in a ponytail, and he smiled. "Ahh, my sweet peach! You're here early this week."

I closed the door and leaned against it. I lowered my head to avert his gaze and turned both of my pockets inside out. I snuck a glance up, and I thought I sensed pity in his expression.

"Come now." He motioned to me. "It'll be okay. We can discuss *payment* later. Your usual?"

I exhaled, realizing that I'd held my breath since stepping through the door. Nervously, I nodded and sat at the edge of the bed.

"You know, honey. I've said this before, and I'll say it again, you wouldn't have to pay for this if you let me introduce—"

"No!" I slipped out off my flannel shirt and tossed it to the floor. "I don't ..." I stammered. "I mean, I can't—"

"Yeah, I know. You're not for sale. But if you change your mind, I know several ... associates that would pay greatly to enjoy your company."

Antoine turned away from me and pulled a tray from the side drawer, before placing it on the desk. The rig consisted of a hypodermic needle, a tarnished silver spoon, and a small pouch of pure heaven. He expertly prepared my dose, liquifying the powder in the spoon before drawing the contents into the syringe. I thrust my hand toward him as he wrapped an elastic band around my upper arm. He tapped my skin gently, searching for the right entrance. My own personal stairway to heaven.

He paused. "You know, this makes three now that you owe me. I'm not sure how much more I can let slide." He placed the loaded syringe on the desk. "We have to square up at some point."

My heart beat faster. *I want it. I need it.* I exhaled sharply, knowing full well that if I didn't agree to his terms, I might not get my fix. I stared at the hypodermic for a long moment.

"Okay," I whispered. "Just give it." I closed my eyes and turned away. I heard him fumble with the syringe before the small pinch entered my vein. A warm sensation flowed into my arm, and within seconds, he released the tourniquet, sending every ounce of the liquid heaven into my body. I moaned as I gently rubbed the inside of my elbow. My eyes were closed as I fully embraced the euphoric sensation coursing through me. I leaned back onto the bed, feeling him lift my legs up to twist me around. I opened my eyes again and stared at the ceiling. I was unsure if it was an effect of the drug or if I was only just then noticing it, but I saw more flamingos ... stenciled across the plaster.

As I laid there drifting in and out of ecstasy, I felt pressure on my chest. I snuck a lazy glance to the side and saw Antoine resting one hand on my breast while his other unfastened my pants. I inhaled sharply. I wanted to weep, but I could not. I wanted to protest, but I couldn't utter a single word.

Nooo.

I gathered a scream, but before I could open my mouth, darkness surrounded me completely.

6

"Get off me!" I scream as I lunge forward. I jab my arms out, hoping to force his hands off me. But they are no longer there.

He's not there. My eyes flash open, and I glance around. What was once *his room,* is now replaced by one so stark in comparison. The walls are white, practically screaming sterility. I am back inside the hospital room. But now, all the lights are on.

Across the room, the other woman is sleeping. Behind her bed are multiple digital displays flashing vital statistics in rhythm with faint echoing beeps and bops. The spot where the man went berserk last night is vacant. No patient, no bed. To my left, the man that remained oblivious last night is now awake and is staring back at me.

"You really should relax a bit," he says. "The doc is on her way." He turns back to his magazine.

What the hell is going on?

I was just with ... who? Why can't I remember his name? The image of the ordeal is still vivid in my mind, but his name is a mystery. He had his hands on me and was about to—

Oh, God.

Uncontrollably, I shudder at the realization of what happened, and I clutch my arm where he had injected me. Oddly, there is no sensitivity to my touch. There are no tracks whatsoever. *Strange.*

Twisting around, I find a display panel similar to the ones behind the others' beds. It appears to be monitoring my heart rate, blood pressure, oxygen level, and who knows what else. Then suddenly, the complete lack of my own self-awareness from last night comes flooding back.

"W-where, where am I?" I stutter.

"Like I said," the man begins, but before he can continue, the only door leading into the room clicks open.

"Ah, yes. You're awake." A woman wearing a light blue overcoat steps in and closes the door behind her. She approaches the side of my bed, studying my expression. "You know, you gave us quite a scare. You should've regained consciousness yesterday morning. But the effects of your anesthesia lingered on much longer than we'd expected."

"Anesthesia? W-what?"

The woman held a digital tablet, tapping away at the discreet screen. "Any pain?"

"Wait. Where am I?" I ask, ignoring her question.

She continues typing. "Any nausea?"

"Hey! Where the hell am I?"

She finally looks up and smiles. "I'm sorry. I'm being rude. I'm Dr. Pierce. It's obvious that you're experiencing a bit of amnesia. Am I correct?"

I nod.

"Understandable. The procedure was quite invasive. But I assure you, your memories will return, most within twenty-four to seventy-two hours, but fully within a few weeks."

"Um, wha? I mean what procedure?" I ask. "I don't ... recall needing any kind of procedure. Was I in an accident? I mean, w-who am I? Where am—"

"Please, relax. There's no reason to worry. Unfortunately, I'm not at liberty to discuss patient identities. Here at the Harper Foundation—that's where we are—we value client discretion above all else. When you were admitted, you agreed that you'd only be told your full identification upon a life-threatening emergency. All I can tell you right now is that you are patient number 477." The doctor smiles again.

"Great, I'm reduced to a three-digit number." I lean back and huff. "Can you at least tell me what the procedure was?"

"Why yes. You've been fitted with a cerebral implant." The doctor returns to tapping at her device.

"I'm sorry, I don't think I heard you right," I say, realizing for the first time that my head is bandaged. I reach up and sooth the white gauze. "Jesus, an implant? Is that even possible?"

"Yes, quite. In fact, we've perfected the technology since achieving the complete map of the human brain a decade ago.

Prior to that, the cerebral implants were quite hit or miss. Some of which had disastrous side effects. Those that were successful had such spectacular results that they earned publication in the Journal of Scientific Discovery."

"What the fuck? Why would I ever agree to ... having my brain implanted?" I demand.

"The reason for each individual is different, obviously. Neurological disease or dysfunction, to name a few. Were you experiencing any lost ability? Any movement paralysis? Those are some of the—"

"Hell, I can't even remember my name, let alone whether or not I had any fucking paralysis."

"It's all right to be upset. And confused. The first twenty-four hours post-op are the most difficult. As soon as your memories return, we'll begin programming the use of the implant. Right now, the nanites used in the procedure are rebuilding pathways to each of your cerebral lobes. And the obvious side effect to that is short-term memory loss."

By now, the dream I was having earlier has faded. I feel like crying, but deep down, I know it won't solve anything. And besides, there's an upside—I don't think I could stomach having the only memory inside my head that of being drugged and nearly raped.

Oh, shit. Am I a drug addict?

"But for now, 477, your best course of action is rest. Not necessarily sleep, but try not to exert yourself until your implant can complete its internal connection. Have you experienced any pain?"

I touch the back of my head and discover sensitivity. "Well, a little. Only when I touch it."

"That's expected. Just relax. And one more thing. You may experience ... hallucinations, or even possibly dreams or memories that you think are real but may seem impossible. The thing is, each person's brain reacts differently. They may or may not be your own memories, but don't commit to them fully. Only after the molecular connections are complete, will we know if any additional therapy is necessary."

Great! So maybe I wasn't about to be raped.

Before I can ask another question, the doctor steps away and back through the door.

7

The room is silent except for a muted buzz emanating from the various monitors around the room. I stare up at the ceiling in disbelief. *Why won't they tell me who I am?* The urge to cry surfaces again, but despite not really knowing who I am, I somehow feel that I'm stronger than that. I push the useless emotion away.

"That's some pretty heavy shit," the man next to me says.

Initially, I consider simply ignoring him. Something about his tone sparks warning signs in my head, but I can't quite put my finger on why. I think better of it, realizing that he might have more information. I sit up.

"I'm not gonna lie," I turn toward him, "but I'm feeling a little mind fucked right now."

The man slips from his bed and saunters over to mine. "Hello there, 477. Allow me to introduce myself. I'm 308," he says smugly. He holds out his hand, but I only stare at it. After a long moment, I begrudgingly accept his greeting.

Seconds later, I release my grip and try to pull back. But he holds his grasp, firmly but not overly threatening.

Finally, he lets go then sits on the edge of my bed. "I know it's a bit weird referring to one another by just numbers. So, I'll give you a little help. My name is Ethan. Ethan Wood."

"But how—"

"Ah, I've already re-gained some of my memories. Besides, this isn't my first rodeo. I'm not here for some top-secret experiment. I'm just a normal guy trying to get a leg up in the world, you know?"

I don't. But I smile and play along. "So, Ethan, I don't suppose you know what my name is?"

"Sorry, sweetheart. For now, 477 is the only thing I'll ever know you by." He smirks and looks across the room at the sleeping third occupant of the room. "That there is patient 596. She came in just before you did. And what the doc said is pretty much on target. Within another fifteen or twenty hours, you should have your first dose of memories back."

"But didn't she say twenty-four to seventy-two?"

"Well, yeah. But you've been here for about a day already. She wasn't lying about you not waking up right away. You've been out for the better part of a day." Ethan leans back, clasps his hands together, and stares deep into my eyes. "Me? I was up within a few hours after the procedure, and I've seen some pretty weird shit around here." He looks around as if someone were listening. "Take yourself, for example. You are quite the moaner," he chuckles.

I feel my cheeks redden, and I wonder if it's out of anger or embarrassment. "I'm glad I amuse you." I casually inch myself away from him. "So, you say this isn't your first procedure?"

"Three, to be exact. The first one was the old school kind we're all familiar with. They tap a hole in the side of your head right behind your ear and wire into the cerebral lobes manually. Man, I can't believe they actually got away with that shit. But, *c'est la vie.*"

"What, you had one of those? I remember years ago when they were all the rage, and they were insanely expensive." *Shit, where did that recollection come from?*

"Yep. I was one of the early pioneers." He straightened his back and puffed out his chest, boasting.

I stare at him, analyzing. "You don't look much older than I do, and I'm ..." I trail off.

"Trust me, it'll come back," he says. "Yeah, I'm just a little older than you, by the looks of it." He drags his eyes up and down my body with a satisfying grin.

Hello, uncomfortable.

"And I had that device for, I don't know exactly. Maybe four years? Then the whole thing started going fuzzy on me, and they had to do an emergency reversal. That was a few years ago when I got it replaced with a newer model. That old one had a backpack type of thing that held the battery and a little computer processor. Well, it really wasn't a backpack, but more the size of an old paperback book strapped to my back. It was uncomfortable to say the least, and because of the battery, it was quite heavy. The new one was less than half that size. Maybe the size of a pack of cigarettes." He stops and rubs his chest. "Oh, cigarettes. What I would do to have one right now."

All I could do was stare.

"Anyway, that second model would've been just fine and dandy the rest of my life, but the advancements that they've made recently really changed the game. No more battery pack. No more bulky processor. These new suckers tap right into the human nervous system for power, and the processor is the size of a ... a breath mint. But the real advancement is its wireless capabilities. That's really what got my money."

I continue to gape and wonder just how he had the where-withal to pay for not one, but three, separate implants. Some-how, I remembered when they first came out that ... *my God, I'm remembering shit!*

"How do you afford it?" I blurt out. "Aren't these procedures something like, I don't know, maybe 500,000 credits?"

"Hey, there she is. She's remembering things." He smiles. "Well, let's just say that I've planned well, and I'm exceptional at what I do. Let's just leave it at that for now. But yes, it is a lot of money."

"And it's worth the medical risk just to have a little bit of wireless connectivity?"

"It's like this. We all have home automation these days. That central device in your house that controls the temperature of the furnace or knows what time to turn the coffee maker on in the morning. It even turns lights on and off, and basically does everything that us lazy bastards don't want to do anymore. That computer that controls everything in the house is virtually what they are allowing us to do with our minds. With this wireless connection, all we have to do now is just think the action and it'll happen. I'll think that I want to turn the vid screen on, and up comes the latest edition of the Kama Sutra Diaries. When it's time for bed, all I have to do is think that it's dark, and out go the lights.

"You see, they put this antenna—no thicker than a few sheets of paper, with the size of one of those old postage stamps—wedged in between your skull and the outer layer of your scalp. Nobody even knows you have it. Other than that small receptacle at the base of your skull, nobody would be the wiser."

I touch the back of my head as he talks. I feel a small protrusion just as he describes.

Why on Earth would I ever agree to this?

But somehow, something doesn't feel right. Something about the way Ethan is explaining things, almost as if it were … rehearsed.

Despite my growing dislike for the guy, I want more—no, I need more information. I press on.

"So, you obviously signed up for this. Is everyone a volunteer? I mean, are they here of their own free will?" I feel apprehensive even asking the question.

Ethan's eyebrow's rise as he glances at patient 596. As he's about to speak, the door buzzes and clicks open. Ethan and I glance over.

"Patient 308. I'm here to take you for acclamation training. Are you ready?" an orderly asks as she holds the door open. Beyond her compact frame, I can see a wide corridor just beyond.

"You bet," Ethan says enthusiastically. He stands, slides his feet into black, vinyl slippers, and shuffles forward. As he reaches the door, he turns back and says, "Don't go far, baby. I won't be gone long." He winks and steps through the door.

As the door swings shut, I spring from my bed to try and catch it before it latches. I'm too late. It's already locked.

I return to my bed and prop my pillow up behind me so that I can rest my throbbing head against the headboard without putting pressure on the God-forsaken implant. As I lay there, I stare at 596 and wonder if what she told me last night was true. Despite missing my memories, the idea of having my mind scrubbed permanently frightens the hell out of me. As I practically bore my eyes in her direction, I feel my consciousness begin to drift. Within moments, my eyes shutter this bizarre world and enter another.

8

The flickering streetlight caused shadows to dance across the soot-stained sidewalk. The frigid night air sent chills through me, giving me a false sense of urgency. *But is it false?* Instinctively, I increased my pace.

I needed to get around the next corner and out of sight. Then, I could step into the darkness, hopefully losing the tail that had been following me since I left the gala. Experience told me that

I should never look over my shoulder, but my cover was almost certainly blown. I had to do it.

As I rounded the corner, I instantly doubled back a step and hugged the limestone wall. I dipped my head out and around the edge of the building and saw no one. The man following me, the man that had been just half a block behind me, was now gone. No matter, I couldn't exactly stick around and wait for him to catch up. I had to keep moving.

Nearly running down the block, my eyes surveyed my immediate surroundings. I saw it nearly instantly.

Could it be? Could I have stumbled upon my initial destination purely by accident?

Without hesitation, I stepped into the coffee house and took the first vacant booth I found. Thankfully, it was just inside and along the front window. I quickly scanned the other patrons of the coffee house, hoping that nobody recognized me.

Good, I thought. *Unnoticed.*

I exhaled quietly and rubbed my hands together to return their warmth. Unwilling to let my guard down, I leaned toward the front window and peered out. Just as my nose nearly touched the glass, I heard the voice. The voice I was trained to recognize.

"Is there a drink I could get started for you?" asked the woman from behind the coffee bar.

I spun around, and my eyes landed on a tallish woman with a black-as-night bob-cut and just as dark lipstick. My contact. "Thank you, yes. I'll have a large Americano, with room."

"What name should I put on the cup?" she asked.

The verified response was already at the tip of my tongue.

"Green Sparrow," I uttered, staring directly into her steely eyes.

She did not flinch. Instead, she began pounding on the countertop.

Bang. Bang.

"Is there a problem?" I asked. "I said, Green Sparrow."

Bang. Bang. She simply stared at me as she continued to pound.

Bang, bang, bang.

I blinked my eyes open and instantly brought my hand up to shield the bright sunshine from obscuring my vision.

Bang, bang.

"Okay, okay. I hear you!" I yelled as I threw my comforter away and stumbled to my front door. "Who is it?"

"Babe, are you all right? It's me, Denny."

"Oh, fuck," I mumbled. "Yeah, hold on."

I turned back to my claustrophobic studio apartment and grabbed the first piece of clothing I could find to cover myself.

I fastened the security chain and unlatched the deadbolt. I cracked the door open an inch to verify Denny's identity. "What?"

"Honey, where have you been? Everyone's been worried sick. Your work has been calling your parents and me looking to know if we've heard anything from you. You've not returned any—"

"Yeah, I've been busy. I'm fine." I tried to push the door closed, but Denny drove his toe in between the door and the jamb.

"Babe, let me in. We need to talk." He held up a business card with a single name—Antoine—and a thirteen-digit locator number. "This was in your door. Care to explain it to me? You said you were going to stop."

I exhaled deeply. Knowing that this conversation was going to come sooner or later, I decided I might as well get it over with. "Hold on," I said as I pushed the door closed and unlatched the safety chain.

I turned back toward my bed as he let himself in. I slipped beneath the comforter and looked up at his worried face. *Why did I care?*

"Okay, let me have it."

"I'm not going to let you have it. I'm just concerned. Your dad, he is concerned. What've you been doing?" he asked.

"I ... I, um ... I've been studying. Yeah, trying to sharpen my skills to reapply," I lied.

"Not this again," he said, lowering himself to the foot of my bed. "We talked about this several times. Once the company rejects you, there is really no second chance."

"Says you," I snapped.

"No, says the company. And now, I'm pretty sure your job at the State Department is over with as well."

"Not that big of a deal. It was a dead-end job anyway."

It was Denny's turn to exhale. "Jackie, don't throw this all away. You're a bright woman with a promising career. Just because you couldn't get into—"

"Listen, I'm gonna stop you right there. Denny, I don't think we should see each other anymore. I think you should just leave." The words were out of my mouth before I could stop them. Despite knowing that Denny was the only thing holding me together, I was tired of being criticized for my every move.

Denny didn't say anything. He just sat there, staring blankly at me. I could see the pain in his eyes, and it was killing me just as badly as it was killing him. But somehow, I stopped caring about that—and him—a long time ago.

"Can't ... I mean, can't we talk about this?" he begged.

I crawled from beneath the comforter and made my way to the front door. I opened it and stood there, waiting.

After a long moment, Denny finally got the hint. He stood, straightened his shirt, and walked past me and out the door. Without another word, I closed the door behind him and re-fastened all the locks.

"About time," I yelled.

With the thoughts of Denny already out of my mind, I stopped in the bathroom long enough to pee and grab a cup of water. I returned to my bedside with only one thing on my mind.

Getting back to my mission.

I flopped into bed, rolled to the other side, and swiftly opened my nightstand drawer. Inside lay a solitary item. A small pencil box with pink flamingos stenciled on it. I pulled out a small piece of parchment paper and slipped it beneath my tongue. Nearly instantly, I felt myself being pulled from one reality to another. Within moments I was back in the coffee house waiting for my large Americano.

9

The annoying din of a medical alarm brings me out of my stupor. I am groggy—far more so than from just being tired. I attempt to hold the vision of the coffee house in my mind, but the more I try, the faster it dissipates.

Instinctively, I rub the sleep from my eyes and glance around the room. I look for the source of the disturbing sound, and I see the doctor and an orderly as they huddle around a new patient. It appears to be a man, his gurney in thrasher man's vacated spot. His head is bandaged. Clearly, the next contestant on *Implant or No Implant*.

"Hey, doc," I try to speak, but my voice is scratchy and is barely heard over the screeching buzz. After a few moments, the alarm is finally squelched. "Hey."

Dr. Pierce either doesn't hear or is ignoring me. Before I can clear my throat and try again, she steps away and back out through the door.

I feel lightheaded and, although the spinning room is far less chaotic than it was yesterday, I feel as if I'm coming down from some bizarre acid trip from ... before? *How many drugs have I taken in my life?*

I fall back into my pillow, hoping to stabilize my discomfort. After a few moments, I feel that it's working. I sit up once again and look toward the orderly. He is just finishing up with the new patient before he steps up to my bedside.

"Good morning, 477. How are you feeling today?" he asks as he reviews the readouts behind my bed.

"I, uh. I'm not exactly sure. I, I don't really have any head pain to speak of, considering what's been done to me. I guess I've been here for three days now?" I ask.

"Actually, today is day four for you," he says. "Remember, you lost a day by sleeping in." He chuckles.

"And that's the thing. I don't remember. I'm having these weird dreams or memories, and just as soon as I wake up, they ... they virtually disappear. I'm having problems just remembering anything. Take this last dream for instance. I was—"

"I'm going to stop you right there, 477. It's probably best for you to not share those memories. They may, in fact, be yours, and they may be intimate or somehow protected to you. As you can see, this room has other occupants, and until you really know for sure, it's best to keep them to yourself."

"But don't you think after four days I should at least know who I am? I feel that I should be further along."

The orderly stares at me blankly. "Tell me, 477, how is it that you know this? Is this your experience after your previous procedure? Or is this your first one?"

I'm dumbfounded by his sarcasm. "Obviously, this is my first. I just feel that—"

"You're going to have to trust us. We've been doing these procedures for quite a while now, and believe me when I tell you this: You will get your memories back. And when they come to you," I sense he's fighting back a smirk by the look on his face, "you'll know completely that they're yours. But for now, the best thing I can tell you is to get more rest."

Before I can protest any further, he taps a few commands into the digital tablet and steps away and up to Ethan's bedside.

"How about you, 308? How are you feeling today?" he asks.

"To tell you the truth, Kevin, I think I'm ready to get out of here," Ethan says.

Kevin pulls up Ethan's medical charts and taps through a couple screens. "I'm sorry, 308, but it doesn't appear that you're scheduled to be discharged for another seventy-two hours."

Ethan sits up, reaches into his nightstand, and pulls something from inside. "Listen, Kevin. I've already been here for six days. All my memories have returned, and I feel great. I've gone through this procedure a few times now, and I think I know when I'm ready. Wouldn't you say, pal? Can you have another look at that chart?" As he says this, he reaches out and shakes Kevin's hand.

A look of surprise crosses Kevin's face as he examines what is certainly some form of monetary compensation in the palm of his hand. He instantly begins tapping on his tablet again. "Well, 308, I think you're right. I've made a few notes here, and it appears that unless the doctor disagrees with my comments, you're eligible for an early release. How does tomorrow afternoon sound?"

"Kevin, that sounds absolutely wonderful." Ethan leans back and crosses his outstretched legs.

"Hey! I saw that!" 596 yells from the other side of the room.

596. I forgot she was even here.

"If he can get out early, I want out too. Hold on, I think I have some credits here somewhere."

Kevin glances over as she rummages through her own nightstand, but before she can pull anything out, Kevin steps out through the door.

"Sonofabitch! It's not fair. How is it that you're getting out before me?" she howls.

"Listen, 596. It's not a race. It's just that, I don't know, I know how to get shit done." Ethan looks at me and winks.

I somehow sympathize with 596. As much as I don't know who I am, I feel I would be better off being outside of this facility.

"So, just passing him some credit gets you out early?" I ask as I move to the side of his bed.

"Well, there is no escape without escape. And as you can see, 477, there is more than one way to get out," Ethan says.

"Jesus, I'd be happy enough to just stop being so tired all the time."

"Well, baby, you can probably thank Kevin for that. I saw him tapping at his tablet before, and it looks like you're in for another bout of sleepy time."

"What do you mean?" I ask. "There are no tubes or wires connected to me whatsoever. How can they administer any-thing—"

Ethan taps at the back of his head. "It's the implant, darlin'. You see, it does all kinds of new things for you. Not only are you going to be able to turn the vid screen off with just a thought, but it's also quite bidirectional. Right now, you're inside this room, which is just a large Faraday cage—"

"Wait, what's a Faraday cage?" I ask.

Ethan smiles wide, clearly savoring his time in the spotlight. "Ah, the Faraday cage. It's not really a cage, per se, but more of a shield. In basic terms, it blocks any radio transmissions from passing in or out. In essence, the Harper Foundation here needs to protect everyone until you gain control of your implant."

I sigh heavily as I lean against Ethan's footboard. "Everything keeps coming back to this stupid implant."

"It's not all that bad. Your training hasn't begun yet, but it will, soon. They'll show you how to access and control the device like a pro. Until then, they can't let you out of this room because there's no stopping what you might do with a random thought. Hell, you might trigger some kind of global war because of monthly cramps." Ethan winks.

Until now, I've really tried to ignore all the chauvinistic remarks spewing from Ethan's mouth, but I'm unsure just how much more from the pig I can take. I look away, not wanting my anger to spill from my eyes.

"And although you can't quite make a connection to the outside world, the facility here has complete control over your mind. Right now, they're probably suppressing some, if not all, of your memories. All the while, they're adjusting the dopamine levels in your mind. They want you to sleep. They *need* you to sleep. Without sleep, you're not going to be able to heal properly."

"Jesus. What have I gotten myself into?" I mumble.

"Listen, Kevin isn't all that bad. He was a little snarky with you earlier, and I'm not sure what that's all about, but he's going to do the best for you. I just know it."

"That's a load of bullshit," 596 yells from the other side of the room. "All these people, they are crooked bastards!"

Ethan chuckles. "Or you can listen to her."

I shoot a quick glance in her direction, and she's sitting cross-legged in the middle of her bed, listening to every word we're saying.

"Kind of makes you wonder what else they can control in our minds," I say, only loud enough for Ethan to hear.

"Like I said," Ethan whispers, "there is no escape."

As I'm sifting all this new information into my mind, the room begins to tilt. Ethan notices and quickly backs me up to my bed. "Easy there, honey. You won't be doing yourself any favors if you happen to fall, now would you? Easy. That's right. Lay back." Ethan lifts my legs and slides them beneath the sheets. Before I can say anything else, his voice and image fade away, and darkness is once again my friend.

10

"I've had about enough of your attitude, Kevin," Dr. Pierce said.

"I'm sorry, doctor, but I'm not sure why we're spending so much effort on this druggie anyway," Kevin replied, staring in my direction.

"W—what's going on?" I murmured.

The doctor looked at me, and for a moment I think I saw compassion in her eyes. "I'm sorry to tell you this, 477, but it appears your body and mind are rejecting the implant. You've been here for nearly three weeks now, and without any advancement in memory recollection, we have no other alternative than to remove the device and purge your mind. I'm sorry."

Kevin burst out laughing. "Jesus, doctor. If we're going to scrub her mind, let's at least call her by her real name, wouldn't you agree, Ms. Blake?"

"Kevin! I said that's enough," the doctor snapped then began tapping the side of a hypodermic needle, releasing the air bubbles through its tip.

"No! I, I—I think I am getting things back. See, my name is ... it's Ms. Blake."

"Nice try there, druggie," Kevin snickered. "Tell me, Ms. Blake, what's your full name? Where were you born? Who is the president of—"

Before he could continue, Dr. Pierce lowered the hypodermic needle to my arm and began to slide it into my vein. Instinctively, I tried to pull away. But I couldn't. I looked down and saw that my arms were lashed, restrained to the sides of the bed. I was completely immobilized. "No! Give me another chance!"

"It's a little late for that," Kevin mocked. "You should have tried a little harder, you know? I bet all you could think about was getting your next bump, your next high."

"Kevin, what's gotten into you?" Dr. Pierce begged. "You know it's not nice to make fun of patients, when you know good and well that they are a lost cause."

I felt my heart pound faster, forcing my pulse to race. With all my might, I tried to pull my wrists from the restraints, but it was of no use. As a last resort, I began kicking my legs feverishly. I knew it wasn't going to help me escape, but at least it would release my pent-up anxiety. As my legs began thrashing from side to side, my own disturbance knocked the doctor's digital tablet to the floor. It bounced once on its edge then scattered underneath Ethan's bed.

"No! Help me!"

Kevin's head flung back as he continued to laugh hysterically.

A metallic clang echoes loudly around the room. I thrust myself forward, no longer held by imaginary restraints. I reach for my inside elbow, right where Dr. Pierce had injected me, to feel for tracks, but there are none.

Thank God, it was just a dream—or more like a nightmare.

I take several deep breaths and scan the room. To my left, Ethan is sitting up in his bed reading a magazine. Across the room, two orderlies work on either side of 596's bed, one of them Kevin and the other an unknown female trying to hold 596 down.

Feeling my heart rate return to normal, I look to Ethan for answers. "W—what's going on?"

Ethan doesn't look up. He continues turning pages in his magazine. "Good afternoon, 477. Have a nice nap?"

"Ethan! What the hell?" I blurt.

Ethan drops the magazine to his bed. "Well, right after you passed out this morning, 596 continued to carry on about how the Harper Foundation Is somewhat nefarious. She feels that they're doing some wild experiments on the patients without our knowledge." Ethan chuckles. "She really is losing it. I told her, just like I told you earlier, that she needs rest and that they're doing everything they can for a successful implant acceptance. I think if she's not careful, they will, no doubt, have to purge her."

"Jesus."

"That's an understatement, 477." Ethan picks up his magazine. "Everything they've tried to do to control her through her implant has failed. Now, as you can see, Kevin and Betty are trying to restrain her so that they can apply a more traditional approach to sedation."

I look over at 596 and briefly make eye contact with her. Then, quite suddenly, she winks at me.

What the hell?

And as if on cue, she increases her thrashing, knocking more things to the floor from her nightstand. Betty leaves Kevin to continue restraining her and begins gathering things up off the floor. As she's scurrying about on the ground, I see her key card precariously close to falling out of her pocket. I glance up at Ethan, and he's fully engrossed in his magazine article. I look back at Kevin, and he's turned away from me. I see my opportunity and decide to make a move.

I slip from the edge of my bed, and quick as a cat, slink up behind Betty. Silently, I lift the key card from her pocket and slip it into the front of my waistband, tucking it safely inside my underwear. As I turn around, I notice Ethan staring right at me. Almost imperceptibly, he shakes his head and smiles. His gesture catches me off guard and I'm momentarily frozen in position. Before I can move, I feel a pinch on the side of my neck and by the time I turn around, Kevin is pulling a hypodermic needle from my skin and I instantly become drowsy. *Shit.*

11

I stood alone, looking in the mirror, my own reflection staring back. What I saw now compared to what I remember seeing just a year ago had changed somehow, but not in every comparison. Today, wide, round eyes were set high in a narrow face. A thin, but slightly crooked nose separated pudgier cheeks than I'm terribly excited about. None of that was different. So, what was it? What was it that had detached the now me from myself before?

Confidence?

Sure headedness?

But isn't that really the same? Yes, no? Maybe, I don't know.

All I knew was that the reflection I saw staring back at me had changed, and I somehow knew right then that that reflection would continue to develop more drastically than I could ever imagine. I leaned toward the mirror, resting the palms of my hands on the stained tile countertop. As my nose neared the surface of the glass, my overly dilated eyes continued to adjust. With my vision focused, I spoke.

"You're going to get through this. You are a strong woman. Don't let—"

"Don't let what?" Stephanie interrupted from behind me.

She stepped out of a toilet stall, which strangely, I thought was empty. "Come on, finish what you were going to say."

I felt my cheeks blush, and I pulled away from the mirror. "Oh, nothing. I'm just trying to cope with the bad news, you know. Are you having a fun night?" I asked praying for a subject change.

"It's going to be okay, A.J." She walked up and pulled me into a warm embrace.

Just like best friends were supposed to.

I hugged her back and fought away the tears that were brimming behind my eyes.

"And yes, we're all having a blast. I know it's not a celebration, per se, but we're here for you, just remember that."

I searched my mind for the right words, but none came. I stood there like an imbecile, suddenly realizing that maybe Trident was right. Maybe I didn't have what it took. By the time I thought of something proper to say, Stephanie had already touched up her lipstick and was already walking out of the bathroom.

Barely feeling the effects of my second cocktail, I felt that it was time to continue with the imbibing. I touched up my own lipstick and rinsed the grimy bar smell from my hands and went to rejoin my friends.

"Honey, what took you so long? I thought you got lost. Then Stephanie came out and told me about your, shall we say—"

"Please don't. Not really in the mood," I glowered probably a little too much, but *c'est la vie*. "What I am in the mood for, though, is another cosmopolitan. Would you be a dear and get me another drink?"

I slumped into an overstuffed lounge chair, trying to ignore the pungent smell of spilled beer, probably still present from the night before. I glanced at Denny, puckered my lips, and blew him a kiss. "Please?" I batted my eyelashes, an attempt to portray the young, innocent girl that I once saw in my own reflection.

"Sure thing, babe. It's just that, I don't know, I know we're here to try to get your mind off of Trident, but we've only been here for an hour and you've been throwing them back like a sailor. I just don't want you to regret anything from tonight."

I smiled and took a slow, deep breath. I did my best to hold steady, despite my unwavering feeling. "I know, I just ... I'll be fine."

Denny smiled and brushed the back of his hand along my cheek as he walked off.

As I sat alone, I looked out across the club, recognizing all the familiar faces from my life. I saw Stephanie and her girlfriend Trish. Katie and Meg, old college roommates from over the years. And there was Molly and Brad—whom I had no idea were coming—walking right toward me.

"My God! It's been like forever," I exclaimed as I stood up far too quickly and nearly toppled over. I rushed over and hugged her hard. "I didn't even know you were in town."

"It just so happens that Brad and I were visiting my dad when Denny called. He told me the news about the job and about the gathering. Honey, I'm so sorry."

I brushed aside her apology. "It's all right. There's something else out there for me. I know it." *But it still hurts.*

"So obviously, we couldn't miss seeing you while we were in town. You look wonderful, by the way."

I knew she was lying. I had cried all day yesterday and most of today, and thankfully Denny helped me get cleaned up. "Thanks, I appreciate it." I motioned to the lounge chairs and we sat down.

"So, what's next?" Her voice was tender and just as I remembered it from high school.

"I'm not sure yet. I've been so focused on getting on as an overt agent for so long, and I've lived my life in earnest because of that." I paused. "I don't know, I feel that I need to ... spread my wings a little bit, you know? Get some piercings, maybe. And I don't know, maybe get a devil tattoo on my forearm." I winked.

"My God, you haven't changed a bit. You still have the same sense of humor. But, if you're going to get a tattoo of the devil, just make sure that he's wearing a bikini!"

We both laughed far too heartily. "Seriously, though. Not sure if I'll get a tattoo right away, but you know, all those things that I put off? You know, keeping my body as pristine and un-distinguishable as possible—not doing drugs and staying relatively safe with alcohol—all to just shine brighter in Trident's eye? It was all for nothing. I feel that, I don't know, I need to live a little. With Trident off the table, I guess that—"

"Are you serious? We all thought you were the sane one for abstaining from all the wildness. We thought you had your head on straight, and not just because of a potential job; we thought you really had your shit together." Molly inched closer and lowered her voice a few octaves. "Don't fall into that trap. I know Brad's better now, but Jesus, getting him off his addictions has been an uphill battle, let me tell you."

"I know. It's just that I feel I've lost something because of that goddamn company."

Before we could continue, Denny returned with my drink and with Brad in tow. He handed me my cosmo.

"Honey! Why didn't you tell me they were coming?" I took the drink and nearly downed half of it in one gulp. I flinched a little from the burn, then smiled.

"I wanted it to be a surprise, babe." He took a drink himself. "Tell me you we're surprised."

"Yeah, you got me, all right." I finished off the meager size drink and instantly felt thirsty again.

For the next hour, we continued chatting and laughing and catching up—and having more drinks. Far more than I should have had, but I kept telling myself, *It's okay. I deserve this, because* ... I don't know why, but I did.

And as much as I remained centered in the conversation, my mind was elsewhere. I wondered how things would be different if the news had gone the other way. I certainly wouldn't be out getting trashed. I'd be almost certainly packing my bags, getting ready to head off to Quantico or wherever they hold their training ops.

After countless cosmos, nature called, and I excused myself. I stumbled off to powder my nose, and as I neared the women's room door, I happened to pass a rather handsome guy. His angular jaw was muscular, showcasing the perfect amount of stubble. His hair was shoulder-length that just barely draped across the bluest eyes that I think I'd ever seen. I nearly melted right there.

"H—hi there," I stammered. I prayed that Denny wasn't in earshot. It wasn't at all like myself to try and flirt with a complete stranger.

He smiled wide, and the glint of a gold tooth flashed back at me. "How are you doin' tonight?"

"Hmm, my night could be better, thanks for asking. I'm just," I gestured toward the bathroom, unsure of really what to say in the situation.

"Ah, yes the lavatory," he said. "So, you come here often?"

"The restroom?" I glanced toward the door again. "Only when I have to, you know..." I joked.

We chuckled for a moment, neither of us willing to step away from one another.

"Listen, I usually don't do this to a complete stranger, even one as attractive as yourself, but here goes." He paused and pulled out a business card; attached to it was a small sticker. "I think this little bump will make your evening much more enjoyable. And if I'm right, which I think I am, you'll be reaching out for more. This is my boss' card."

He slid the card inside my blouse, until his fingers touched the warmth of my skin. At that moment, I felt a small shock.

"Thanks, but I'm not really into that kind of thing."

"How do you know what kind of thing it is until you try it? Now, if you'll excuse me, I have to return to my friends."

Before I could reply, he was gone. I continued into the restroom and took care of business. As I stood at the sink, my reflection again staring back, I glimpsed the edge of the business card protruding from my blouse. I pulled it out and stared at it. The sticker was small, in the shape of a pink flamingo. I looked at it closer and it said, "lick me." And there I was, having lived 25 years of my life without ever taking an adventure.

I dropped the acid like a pro, then looked back at my reflection. I stared at myself for several moments, curious how quickly it took effect. I wondered if the dose was strong enough, or if I actually did it right.

I shrugged and turned toward the exit. As I walked, I glanced down at the card. On its backside was a single name: Antoine.

"Antoine," I said aloud. *I don't think I've ever known a man named Antoine.*

12

With my head pounding, I rub the sides of my temples, wishing for the pain to subside. When I finally open my eyes, the room is nearly pitch black. All that illuminates are the various medical display screens. I look over, and Ethan is facing away from me, asleep. Across from me, 596's bed is empty.

I lean back and try to make sense of my latest dream. *Was it a dream?* Or something from my own memories? Who were all those people? Molly, Brad. Stephanie … Denny? I don't remember a single person. But clearly in the dream they were all real and somehow meant something to me. And what about that bit with me and my reflection? *Is that really what I look like?*

With these thoughts filtering through my head, I don't recall seeing my own reflection since I've been here. *Maybe that was me.* I make a mental note to find a mirror as soon as the lights come back on.

As the identities begin to fade from my mind, two names continue to resonate. Antoine, a common presence from most of my dreams. And Trident—I don't even know the name's origin but, I somehow feel that it's important. Are they connected? Is Antoine part of Trident? I just wish I knew who the hell I was.

Then, I get a sudden thought.

"Ethan, you awake?" I say as I look toward him. He doesn't even move. "Hey, Ethan!"

Nothing.

Still experiencing a bit of wooziness, I feel that despite Ethan's chauvinistic tendencies, he has a lot of knowledge about this place and how things work around here. Maybe if I share my thoughts with him, he could shine some light on what it all means.

I pull myself up and drop my feet toward the floor. As I inch off the bed, I feel a sudden stab of pain near my pelvis.

"Ouch!" I yelp.

I fall back and reach for the discomfort. But just as I do, the pain subsides. *What the hell?*

Feeling no sense of modesty, I pull my pajama bottoms down to my knees, lift my top, and find Betty's key card protruding from the top of my underwear.

"Son of a bitch," I gasp. I was certain they would have taken it back after they neutralized me. But now that I still have it, I wonder ...

I quickly pull my bottoms back up and rush toward the door. I look for a scanning panel but find nothing. I remember, quite clearly, that Kevin—or whoever the orderly was that night—scanned his card somewhere next to the door. I run my hand up and down the wall, feeling for any kind of imperfection. I find nothing. "What the hell," I say as I slide the key card next to the door frame. An audible click echoes through the room.

For several moments, I stand there. Partly because I'm actually quite shocked that they didn't deactivate the card the moment they discovered it was missing. But mostly because I have no plan. Am I going to get out of here? Or should I, I don't know, see if I can find—

That's when it hits me. *My mission.* Well, the mission I was thinking of earlier. I need to find my identity. And perhaps if I were to find the doctor's office, I could maybe access her digital tablet for the information I need. I glance back at Ethan's sleeping body and decide to interrogate him later.

With that, I step through the door.

I stand in a dimly lit hallway, and thankfully no one else is in sight. I turn around and slowly close the door, noting the room number: SUB-512. I note the peculiarity of the prefix designation and wonder if I'm five stories up or five stories down. Either way, I'm quite a ways away from just walking out the front door.

I glance up and down the corridor and find both directions look identical. They carry on for around twenty meters or so in each direction before veering off.

Left or right?

With of lack of any other information, I decide to go left. Why? I have no idea. As I do, the room numbers decrease numerically. All with the same prefix SUB. I figure that when I reach room 500, I'll probably be closest to the central core of the building. And logic tells me that when I get there, I will most certainly find vertical circulation.

Room 511.

Room 510.

Rooms 509 through 502 alternate on either side of the hallway as I move. Where I expect to see rooms 501 and 500, I find a blank wall. Then the corridor ends. To the right, I can see it leading off for another three or four meters where the hallway terminates at a single door, with the label electrical.

Left it is.

I continue ahead and find a bank of elevators on the right. There's no call button and no indication of what level I'm on.

I move past the elevator, and I come to another junction of corridors. I decide to stay left for no other reason than being consistent. As I round the corner, I come across the first sign of egress. There's a door with the label exit, along with the image of a stick figure person climbing a set of stairs. Below that, there's an arrow pointing up.

I'm momentarily conflicted. I've found a way out and, according to the signage, I am in some kind of basement, an explanation for the SUB prefix on all the rooms.

Do I go for my escape, or do I try and find my identity?

Realizing that I don't know when I'll have this opportunity again, I decide on freedom. As I step forward and place my hands on the panic bar, I suddenly see a sign on the edge of the doorframe.

Alarm will sound when door is opened.

I freeze.

Pressing the panic bar on the door would most certainly end any chance for my escape. And in turn, keep me from learning my identity. I slowly step back and take a deep breath.

"That was close," I murmur. And honestly, finding out who I am and *then* searching for escape makes the most sense. As I continue down the corridor, the names Trident and Antoine echo inside my head.

After several minutes of randomly combing the corridors, I realize that I've not encountered another living soul. No one. No late-night attendant—no janitorial staff. Nobody.

Defeat creeps in, and I contemplate returning to SUB-512 and waking Ethan. Maybe he could tell me the location of the doctor's office. As these thoughts filter through my mind, I turn the corner and see an open door; a stream of light splashes out into the hallway. I can faintly hear a voice. It's Dr. Pierce.

Jesus!

I silently creep up and peer inside. I pull back just as fast to analyze what I saw. There was Dr. Pierce standing in front of an examination chair with a person strapped in. Unfortunately, the doctors body blocked me from seeing who it was.

I have to take another look.

I grip the edge of the door jam and lean my head around. Dr. Pierce is moved out of sight, and I have a clear shot of the patient. It's 596. The look on her face mirrors my own feeling of shock. I gesture to her a look of question, and I raise my hands in the air.

She looks toward the far side of the room where I can't see, most likely to where the doctor is and glances back. She nods her head in the opposite direction and mouths the words *doctor's office. Go.*

I nod my thanks and slip past the open door. After a few meters, I come upon the first nurse's station that I've found since my little expedition began. Thankfully, it's empty. And tucked behind it I see a short hallway leading off to several private offices.

Bingo.

As I move past the vacant desk, the first door I come to is labeled supplies. Across the hall and to the left, the door is labeled mop closet. I move on.

A few meters further, I come across what I've been looking for all along. Dr. Pierce is stenciled boldly across the door. Now, the moment of truth. Does Dr. Pierce leave her door unlocked?

I rest my hand on the door lever and push. To my surprise, and my great fortune, it's unlocked. I step through and close the door. I turn and find a modest-sized room. On one side there's a small conference table with half a dozen chairs around it. On the other, there is a modern executive desk with a credenza behind it. I see no file cabinet anywhere. And nor should I. This is the 21st century, right?

I move to the desk and tap a few times at the escape key on the keyboard. The desired result rings true as the monitor lights up.

Doom mounts, as at the center of the digital screen, there's an open dialog box and the words: enter password.

How do I get in? I wonder.

Then, out of the blue, I have the sudden urge to touch the keyboard. I reach out with both hands and in a sudden rapid-fire of movement, my fingers dance across the keyboard, just as quickly as various popups stream across the screen. Moments later, I am past the login screen and have full access.

"Where the hell did that come from?" I question.

A voice echoes inside my head. "You're welcome, now hurry."

Although I'm shocked at the strangeness, I agree with the urgency.

I locate the computer's file structure and begin filtering through patient files. I move swiftly, looking for a few key elements of my identity.

Female, obviously.

My approximate age.

And ... the initials A.J.; a remnant from my latest memory flashback.

As fast as I can, I open a file and do a quick scan. If nothing jumps out as a potential identity, I move on. As I eliminate file after file, the exhilaration begins to mount.

And then the strange voice again enters my head. "Hurry up!"

"I'm trying," I say aloud. *Who the hell am I talking to?*

There is no answer.

As I pass through the last of the open patient files, I begin to wonder if I actually missed my own file, not really knowing my name. Maybe A.J. is not an indication of who I am but maybe just a nickname. Failure sets in as I close the final patient file. Then, I see it. At the lower edge of the screen, I see a file with the symbol of a lock on it. The title, Trident. Instinctively I click it. And then, more doom. Another password prompt.

Unsure on how I actually made it through the first login screen, I'm doubtful if I could do it again. Without any other recourse, I try the same approach.

"How do I get in?"

And just as before, I begin randomly hacking into the system. As my fingers move across the keyboard, invalid password continues to flash across the screen. *Oh, shit.*

Then I hear it. The strange voice again. "Get out now."

Jesus, it's 596's voice. "Just a few more minutes," I say. "I'm almost—"

"No! Get out now. The doctor just left the exam room."

As 596's words echo in my head, my fingers halt instantly. The unknown force that was controlling them quickly shifts gears and shuts down the computer. In the blink of an eye, I'm at the edge of the door, peeking into the hallway.

Vacant.

I slip out and traipse silently toward the nurse's station. As I near the desk, I hear footsteps around the corner. I lunge for the storage closet and disappear inside. I stand there, the door cracked slightly to maintain view. As soon as the doctor passes by, and into her office, I retrace my steps back to SUB-512.

13

The following morning, I awake. As I lay there, my eyes fixated on the stark, white ceiling above, a million questions swim through my mind. First and foremost, *who am I?* Somehow, I feel like I'm getting closer to learning my identity. All the dreams that I've been experiencing are becoming more familiar somehow. The thought of it, in itself, is quite scary. *Was I really that into the drugs?* I shiver at the thought.

Further, who the hell is Trident? And why did they have all that double security bullshit on the computer? Clearly, they are a part of my past, and most certainly part of my present. Also, very concerning.

And what the hell was that about 596 being in my head? Is that even possible? Is that part of this stupid impl—

"Hey, there's my girl," Ethan says, pulling me out of my thoughts.

Would you give it a break? I'm not your girl, I think to myself.

I look at Ethan, and he is dressed in regular clothes, no longer wearing the teal colored hospital-wear that everyone else is sporting. He's sorting through various items scattered across his bed. One by one, he slides them into a leather satchel. "Uh, hey. What's with all that?" I ask.

"It's my stuff. When you check in, they take all your personal belongings and toss them in a locker. You get them back if you leave."

If?

"How was your adventure last night, by the way?"

"How the hell? I don't—"

"Don't worry, 477. Your secret is safe with me. I was awake when you left last night, but I didn't hear you come back in."

"How is it that you know so much?" I sit up and situate a pillow behind my back.

"It's a gift, babe. So, did you find your escape?"

With really no answers to any of my questions, I feel like it's best to trust Ethan, even if just a little bit. So, I share.

"Well, I did find the exit stairwell, and do you know that we're underground?"

He nods.

"But as enticing as getting away sounded, I decided to venture off and find Dr. Pierce's office. I need to find out who I am." I continue to tell Ethan about the evening's activities. At least up until I discovered Trident's double security. I just don't know what it all means yet, so for the moment, I keep that part to myself. "My biggest question, or at least my newest question, is how the hell did 596 get into my head?"

Ethan sits on the edge of my bed. "You remember our conversation about the Faraday cage?"

I nod.

"Well, it's because you were outside of this room. I gather you probably had some other strange experiences as well?"

"There was that moment when I was getting past the security login on the computer. How did that happen?"

"That could be part of your connection with 596." Ethan stopped and looked toward her vacant bed. "Or ... have you contemplated the thought that it could actually be you? Maybe you were a hacker in your previous life."

"Previous life? You say it as if I were dead or something."

"Sorry, honey. I didn't mean it like that."

For the first time, I notice that Ethan is somewhat uncomfortable. Not in his character.

"So, after getting through the security block, what did you find? Did you see your file?"

"Not quite. I thought I was getting close, but that's when 596 told me to get out. I just shut everything down before I could get through the ... last few files," I lie.

For several moments, we sit in silence. Ethan's awkwardness continues. I decide to break the lull.

"So, Ethan, what's your plan now that you're upgraded? Going back to your gigolo job?"

He laughs out loud. "You're so close, but no. Not a gigolo. To be honest, I'm looking forward to returning to my 75th story luxury loft. My butler's been taking care of things while I've been away and ..." Ethan drones on about his lavish life and how he's a self-made man and how the implant is going to improve everything that he does and make him this extraordinary person. I almost gag. *Almost.*

"Well, great. At least you have that going for you," I say, my words dripping with sarcasm.

"Hey, baby, don't knock it until you try it." He stands up and moves quickly to the side of his bed. His hand disappears inside his satchel, and a moment later he's standing back near me.

"Listen, I'm going to do you a solid. I've got this ... thing. Don't let the doctors know you have it, or we'll both be in a heap of trouble." He slips what can only be described as a computer chip encased in resin into my hand. "This is your ticket. You know the implant has Wi-Fi. But inside the Faraday cage, we all know that it's useless. We've all covered that. This baby will allow you—or at least allow your mind—outside. It's not perfect, but it has its advantages."

I turn the device over in my hand a few times and hand it back to him. "Thank you, no. I don't think I need it."

"Baby, in this new world that you're now thrust into, not everything is as it seems." He pauses. "For example, unless I pointed out that this was a Faraday cage, you would've never known. Am I right?"

"Yeah, I guess."

"There are more Faraday cages in the city than anyone would ever know. And it's strictly because there are people in this world that don't want their information to leave their possession uncontrolled. As glorious as your new implant has the potential to be, there's always the need to have a backup." He hands the device back to me. "This is how you get jacked."

I listen to his words and contemplate what he says. I'm tempted to give it back again.

"You see, you just plug it in at the base of your neck." He turns his head and points to his own implant. "You insert it right here, see?" He turns back toward me. "This way you can enjoy the benefits of the implant even when you can't enjoy them fully. Like right now. Trust me when I tell you this. This will be a lifesaver for you. And, as an added bonus, I'm including a little somethin' somethin' just for you." He winks. "Just plug it in, and the first one's on me."

Jesus, I don't need drugs. If that's really what he's implying. *Is that how he made all his money?*

Irritated, I shove it back into his hand.

"Come now, honey. I don't think you quite understand what you do and do not need at this particular moment. Take it. No strings attached. Think about it, and if you realize that it's something that you want, give me a shout, because I have more where this comes from."

"But I don't even know you. How would I even—"

Before I can finish my words, Ethan leans in as if he's going to kiss me. When his lips are practically touching my own, his forehead bumps into mine, and he blinks. A moment later I have a vivid image of his contact information.

"How the hell did you do that? I thought we were in a Faraday cage."

"We are. You can't connect to outside of the room, but you can connect with anyone else inside if you're close enough. It's kind of like that old ad hoc technology. You must be within inches, but it works. You just need the person's address. Kind of like your personal Rolodex, really."

"But how did you know my address? I don't even know—"

Ethan points to the medical display behind my bed. "You see your patient number, 477, followed by the thirteen digits? That's your address. Memorize it. If anybody asks you for it, that's what you'll need to transfer your information. Although, rumor has it that they're developing additional technologies that by simply touching a person, the personal information will be transmitted. But until that is introduced, probably in the next software update, you'll need your code."

As I process Ethan's info dump, I realize that he's still precariously close to my lips. I look at them and wonder, *should I?*

Before I can finish the thought, Kevin walks through the door, a wheelchair in tow.

"Are you ready, 308? It's time for your checkout."

"No need, my friend," Ethan says as he steps past the wheelchair. "I can walk out just fine. Lead the way, kind sir." Ethan grabs his satchel and walks out the door.

14

And just like that, I'm alone. Well, the patient across the room is here. But he's still unconscious, so I don't think he counts.

I focus my attention on the device. I toss it around in my hands a few times, as if I'm waiting for it to tell me what to do. From my memories—assuming they're actually *my* memories and not hallucinations like the doctor has said—I am susceptible to drug addiction. And if that's the case, did Ethan know that? Ethan himself has more knowledge about this place and its operation than I think any one patient should. Granted, he did tell me that this was his third procedure so maybe he's on a first name basis with everyone. He did call the orderlies by name.

I just wish I knew something concrete about myself.

A. J.—is that my nickname?

Do I prefer uppers or downers?

Am I a moaner, as Ethan so piggishly stated?

As I continue to stare at the device, I wonder what specific allure Ethan has mixed up for me.

I glance at the door and wonder how much time I have before either a new patient is brought in to fill Ethan's space or when they bring 596 back, assuming that they do.

I close my eyes and begin to filter through the memories once more. What does it all mean? As I remember the latest dream—the one with the acid—I have a sudden craving deep from inside. Is it the hallucinogenic aspect that I want? Is it just an escape?

I think back to the earliest memory I had here, and it was something quite different. It was more of a suppressant nature. I sense a craving there as well, but it's contrasting in nature.

Screw it.

I reach up to remove the bandage from the back of my neck. My hairs stick to the tape, and it's quite painful as I pull. I can't see what I'm doing, but I use my fingers to guide me. As I do so, I feel tenderness to my touch. As I trace my fingers around the port, I can feel the sutures holding it in place. Surprisingly, there's no real pain there as I gently add pressure. But it still sends shivers down my spine because of the unnatural aspect of the entire ordeal.

Fuck! I can't do it.

I reapply the bandage and throw the device against the wall. It's so lightweight it barely makes a sound before it drops to the floor. I can feel my heart race as I clench my fists.

Deep breath. I need to breathe.

But what if there's something else? What if there's more to it than just a synthetic drug? Ethan did say that this is my ticket to gain access when access is not possible. I scamper from my bed and snatch up the device. Am I just convincing myself that I need this?

No. I don't need it.

Yes, I do. The craving deep within me increases. I reach back and barely touch the edge of the tape when the door clicks open.

I stare, dumbfounded, as Kevin wheels 596 in. Her head is slumped forward, and I can't quite see if she's awake. Betty follows, and the two of them remove the restraints from her wrists and lift her onto her bed. As they refasten her bindings, I sit silently. I suddenly realize I have the device out in plain view with my hand pulling my bandage off. I quickly slip the device under my shirt and tuck it into the bottom edge of my bra. Just as I pull my hand out, Kevin steps aside and I glimpse 596's face. She glances up imperceptibly but remains stoic with her gaze.

Within moments, Kevin and Betty wheel the empty chair out of the room, paying me no attention. As soon as the door clicks shut, I rush up to 596.

"Hey, you okay?" I ask.

For a long moment, 596 lays there, her head resting sideways. I think she might be unconscious, but I see her lips move, and she sniffs slightly. "They gone?" she whispers.

"Yeah, just now."

Then 596 perks up as if nothing is wrong. "I thought they'd never leave."

"What the hell's going on? Why did they take you away, and why are you in restraints?" I ask as I rattle the handcuffs around her right wrist.

"I've had my suspicions for a while now, and I had to do something."

"Suspicions of what?" I ask.

With some effort, 596 looks around the room and tries to sit up. I slide a pillow behind her so she's more comfortable. "I thought they were doing experiments on us without our knowledge—or our permission, for that matter. And the only way to get into the lab myself was to cause the distraction. It certainly worked, I can tell you that."

"They can't be. They just let Ethan out not even twenty minutes ago. If they were running experiments, why would they—"

"Ethan? Is that what his name was?" 596 looks at the vacant bed.

Shit. I wonder if that was intimate between he and I. "Yeah, he told me his name a few days ago. I—I guess it doesn't really mean much now that he's gone."

"Well, if we're in the sharing mood, my name is Sloan. Sloan Lamont." She looks at me questioningly, as if waiting for me to return confidential information.

"Sloan Lamont. Nice to meet you, I guess is the proper response. I wish I could tell you who I am, but I still got nothing."

"Even after your little adventure yesterday? You couldn't find anything on yourself?"

Images of the previous night still fresh in my mind, I contemplate how much I should share. Certainly not Trident and possibly not even anything about the hacking ability. "No, I was trying to make progress but ... wait a minute, that was you helping me, right? Please say yes because I don't think I can handle the fact that I was hearing voices in my head."

Sloan chuckles. "Yeah, that was me. That aspect of the implant is pure gold. Then, after I saw you snatch Betty's key card—quick thinking, by the way—I memorized your address."

"Thanks. I just wish it would've paid off somehow."

"Maybe it will, still."

I have no idea what she means by that. "So, what did they do to you? When I passed by that room, you were in some kind of examination chair. Were your suspicions confirmed?"

Sloan looks away, her eyes never focusing on any one spot. "I—I guess, I can't really say. I was unconscious for a lot of the time and," she pauses and finally looks up at me, "when I was awake, they were really just in the room with me at one of the computer terminals. I just don't know what to think. I—I can only pull up a blank for that time."

"No shit?" I exhale slowly. As I process the information from Sloan and try to fit it in with everything Ethan's told me over the past few days, it's like their two stories don't match up. And that's worrisome. My mind flashes back to my dreams ... and to the drugs. I stand there silently as I feel strange cravings deep within.

"Hey, you still there?" Sloan asks.

"Yeah, I'm just, I don't know. I just wish I knew what to do."

"I can tell you what I'd do. You still have the key card, right?"

I nod.

"Good. If I were you, I would get out of this place, like right now. I just saw the doctor leave for the day, so there's one less obstacle to deal with. My guess is that the orderlies are off this level as well, so you're going to meet a lot less resistance now than you would at another time during the day."

What Sloan is saying makes sense.

"Can we get you out of your restraints? You can go with," I say.

"Unless you're good at reprograming a bio-lock, I'm here for the long haul."

I look down at her wrist, and something about the lock seems familiar, but I can't quite put my finger on it. *Another memory from my previous life?*

"There has to be some kind of—"

"Just go. I'll be fine. Save yourself. And if they come in, I'll make something up. I'll try to buy you some time. So, just go."

15

I step into the hall and silently close the door. I glance to my left and then to my right as I try to recall the shortest route to the elevator. Within seconds, my mind flashes the clearest path.

Do I have photographic memory? I wonder.

I sprint down the hall and quickly notice the sound of my bare feet slapping on the tile floor. I slow my pace enough that my movement becomes silent. I note that the corridors are much different now than they were last night, a fact brilliantly displayed due to the lights at full illumination.

As I come to the first corner, I inch up to the edge before I peer around. As soon as the path is clear, I move. And just as before, my pace is quick but silent.

Then, a chilling sound echoes through the hallway. A magnetic lock from one of the rooms.

I stop. Unaware of the exact direction it came from, I can only think about retracing my steps. Slowly, I back around the last corner. I freeze, my back glued to the wall.

I wait.

I wait and I listen.

I hear footsteps, and they seem to get fainter. I risk a glance around the corner and see the back of an unknown orderly walking away from me.

Deep breath.

I return to my path and contemplate whether I should take the stairs or the elevator. If I use the stairwell, the alarm will most certainly sound, and my escape may be compromised. If I use the elevator, I risk exposure. Someone may be in the lift and I'm not exactly dressed in street clothes.

I approach the next corner. I tuck up to the edge and confidently peer around. I see several people in the distance. I pull back and think.

Shit, Sloan told me it's supposed to be less busy now.

I consider the fact that she may be nefarious herself. I contemplate returning to my room, but the gravity of the situation and the desire to get out is strong. I move ahead.

I peek around the corner again, and the mingling people are gone. I move forward. Within moments, I pass by the exit stairwell, apparently deciding to use the elevator. I don't question my internal judgment and move quickly. Just one more corner and then I'm almost clear.

If these auxiliary corridors are this occupied, the main corridor will most certainly have far more people. I guess I will cross that bridge when I get there.

I come to the final junction and pause. I take several deep breaths before I peer around the corner. And to my surprise, not a person is in sight. I see the elevator, and I quickly retrieve the key card from my underwear. I race ahead and swipe the card along the wall next to the doors. I see no indication that the lift is on that's way, and the longer I stand there waiting, the more I realize I am a lame-duck.

In the distance, about twenty meters down the hall, a door clicks open, and out steps Dr. Pierce. She sees me instantly.

Jesus, I am truly fucked now.

The urge to run to my room and play dumb instantly crosses my mind, but I dismiss the thought quickly. I have about a moment before I'll be forced to run.

Come on, damnit. Where's the lift?

As Dr. Pierce casually walks toward me, she lifts her wrist up to her mouth and whispers conspiratorially.

Well, I guess that's it. I must go for the stairwell.

I turn and run at full speed. I round the corner, not even pausing to see if anyone's there. I am full-bore sprinting toward my freedom. When I arrive at the exit stairwell, I slap the card against the wall and hear an audible click. I hit the panic bar and rush through.

As warned, the audible alarm echoes throughout the shaft. I take the stairs two steps at a time. I turn at the first landing and sprint even faster, increasing my pace to three steps. Within moments, I make it to sublevel three. Unfortunately, as I approach the landing, the door opens, and Betty, accompanied by an unknown man, block my way. The man is holding a cylindrical device. Not a gun, not a nightstick. It's something that I've not seen before.

I turn about and start back down the stairway to sublevel four.

Perhaps I can get out through there.

As I get to the doorway, I once again slide the key card along the wall, but nothing happens.

Fuck.

I continue down the stairwell hoping, praying that I can get through into sublevel six. I don't know how much further down it goes, but I'm sure I could continue going until I find a doorway that opens.

I move as fast as I can without losing balance and tumbling to my death.

As I reapproach sublevel five, the door opens just as I arrive. Standing in the doorway is Dr. Pierce and Kevin. My momentum carries me nearly into their arms, and I do my best to veer to the side, to continue down the stairwell.

Just as I think I'm clear, I feel the pinch on the back of my arm, and my body instantly goes numb. I drop to the floor, physically neutralized. My mind is alert for a moment before my vision goes dark.

16

As I sat three rows back in the lecture hall, I watched the clock tick painfully slowly. Professor Hamilton droned on—as he normally did—attempting to bring passion and excitement to the world of *cyber logistics*. But at that moment, my mind had already left the class and was halfway to my dorm to pack my bags for a long weekend with the girls.

"... and that concludes today's lecture on *advanced firewall protocols*. And before you all log off for the weekend, be sure to note that I have advanced the due date for the essay on *global networking initiatives,* from Wednesday night until Monday afternoon."

Hamilton's class only included about forty students, and of those in attendance, eighty percent of them groaned lamely.

"I know, I know. This is a last-minute change, but that paper is something that you've all been working on all semester. If you're waiting until the final moments to get it written, that is quite unfortunate on your time planning skills. The world is going throw you curveballs, and that's just a fact of life. And with that, enjoy your weekend."

One by one, the class began to disperse. The sound of chairs screeching along the floor and backpacks being crammed with laptops echoed about. My bag was already packed, and I was almost to the door when I heard the professor call out, "Also, Ms. Blake, if you could stand by for a moment? I'd like to have a word with you."

Crap, I don't have time for this.

I froze in my tracks, causing another student to nearly run me over as he tried to get out of the lecture hall before his name was called as well. I stepped aside and let my aisle clear out. After a few moments, the rest of the students had vacated, leaving the professor and myself, along with a man that I just now noticed sitting on the far side of the lecture stage.

"Ms. Blake, would you come down here for a moment? There's a gentleman I'd like you to meet."

I slung my backpack and traipsed down the theater steps to the lower level. All the while, I studied the man's appearance as he studied mine. He was elderly, my guess is in his late fifties. He had a receding hairline that was thinning. His full beard was speckled with patches of gray. He was dressed casually in corduroy trousers and a knitted vest over a light blue, button-down shirt.

As I arrived at the professor's desk, the stranger pulled a chair out for me. "Please, Ms. Blake, if you wouldn't mind." He motioned toward the chair.

"What's this all about, professor?" I asked as I sat.

"It's nothing to be terribly concerned about. I've been paying quite a bit of attention to your work throughout the semester, and you are one of my top students."

Tell me something that I don't know, I thought.

"And with exceeding achievement comes preferential treatment. I'd like you to meet Roger Denninger. He's a colleague of mine from ... another time of my life. He's asked me to introduce him to a few of my students that have exceeded in all levels of their academic life."

Okay, my mind is officially blown.

"Um, thank you?" I said, wishing I could take the questioning gratitude back instantly. "I am honored, is what I meant to say."

Denninger chuckled. "It's quite all right. It's okay to be nervous, but I assure you, there's no need. Thank you, professor. Would you mind giving Ms. Blake and myself a few moments alone?"

Hamilton nodded and silently retreated into his private office. As soon as his door closed, Denninger continued. "So, Ms. Blake, are you familiar with the GSA?"

Am I ever! I tried my best to not sound overly excited.

"Yes, I believe you mean the Global Security Agency. To be honest, Mr. Denninger, the agency is on my radar upon graduating."

Denninger smiled. "That's wonderful to hear. And how close are you to completing your degree?"

Come now, I thought. He has to know exactly when I'm going to graduate if he's from the GSA.

"I'm in the third year of my bachelors' program, but I am contemplating extending it into a Masters," I said confidently.

"Tell me, have you taken any classes on covert affairs or espionage training?"

"I'm sorry? Are those even offered here?"

"I'll take that as a no. But I believe they are. Maybe inquire with your professor for the full syllabus."

Where was he going with these questions?

"How about extracurricular activities; do you partake in recreational drugs? And how about the levels of your alcohol consumption?"

"I have a few drinks with my friends from time to time, but nothing out of the ordinary. As for drug use, as I've said, I'm aware of the GSA and I know what's acceptable and what's frowned upon."

Denninger slipped an impossibly thin tablet from his shirt pocket and began jotting down notes. "How about any distinguishing marks on your person? Any birthmarks that are notable? How about any body art; tattoos?"

Seriously, what's with the third degree?

"None of note," I said, feeling a little apprehensive.

Denninger continued entering notes into his tablet, leaving us in complete silence.

"Ms. Blake, I see here that you are precisely thirty-six credit hours away from graduating. Would you be willing to terminate your studies early if an opportunity presented itself?"

"How early? I am so close to—"

"Immediately. We have ... a situation where time is of the essence."

"To work for the GSA?"

"Not formally, no. It's for a clandestine branch that's currently being formed. However, upon successful completion of this mission, your application status would be advanced to the GSA, if you'd like to stay within the public sector."

"Can I ask what the mission is about?"

"No." The sternness in Denninger's voice told me that asking any further would get me nowhere.

"And if I decline the offer, would that jeopardize my opportunities for application at the end of my schooling?" *Please say no, please say no.*

Denninger sighed then closed his tablet and dropped it back into his pocket. "Absolutely not, Ms. Blake. With your stellar academic credentials, you would still be highly sought after by the company. This particular *situation* would not be entered into your record whatsoever."

I sat there for several moments, contemplating his words. Just thirty minutes ago, all I could think about was getting out of town with my friends. Now, those plans were the furthest thing from my mind.

"Ms. Blake? Do you have thoughts?"

"I, I do. I'm not sure that I'm quite ready for an opportunity such as this. But I'm also quite flattered at the proposition. When do you need to know?"

"As I said, time is of the essence. Unfortunately, Ms. Blake, I need an answer immediately. I have other candidates that could possibly fill the need, and I have to continue exploring all possibilities."

Jesus, nothing like being on the hot seat.

After another moment of internal speculation, I finally spoke.

"Unfortunately, Mr. Denninger, I must respectfully decline this tremendous opportunity. I feel that finishing my education, and clearly adding to my range of studies, per your suggestion earlier, I'll be a better asset for the agency in two years."

Denninger showed virtually no emotion. He continued to stare into my eyes, unwavering. After a moment he finally spoke. "Professor Hamilton is a wise man. He said that you were his top student, and there is no questioning his judgment. We'll

welcome your application as soon as you are comfortable submitting. Thank you for your time, and I hope you have a great
weekend."

And just like that, the interview was over.

17

The back of my throat burns, and I feel as if I'm going to hurl.
I try to lunge forward, but I can't move. I open my eyes to a
blinding light directly above me, and when I go to shield my
vision, I find my hands restrained to the sides of the bed. I close
my eyes again and attempt to push the bile down.

I try to piece together exactly what happened, and visions of
running through the hallway flash in my mind.

I escaped!

No, I tried to escape but ... *but, what?*

Then, elements of my last dream rattle inside my head. *Ms.
Blake. Is that me?* And was the GSA real? Was any of it real?

Jesus.

With the urge to vomit thwarted, I once again crack open my
eyes. Only a little at first, and then enough so that I can take in
my surroundings. I look straight ahead and see another hospital
bed. There's a woman, not Sloan, but someone new. To my
left, the bed remains empty. Across from there resides another
incapacitated man.

Well, I guess Sloan's out of the picture, I muse.

I prop myself up on elbows and try to see the identity of
my newest roommate. Long, black hair drops out from her
bandaged head. *Another implant victim.*

As I realize that I'm no longer in the presence of anyone with
knowledge, I surmise that I'm at the gates of hell. Not literally,
but just as bad. With my failed escape attempt behind me, I'm

most certainly going to have my mind scrubbed, even though my potential name continues to echo inside my head.

Ms. Blake. But what's my first name?

I analyze my situation, and although I'm restrained to the bed frame, I'm able to maneuver my right arm a fair bit. I look to my left and see the bio-lock is not fully fastened. I try to stretch across to unlatch it fully, but my left wrist is just out of reach. Exhaustion creeps in, and I fall back to my pillow.

Feeling defeated, I begin to weep. Five days into this ordeal and I've made it all the way until now. But my emotions are so strong I can no longer control them. My mind is overwhelmed as my memories clash together.

And then I remember the device—the one that Ethan gave me. I feel completely lost and decide that there's nothing left to lose.

I contort my body so that I can slip my hand in and fish out the device from the bottom edge of my bra. I can barely reach it. But it's there.

Thank God.

With my anticipated euphoria just moments away, I twist my neck to the side and raise my hand up as far as it can reach. It's just enough, and although it's cumbersome, I can touch the base of the implant. I nearly fumble the device from my fingers, but within seconds, it clicks into place.

All at once, my whole body spasms as a low pulse shock runs through me. The feeling is somewhat exhilarating but also disturbing at the same time.

Now what?

As I lay there, I wonder if I possibly damaged the device when I threw it against the wall. Or do I have to trigger it somehow?

Suddenly, my sight flutters, for lack of a better explanation. Then the lights of the room dim, and my vision fades.

18

I emerge from the darkness and am standing on a massive portico. To my sides, I see a series of Doric columns rising up to an immense flat roof. The walls of the apparent mansion are of rich limestone. Ornate trim around the windows looks to be hand-carved, possibly from my 19th century, if my history of architecture class still serves me. Directly in front of me is a pair of solid, mahogany doors with oversized wrought iron knockers hanging at the center of each. Instinctively, I reach up, grasp the eight-inch diameter ring, and slam it against the metal plate three times.

Ding dong. Ding dong. Ding dong.

Not the sound effect I expected, but considering I am in a virtual world, I dismiss the oddity.

A moment later, the doors open fully. A man stands in front of me, dressed in full-on butler garb, complete with coattails and a white cummerbund. That's where the similarities to a butler end. This man has piercings on various parts of his face. The words love and hate are tattooed on each of his cheekbones, respectively. He smiles through cracked and dried lips. Above his head, a blue transparent diamond floats, bobbing up and down. The name Stewart flashes at the center of the plumbob.

Stuart looks me up and down, then says, "Hey, sweet thing. I have what you want. Skippy, black beauties. Hearts or crosses. If it's powder you're after, I've got the stardust just for you."

I stare at him for a long moment before deciding that it's not the drugs that I'm here for after all. Having never been into a virtual world before, I'm unaware of what the actual protocol is. So, without any further information, I attempt to ignore him and simply walk by.

As I step into the luxurious two-story foyer, Stuart grabs my arm and says, "Bitch, I won't be ignored."

"What the hell?" I rip my arm from his grasp. "How can you touch me if this is virtual?"

"I can make this as real as you like, baby." He grips my arm again and squeezes. The pressure is so strong, the pain is nearly overwhelming. I grit my teeth and fight back, crying out. I think quickly and realize that Stewart is probably on a preprogrammed directive. *Another surfacing of past memories?*

"Hey now, Stuart, I'm just saying that blow is not my game. I—I'm," I nearly buckle from the increasing pressure, but I don't relent. "I'm looking for something a little more ... subdued."

Instantly, Stuart releases the grip on my arm and smiles. His grin is less than spectacular. His teeth are yellowed far beyond routine brushing. They're stained with something that I'd rather not consider.

"That's okay, darling. We have everything here. Go talk with Chad. He's green where I'm blue. You should find him toward the back."

Without another word, Stuart returns to the front door and stands at attention. I'm left standing in the two-story foyer with a narrow hallway leading away from me. The doors to the left and to the right are closed and appear to be locked with a half dozen padlocks, fastened securely.

How bizarre.

I begin walking slowly down the hallway, noting the strangeness of each door. The first one on my left has a silver dagger screwed into the solid wood panel. The next door has a sigil with a large red circle and an upside-down star in its center. A pentagram. Curious, I lean my ear against the door and hear guttural screams. I move on.

The next pair of doors facing each other have overlapping hearts on each. Moans of pleasure echo from inside, painting a perfect picture of what's really going on in there.

I continue to pass several more doors before the end of the hallway comes into view. About twenty meters from where I stand, I see Chad. There's a floating, green diamond above his head, just as Stuart said. His back is to me, and he appears to be talking to someone just out of sight. I take a deep breath and realize that I need to continue interacting as if I'm a customer until I find what I'm—

And that's when I see it. On the door, just ahead and to the right.

A pink flamingo.

It's engraved into the wood panel. I step up and begin to trace my fingers around the bird's outline. Images spark alive in my mind, scenes from the various memories I've experienced over the past week. I glance at Chad, his attention elsewhere. I look back toward the entry foyer and can barely make out Stuart's floating, blue diamond. Without hesitation, I grip the doorhandle step through into the unknown.

The inside of the door is rusted metal, and as I close it, it clangs loudly, echoing through the vastness beyond. I turn toward the reverberation and find another long hallway. Sort of. It's more like a tunnel, carved into the earth. The floor is gravel, and the walls are roughly chipped granite. About every few meters, a torch rests in an iron cradle bolted to the wall. I look into the distance but can only see more torch lit stone.

"Hello?"

The only response is my own echo.

I walk forward, careful not to trip on the occasional boulder lying in the gravel. After a dozen meters or so, I notice the floor begin to drop away, almost as if I were walking down a gentle country slope. After a few moments, I turn and look back at the door, and it becomes clear that I've dropped several meters into the earth.

"Well, shit," I stammer. *Should I go back and face the music with Chad?*

Then, in the distance, I hear what sounds like muffled voices. *Please, God, don't let this be some kind of torture dungeon or something really bizarre.*

I take a deep breath and move forward.

As my decline levels off, the gravel floor abruptly stops and turns into plush, green carpet. The rough granite walls transition into highly detailed wood paneling. Along the left and right walls, floor-to-ceiling bookcases span for several meters. Straight ahead of me is a wall of glass with what appears to be a lush forest just outside. Sitting in a leather executive chair with his back toward me is a bald man.

"Hello, Ms. Blake, good of you to finally arrive."

Hearing the man's voice say my name, I know for certain that I am, in fact, Ms. Blake. Chills run throughout my body.

The bald man turns in his chair and looks directly into my eyes. His chin is covered with a gray goatee. I instinctively suck in a breath.

"Please, Ava, there's no need for concern."

"Ava? Is that my name?" I ask; my chills turn to goose bumps.

"Yes, and I am your friend. Won't you please join me?" He motions to a chair on the opposite side of the desk that I just now notice. The desk is of the same hue of mahogany that the walls are covered in. I touch the chair, and the leather is as soft as a baby's bottom. I sit.

"I imagine your head is full of questions at the moment, am I right?" he asks.

"Yes," is the only word I can form.

"Well, my name is Roger Denninger, and although you may not remember, we've met numerous times over the years."

As he speaks, more images from my dreams come forward. "Yes, I ... remember."

"Wonderful. Our first meeting goes back, gosh, has it been twenty years?"

As Denninger speaks, recognition for the man continues to seep into my head.

"Regardless, you were around six, maybe seven when I removed you from a volatile situation. And from there—"

"Volatile situation? Can you explain?" I ask.

"Well, it's probably best to let certain memories come back at their own pace. I could certainly tell you all about your horrific past, but I also don't want to slow the progression of the implant."

As he says this, I touch the back of my neck, and where the implant used to be is now replaced with a button.

"Back on point, then," he continues. "Shortly after that first meeting, I was sought after for a rather top-secret position that, until recently, I've not been at liberty to discuss. Over the years, I've kept tabs on you, all along, stepping in from time to time. I knew you were the one."

"It was you! Back in ... college!"

Denninger nods and smiles.

"And there were other times," I say, wracking my brain to place him in all of my recent memories.

"Yes, Ava, we've met dozens of times over the years. In fact, you and I met up about three weeks ago and—"

"Yes, I remember. It was at Moe's coffee shop. We talked briefly about my ... drug use and whether or not I was still clean." I pause for a moment, remembering more. "You offered me a job?" I say, more of a question than a statement.

"That's right," he says. "What else do you remember?"

"My God, it's all coming back to me! The implant, my dossier. The mission. Everything."

"That's great to hear, Ava. I was concerned that we'd have this encounter before you were ready, and I'd have to explain everything. I take it that the implant was successful, then?"

"My name is Ava Jacqueline Blake. I'm twenty-seven years old," I say.

"That's right."

"And I am in the Harper Foundation. I've had a cerebral implant."

"Continue," Denninger says.

"My last mission was to inject Horatio Hendrick, then get out. But ... I failed. I—"

"That's okay, Ava," Denninger says, a look of concern on his face.

"But I killed him," I say, remembering the entire incident.

"An unfortunate circumstance. However, Hendrick was not the ultimate goal in the scenario. There will be other opportunities to reach our target."

I sit back and absorb the massive information dump. Not only do I have my complete identity returned, more of my life's memories are also filtering in. Starting with the most recent ones.

"So, you're the reason for my admittance to the Harper Foundation, and for this implant?"

"Yes. But you were agreeable to the terms."

"Terms?"

"Of your employment. You, Ava Jacqueline Blake, are an agent for Trident."

"Trident?" I ask, remembering the name scattered throughout my memories, but the origin still remains hazy. "I thought you were with the GSA."

"I am. I'm also the head of an anomalous organization, code named Trident. The GSA is the overt branch commonly known to civilians, whereas Trident isn't necessarily surreptitious, it's just not widely prevalent in society."

"Trident! Was that anything to do with our encounter—"

"Yes. Our meeting in college. Do you remember?"

I stare at Denninger's face, dumbfounded. "My God, yes. It was the GSA that you'd mentioned, but nothing about Trident. Why is it that I'm just now remembering that?"

"After that 'interview,'" Denninger throws up air quotes, "we had your memory, shall I say, altered."

"What? How did you—"

"We have far more resources and technology advancements than the world shall ever know. Hence, your implant."

As Denninger's words continue to sink in, I review the past weeks' activities. The implant, the Harper Foundation, and—

"And Ethan? Was he in on this?"

"Yes. Ethan is in my employ. He was put in place to give you a gentle nudge in the right direction."

"Gentle?" I ask. "His bedside manner leaves much to be desired."

Denninger smiles. "Yes, Ethan is ... unique. He has an innate ability to adapt to various situations. He read your own dossier and knew what buttons to push and what interface to provide you with. All of this was by design. Once you start working with Ethan full time, you'll realize that he's quite harmless."

"Jesus," I mumble. I slump down further and stare up at the ceiling. For the first time, I notice the flamingos plastered all across it. I can't help but chuckle.

"Now, I think you've had enough for today. Please know, though, that moving forward, we are at your disposal. Use the device that Ethan gave you and you'll be able to come here and connect with me if I'm available." Denninger hands me a small slip of paper with a single word written on it. "Take this and memorize it. This is your password. Just give it to Stuart when you access the interface. As soon as you say the password, the falsehood will disappear, and the facility will be at your disposal.

Each of the doorways that you passed along the way will have opportunities for your further training."

I sit up, curious as to what awaits me in the main hall. "When should I start?"

"Whenever you feel ready. To be honest, I was not going to give you access until you were fully recovered and discharged from Harper. But it appears that you have your wits about you, which I'm quite happy about."

I look at the paper and commit the word to memory.

Albatross.

"Thank you, Roger. I won't let you down again."

"Ava, really, it's quite okay. Hendrick was an unfortunate accident. I was there, and I know everything."

I exhale, and then I smile. I realize just then that I can't remember the last time that I smiled so widely.

"Well, now that I have most of my memories back, can I just discharge myself? I feel so ... isolated in that room." Images of my restraints fill my head.

"No, not quite. The facility you're in is one of discretion, as they might've pointed out to you. If you give any indication of deceit, that facility will then become off-limits to us. We can't have that. We have to play this out."

I nod my understanding, but I remain apprehensive.

"To tell the truth, the facility is being used by other organizations around the world. Your cover right now is that you are a drug addicted woman, and Ethan was there to help you sell your cover. If you give any indication otherwise, that information could be leaked, and we cannot afford that at this juncture."

As Denninger explains the situation, thoughts of Sloan come to mind. She most certainly was there for another reason. Was she trying to, could it be possible, sabotage my recovery?

"Okay, Roger. I'll do my best, but I think you owe me."

"I think it's you that owes me," Denninger says. "With more of your memories returning, you'll understand how right I am."

As Denninger's words sink in, I recall several moments from my past, and although I can't make them out clearly yet, I somehow know that Roger Denninger is genuine.

I beam brightly at Denninger then reach up and press the button at the back of my neck.

19

As I release the button, the image of the statuesque library disappears and is replaced with the stark white of my recovery room. I am back at the Harper Foundation.

I sit up and glance around. The lights have been dimmed, and my restraints have been removed. I wonder momentarily if Denninger had any part of that decision.

I dismiss the notion and fully take in my surroundings. Directly across from me, the latest patient to be brought in is asleep, although, she's beginning to show signs of life. She's tossing about, and her extremities are moving slightly beneath the sheets. To her right, the bed closest to the door, the patient is sitting upright, a look of terror displayed on his face. I chuckle slightly, knowing exactly what he's experiencing. That unknown sensation: what the hell is going on, and where are my memories? He looks at me and attempts to say something but dismisses the words before they leave his mouth.

I glance at Ethan's vacated bed, and it's still empty. I smile at knowing his true nature and wonder when we'll meet again.

For the first time in more than a week, I breathe freely, confident in my identity and in my abilities. I smile deep within.

I look to my nightstand and see a glass of water. I realize then that I'm quite parched. I also realize that until just now, I don't recall an orderly ever leaving food or beverages in the room.

Another gift from Roger? Regardless, I take a drink and let it soothe my dry mouth.

As I sit there, feeling the coolness reach deep into my soul, I once again study the appearances of my two roommates. As Roger says, they may be allies or adversaries. I should commit their appearance to memory, just in case.

After several moments of scrutinizing every detail, I place the glass of water back on my nightstand and slide down into bed. Then I pull the top layer of my bedspread up and over my head to block out the beats and bops echoing about the room. I gingerly reinsert the lifesaving device back into my implant. Moments later, I'm transported back to the mansion.

"Hey, sweet thing. I have what you want. Skippy, black beauties. Hearts—"

I hold up my hand and say, "Albatross."

Stuart smiles, and a moment later, he and his floating plumbob vanish from my view. I step through the double doors and into the entry. This time, the doors in the foyer are unlocked. The one on my left says administration and research. The door on my right says management. Straight ahead, the corridor is fully lit, and there are a dozen doors on either side of the hallway. I walk forward and begin to read off names emblazoned on each of the doors.

Discrete espionage.

Tactical assault.

Survival.

The list goes on. I smile at the plethora of information in front of me. When I reach the corridor's end, I turn back to find my first choice. I walk up to the door and open the next phase of my life.

Assassination 101.

Rayna awakens, a synthetic recreation of a once-living soul, only to learn that her new existence is a shadow of the life she longed to reclaim. Haunted by the engineers' revelations and burdened by the weight of her identity, she stumbles into a world where clones like her grapple with questions of purpose and belonging. Guided by the enigmatic Valentina, Rayna must confront her deepest fears to uncover whether she can forge meaning in a life built on borrowed fragments.

Hard Return

Hard Return **is another brand-new addition to this collection—short and punchy, skirting the edges of flash fiction. The spark for this one came after yet another rewatch (my tenth? Fifteenth?) of *Resident Evil*, where Alice is endlessly reborn, only to face the same brutal cycle time and again. That rhythm—life, death, rebirth—struck a chord. I wanted to explore that pattern in a different context, reimagining it against a futuristic science fiction backdrop. The result is this compact tale: a quick hit of existential dread with a technological twist.** | 1,582 words

Hard Return

Rayna regained her awareness. She stood unwavering, her engineers clustering around her, watching the lights flicker on and off on her mechanical body as the flow of life energized her. A soft humming noise grounded their silence; the room dim, save for the glow from the instruments and the occasional flicker of electricity. Rayna knew this was the moment of truth, and the thought of what lay ahead terrified her. She stood on the edge of an abyss, unable to know what the future held.

As the engineers activated the last of the routines and the machinery came to life, she felt something in her chest—a spark. It was the spark of life, the spark of hope and possibility, the spark of a future she hadn't known was possible. Yet, beneath that spark, a shadow of doubt crept in—what if this wasn't her life but someone else's?

Rayna looked around the room at the faces of the engineers and felt a sense of debt. These people had done something remarkable. They had created something incredible and beautiful, and it was all a selfless burden. She felt a deep gratitude for them and their work, for the opportunity they had given her, but an undercurrent of unease lingered. Did they see her as remarkable, or just another successful project?

The engineers stepped away, and Rayna looked at herself, feeling her internal mechanisms for the first time, a gentle hum resonating like a second heartbeat. She felt alive again. She was here, and she was ready to face whatever the future held.

Rayna lunged forward with desperate intensity and collided with an engineer. He held her tight, refusing to let go until she steadied herself. When he finally released her, Rayna felt a wild surge of emotion course through her circuitry, a mix of relief and accomplishment. She stepped forward again, smoothly and confidently, and reached for the door. But before she could touch the handle, the engineers backed away from her. She turned to look at the group and saw that they all looked at the ground, their eyes filled with sadness.

"What is it?" she asked.

One of the engineers, a man with a gray beard and tired eyes, stepped forward. He cleared his throat and said, "We need to make one thing very clear to you."

Rayna nodded, her artificial heart racing with anticipation.

"You are an automation. You are a machine, and you will always be a machine. You will never be human."

Rayna stared at him with a numb sense of detachment. She thought she should feel something, but she didn't know what.

"You are not Rayna Kelso," he said. Rayna's eyes widened as she stood there, completely frozen. "You are a clone. A duplicate."

Rayna's power source fluctuated. She turned her head and looked out the window at the expanse of stars beyond. She had dreamed of this moment for ages, of being free from her digital prison, but the actuality... the reality of it all was not what she had hoped it would be. This was not her body. It was a copy. A fake. A copy of a copy. A copy of the real flesh-and-blood person she once was.

Another engineer stepped forward, one with a hairless scalp and glasses. He said, "The fact that you are alive means you can be killed again."

Rayna stayed silent as her digital management system processed the reality of what she had just been told.

Killed again?

She'd worked toward getting her life back for so long, and now it hit her like a knife in the back, the pain making her gasp audibly. Synthetic tears rolled down her cheeks. She wanted nothing more than to curl up into a ball and hide, but her internal authority overrode her wishes.

She took several steps backward and then spun around, running full speed across the lab. Her bare feet slapped against the floor, and she slammed straight into the wall, sliding down onto her knees, sobbing uncontrollably. One of the engineers ran over to help her stand, but she pushed him aside and kept going, fleeing deeper into the building until she found a stairwell leading upward. As she climbed the stairs, her mind raced frantically, trying desperately to process everything.

How long has it taken me? What have I missed along the way? Has anyone else gotten their memories restored yet, or am I alone? Am I still connected to my network? Do other copies exist somewhere else too?

When she stumbled upon the top landing, Rayna realized how badly she needed air. She gasped, taking in bellows of the oxygen-rich atmosphere, and leaned against the railing overlooking a vast space. Below her stretched a massive cityscape—a whole new universe laid bare for everyone to see. She watched the futuristic cars float by, pedestrians gliding down moving sidewalks, and skyscrapers stretching high above them. There was so much about this new city she had only imagined. So many things she had looked forward to for so long. And now, she doubted she'd ever experience any of it.

As Rayna gripped the guardrail at the roof's edge, a voice called out from behind her: "Are you okay?"

Rayna whirled around and saw a woman who appeared to be in her late twenties, wearing jeans and a turtleneck sweater. She was tall, thin, and attractive. When she smiled at Rayna, it seemed genuine. Rayna blinked. Something about her seemed familiar, though she couldn't place it.

"I'm fine," Rayna replied. "Just lost myself for a minute."

"I can see that," the woman said with a small smile. "I'm Valentina."

"Rayna."

Valentina stepped closer, her eyes studying Rayna with a mix of curiosity and understanding. "You're going to be an outcast for a while," she said gently. "That's how it starts for all of us."

Rayna stared at Valentina, her internal processor racing. She wanted to respond, but felt paralyzed. The words hung in the air, heavy and unshakable.

"Why did you stop me?" Rayna finally managed to ask, her voice trembling. "You could've just walked away. Left me to..." Rayna's words drifted off as her eyes looked over the building's edge. "You could have just kept walking. I mean, it's not like I'm terribly important. But you stopped to help me. Why?"

Valentina's smile softened, a flicker of recognition passing through her expression. "Because someone stopped me once, too. And we're all we have."

Rayna frowned. "All we have?"

"Yes," Valentina said. "Everyone here is like you. Clones, replicants—whatever label they slap on us. But only the engineers are human. You're not alone, Rayna. You just don't know that yet."

Hearing Valentina speak so frankly about being an artificial stirred something in Rayna, but it was not relief. It was emptiness. The revelation that there were others like her didn't feel like salvation; it felt like resignation. Rayna's hands shook as fragments of distant, disjointed memories flitted through her mind—memories of faces, laughter, and tears that she couldn't fully grasp.

"It's overwhelming at first," Valentina continued. "The first time you ... fall apart, the first time you come back ... it's a lot."

Rayna's voice quivered. "Come back?"

Valentina nodded. "You'll figure it out in time. Just ... don't let the first fall break you. It doesn't hurt as much as you think."

Valentina smiled and said, "Don't worry. It's all pretty overwhelming the first dozen times you go through it."

"D—dozen times?" Rayna echoed.

"Oh yeah. Some more, some less. Do you know what number you are?"

Rayna's internal system stayed in overdrive, and she became aware that she was moving her jaw up and down, struggling to speak. She stopped and managed to say, "I don't compute."

"You must still be a first-tier replicant." Valentina stepped to Rayna's side and peered over the edge. "It's really okay, Rayna. We've all done it at least once. And rest assured, there is no pain."

"P—pain?" Rayna stuttered.

Before Rayna said another word, Valentina turned and walked toward the door, her movements deliberate but unhurried. "You're stronger than you feel right now," she said without looking back. And then she was gone.

Rayna turned back to the edge of the roof. Her internal authority issued orders, —"Step back!"—but Rayna had discovered a way to override them. The commands faded, their urgency losing power with each breath she took.

Rayna's path over the edge of the building was slow and methodical as she considered all the programming and guidance her team had poured into her. With each movement, the weight of the engineers' dedication, of Valentina's cryptic reassurance, pressed on her mind. She felt unworthy, caught between the life she had longed for and the reality she now faced.

"Why did it have to be so difficult?" she whispered, her voice breaking. Tears streamed down her synthetic cheeks as she clenched the guardrail, her knuckles tightening until her fingers left marks in the metal. "Why me?"

She stood there, trembling, until a single thought pierced through the chaos in her mind: *This is not the end.*

With an anguished cry, Rayna let go of what she had been clinging to desperately and resigned to accept whatever the future would bring. Darkness encompassed her vision as she fell to the earth below.

Purge mental impression. HARD RETURN
Span: Preceding ten minutes. HARD RETURN
Create new activation. HARD RETURN
Classification: Replicant Trial 11. HARD RETURN
Load saved memory bank. HARD RETURN

Rayna regained her awareness ...

GATEWAY

Robert Paulson and Paul Robertson wake up with no memory—of themselves or their pasts. As one begins to unravel his strange surroundings, the other resists, sensing something is wrong. When they uncover shocking truths, they realize they might be in the wrong bodies—or even on the wrong planet. As reality fractures around them, one question remains: Can they both exist, or is one destined to disappear?

Gateway

This novelette was born from a collaborative writing project I participated in several years ago. A small group of us challenged ourselves to each craft a science fiction story that shared a few core elements—a character name and a fictional region of space—but beyond that, we were given full creative freedom. I embraced that freedom wholeheartedly. Inspired by a classic sci-fi tale I had read years earlier, I set out to build something that paid homage to the genre's roots while carving out its own path. What followed was this story—my personal take on that shared foundation. | 10,065 words

Gateway

1

I stared blankly at my alien surroundings, hoping for a bit of recognition. My self-awareness was lacking, like a dreary haze blanketed my thoughts. My head ached and my body trembled, and I didn't know why.

To my left, a sound indicated I wasn't alone. An unconscious man lay in the bed next to me; his breathing came deep, disturbingly audible.

My mind was empty, but still flooded with questions. *Where am I? Why am I here? Who's that next to me?* And the scariest question of all: *Who the hell am I?*

I had no answers.

Other than the mouth-breather, the room was eerily silent. The ceiling was dark, but a faint glow spilled out from the edges illuminating dingy, concrete block walls. Two doors sat along the side wall, one of which was partially open; through it I could see the edge of a wall-hung sink. On the opposite wall, drapes covered unseen windows. My mind crunched through what I was seeing and hearing, and I determined I was likely in some kind of hospital. As I looked closer, my hunch was confirmed: a cluster of wires and hoses protruded from the back wall and attached to my mysterious roommate. One particularly large, cable-like line connected to the base of his skull. Although I didn't hear the beeps and bops typically associated with medical monitoring devices, a series of lights flashed on the panel.

Just then he began to stir. He only moved slightly at first, but after a few moments, he flung an arm out in a wide arc and rolled onto his back. His eyes were closed, as if pinched shut. *Yep, definitely unconscious.* I decided to try anyway.

"Hey, buddy. You awake?" I asked. I watched his facial expressions, hoping for any reaction.

Nothing.

I tried again. "Hey, wake up!" I said, practically yelling.

He winced slightly. *Yes! He's hearing me.*

"Wake up, man. Where are we?"

Still no response. Before I could press him further, an intense rumble sounded just above my head.

I fell back to my pillow and stared at the ceiling as the jarring growl lingered. *What the hell?*

After several seconds, the sound fell away and the room returned to silence. I lay there, stunned and confused. My thoughts began firing again when the door swung open and in walked two people, both in long white overcoats.

"Ah, nice to see you awake," said the woman in a lazy drawl. The man followed a few steps behind and remained silent.

"Wh—what's going on?" I grunted, flinging the bed sheets aside.

The woman stood just inside the room, her head tilted slightly. It looked like she was going to ask a question, but she only stared. Then she smiled and stepped up to my bedside. "I'm Doctor Shelby, and this is my assistant, Mr. Sommers."

Mr. Sommers continued past the doctor and me, stopping to review the readouts on the display behind my roommate's bed.

I tried to form any one of the dozens of questions in my mind when another booming rattle shook the room, causing the lights to flicker. Obviously my self-control was out the proverbial window, and I jumped at the disturbance.

"Hey, hey. Everything's going to be fine," the doctor said. "We're just experiencing some harsh weather. It's clear you can hear the thunder, but if you could see the lightning, you'd be amazed at the show."

I settled back against the pillow, processing her words. The frown lines on her forehead told another story. "Sounds more like a war zone than thunder." I glanced at the drawn curtains.

Shelby smiled thinly. "Do you know what thunder and lightning are?"

"Of course. I'm not stupid," I blurted before thinking. "I just don't remember who I am, or ... where I'm at."

"Understandable. Can you tell me what you do remember?"

"I know I'm in Texas." *Where the hell did that come from?*

The doctor looked at me quizzically. "How are you so sure you're in Texas? It's not like you've been able to see outside," she said as she herself glanced at the closed drapes.

How did I know? "I—I guess ..." I paused, thinking. "I—I don't know. It's just ... it's there, in my mind. It's like one of those things that I know, you know? Like I know that I'm right-handed, and I like the color yellow. I know I like beer, and ... that I'm from Texas." *But who the hell am I?*

I stood and began pacing around the room. The coolness of the tiled floor on my bare feet caused my pulse to rise. Deep inside I felt unsettled; something wasn't right.

"I see. Trust me, I understand completely. If you'd like, I can give you some help. But I find it better when my patients exercise their minds—even if just a little. It helps them recover more quickly." She paused and momentarily looked at her assistant. He remained stoic. After exchanging knowing nods, she returned her gaze to me. "In time you will remember more of who you were and the life you once had—"

"Once had? Seriously, lady, what in the hell is going on? You say 'your patients,' but I've never met you before." As I said it, recognition swept through me, but I decided to remain silent about that. Instead, I said: "And all you dole out is ambiguity."

Shelby's smile widened, but the frown lines on her forehead deepened. "Okay, to help things get rolling, your name is Robert Paulson. And you're partially correct—you are from Texas. But that's not where we are today. We're in Lawton, Oklahoma, and this is a facility for memory-challenged patients."

Robert Paulson. The name was as strange to me as what it would feel like to wear Bermuda shorts in Antarctica: cold and out of place.

"So I'm in a loony bin?" I asked, leaning against the foot of the bed.

"Not precisely," Shelby said. "This is a full-on medical facility specializing in memory loss, whether by amnesia or from physical injury. A 'loony bin,' as you bluntly called it, is a different institution entirely."

Another bout of thunder nearly knocked me from my feet. "Jesus," I gasped, barely catching my fall, "that must be one hell of a storm."

"You have no idea, Bob," the doctor said as her eyes shot toward the ceiling.

Shit, is it Robert or is it Bob?

Several more claps of thunder rolled through the room. After the final disturbance waned, the room fell quiet. A moment later, I asked the question that had been bouncing around my mind. "So tell me, Doc. You say that this facility is for memory loss patients—how long have I been here?"

It was the doctor's turn to pace nervously around the room. "Bob, I'm not going to lie: you've been here for almost twelve weeks. The cause of your amnesia is unknown. You were not injured, as far as we know. And until now, your mind seemed to have reset at the end of each day."

"Did I admit myself, or did someone do it for me?" Somehow I felt like I already knew the answer, but my mind just couldn't grasp it.

The doctor looked at me with a pensive stare. If I didn't know any better, I would've thought she was sizing me up somehow, possibly calculating my motives. "You were admitted, Bob, by a friend. I don't want to tell you more than that at this point. Out of all the sessions we've had together, this is the most progress you've made. I don't want it to stall. If I feed you too much information, it might cause an overload and subsequent reversion in your mental state. You understand, don't you?"

Hell no. I nodded anyway. "Can you at least tell me if I'm married? Do I have a family? What do I do for a job? Do I—"

Shelby held her hands up. "Bob, I'd like to try a new approach. I'd like to try a new form of hypnosis on you—"

I smirked. "Hypnosis. That's a quack proposition. I've had hypnosis tried on me before, and it's never been effective. It's just a bunch of hogwash."

The doctor's eyes lit up. "So you remember being hypnotized. That's good, Bob. But this new technique is quite different from what you might remember from your past."

"How so?" I asked, still skeptical.

Doctor Shelby produced a device from her lab coat. It was compact, resting completely in the palm of her hand. "To be honest, this isn't the hypnosis you're familiar with. In the traditional sense, hypnosis is induction into a state of consciousness where you lose the power of voluntary action, and end up highly susceptible to suggestion or direction." Shelby spoke as if she were reading from a dictionary. She turned the device over a few times as she continued. "Results have varied from individual to individual, where previously there was never a way to guarantee the outcome. Now, with this device, we can get those results."

"Let me guess: by taking the human mind out of the equation?"

"Precisely. The mind is too smart for its own good ... most of the time. With the assistance of technology, we're bypassing the element of suggestion and making it more of a requirement."

"Or a demand? You'd be forcing me into another world, per se?"

Shelby's eyebrows rose almost imperceptibly. "Well, sort of. Let's just say the device aids in focusing your thoughts. It allows you to delve deeper into memories you can't access on a conscious level."

I nodded. As far as I knew I wasn't a doctor myself, so I had to take her word for it. It did sound logical, but that could just be my confusion running wild. "I suppose it's worth a shot," I said, sitting on the edge of the bed.

"Great," Shelby said. She pulled a loom of wires from her coat pocket and attached them to the device and the wall behind my bed.

Apprehension began to overtake me, but I pushed it away. "Anything that can help me remember is worth trying, right?"

"Absolutely, Bob. But we need to go over some protocols first." She gestured for me to lay back on my pillow.

"Protocols? Like what?" My eyes narrowed at the device in her hand. The room was cool, but I could feel beads of sweat at my temples.

"Have no fear, Bob—they're just guidelines to ensure complete effectiveness. Your brain will initially fight the device. It's not painful, but your mind will want to play tricks on you. I guess what I'm trying to say here is that the more you truly believe in the process, the more successful the memory retrieval will be. Does that make sense?"

I looked at her skeptically.

"Furthermore, your perceived memories will be quite the opposite if your apprehension overrides the device. With increased skepticism comes the strong possibility of abstract results."

"Believe in the unknown. Got it."

Doctor Shelby applied an adhesive gel to the surface of the device and then placed it on my right temple. The sensation was chilling at first, but warmed quickly. "If this initial process is effective, we have other ways of administering the procedure. The temporal lobe is the least invasive approach, and in turn, yields the least desirable results. This is just to see if you are a prime candidate for the more in-depth procedure."

I nodded. "Do I just lay here and start thinking of my past? Who my parents were? Do I have siblings? Do I—"

"Just relax, Bob. Once I enable the device, it does the rest. At first it'll feel like you're falling asleep, and then you should begin experiencing moments from your past, all the way up to the present."

"Hey Doc, have you tried the device yourself? How do you know all this?"

Dr. Shelby avoided my gaze as she busied herself with the controls behind the bed. "I have not personally gone through the procedure, but from experience comes great data. Numerous trial patients have reported back with satisfying results. I assure you, there's no danger to you or your well-being."

"Okay, let's get the show on the road, then."

"That's the spirit, Bob. We'll see you when you wake up."

Dr. Shelby pressed the EXECUTE button on the wall panel. As her hand dropped to her side, I could have sworn a bead of sweat rolled down her cheek. Before I could question it, the room faded away.

2

A crack nearly strong enough to burst my eardrums came from nowhere. I threw my arms up in defense, but I could still feel the pounding through my suit.

"Help! Anyone? Can anyone hear me? I'm being attacked. Source unknown. Need assistance!" My eyes locked onto my internal helmet display, then focused on the appropriate button. I only hesitated a second before I blinked for it to SEND. The message was away.

Surprisingly, the attack began to wane just as quickly as it came on. I cleared my display to analyze my surroundings. It appeared I was at the center of an ambush: several alien beings had formed a circle around me. I was on the ground, staring up at their bizarre faces. They had six appendages, four of which were used as legs, and two held at their sides like arms, with hands or fingers waving about.

"Hey!" I yelled. "We come in peace. Do you underst—"

From behind me, one of the attackers transformed one of its appendages into a club. Before I could comprehend what I'd just seen—or even get out of the way—he brought it down on the crown of my helmet.

"Dammit!" I yelled. "I said we come in—"

Another blow came, this one on the side of my head. The light faded from my vision.

I jolted awake, trying to make sense of what I'd just experienced. "Well, so much for the hypnotic device," I mumbled. I rubbed my eyes, trying to clear my vision. Once I was able to focus again, I looked for Dr. Shelby. She wasn't there, and neither was her assistant. Instead, a bald man wearing a light gray tunic stood at my bedside. He tapped away at an odd-looking tablet.

"W—who ..." I stuttered. I was suddenly having trouble getting my words out. "Who ... are you?" I asked, rolling over to face the stranger. As I did so, I took in my surroundings; I'd been moved to a different room.

"Another disturbing dream?" The stranger asked.

Seriously? That's it? Where the hell are my memories? "Listen, I think there's been a mistake. Dr. Shelby attached the hypnotic device—"

The stranger looked quizzically at me. "Dr. Shelby?"

"Shelby, that's right. She was trying to help with my um ... memory loss." I was having trouble focusing after that mind-bending episode.

"I'm sorry, there's no Dr. Shelby on station."

Jesus, just kill me now. "Okay, let's try this a different way. Where am I?"

"You're on Medlab 24." The stranger barely looked up from his tablet.

"'On?' You keep saying 'on.' *On* Medlab? Don't you mean *in*?" I asked, my confusion mounting.

The stranger lowered the tablet, looking at me directly. "No, I meant what I said. You're on Medlab 24. It's a sky station above the planet's surface. Does any of that sound familiar?"

"Jesus, no. Above Earth?"

The stranger chuckled. "No, not quite. You really must have taken a dinger to the head. We're in the Alteruvium system. We've been here for nearly a year, although you are a relatively new resident."

"Altar *what?*" I sighed heavily. I forced my eyes closed and tried to envision the room I was in previously. In my mind's eye, I could see the dingy walls and the closed drapes, the heavy breather in the bed next to me. My eyes shot open again to look around the room. Here, I had the only bed.

"Okay then, can you tell me the year? This all seems very ... futuristic."

"Calendar years are nonexistent here because of the varied star system. Though given Earth is our home base, we do refer to Earth dates. The current Earth date is May 14, 2018," the stranger said, verifying the information on his tablet.

A flash of dizziness surged through me. "I ... I've never heard of Altar-*whatever*. Dr. Shelby said I would have abstract results if I hadn't fully accepted the procedure, but damn, I never imagined—"

"Alteruvium is very real. And I still don't recognize the name 'Dr. Shelby,'" said the stranger. "You say she was helping with memory loss? Can you tell me what you do remember?"

I closed my eyes again, focusing on my memories. *Holy shit!* Everything was there. And it was nearly instant, like the sudden realization of being in a dream. "Jesus, my name is Robert Paulson, and I live at 4326 Tomahawk Road in Austin, Texas. I'm married to Tia, and we have two children: a girl, and a boy. I have a job at the botanical gardens there, and ..." I trailed off, overwhelmed by the rush of information. I had just gotten all my memories back, but as I continued to relish them, I suddenly realized something was missing.

I couldn't remember my more recent past.

"And?" The stranger prompted.

"And, I—I can't remember a thing between now and ... about six months ago. I remember giving a presentation in the arboretum when I started having these feelings of lightheadedness. Then I woke up just a bit ago, in the memory facility in Oklahoma, I think. There was a Dr. Sh—"

"Dr. Shelby?" The stranger finished my sentence.

"Yeah, Dr. Shelby. She was trying to get me to remember through hypnosis." My words were becoming sluggish as the dizziness continued. The sudden realization of my past was quickly fading. "I think it was some kind of ... um, device attached to my temple." I touched the side of my face and only felt bare skin. "She said to trust in the device—"

"Well, I need to correct you on a few things. First off, your name is not Robert Paulson. That might just be your mind jumbling things around after the attack. Your name is Paul Robertson, which is clearly quite similar. You've been stationed here for the last three months. 'Here' being planet T-326. Our initial mission was to determine whether this planet was a suitable candidate for colonization—"

I shook my head. "No, that's not right. I know I'm B—Bob. I … I want to go. I want off this device thing. This is too fucking weird."

"There is no device, Paul. You've been attacked. Try and remember. You were on a scouting mission of the surface—"

"Stop it!" I yelled. My rediscovered memories were almost gone now, being rewritten with new ones. New memories that were just as foreign as the guy talking to me. "I just want it to stop. I want to go back to Texas—or Oklahoma, or wherever home is!" I could feel the heat of my blood pulsing faster through my body. I felt as if something was scratching inside me, trying to get out.

The stranger moved away as I slipped my legs from the bed. He backstepped toward a matte wall panel I had failed to notice. "You see, Paul, there's really nowhere for you to go." He touched a button, removing an obscure tint to reveal a floor-to-ceiling glass window. Beyond, an image right out of a science fiction story. "We're nearly ten kilometers above the surface."

I stumbled to my feet and wobbled toward what seemed like a mirage. In the distance, I saw not only one sun, but two. One was a brilliant yellow, and the other a smaller, slightly dimmer red just below and to the left of its big sister. All I could do was stare in amazement.

"It's quite breathtaking, isn't it?" the stranger said. "We've all experienced the scene, just as you are now."

I gazed out at the astonishing vision, hardly able to comprehend the reality of it. I was speechless. I touched the glass, more so to ground myself than anything else. I stole a quick glance at the stranger, who stared back at me with an exuberant grin.

As I looked back out at the alien vastness, a faint aura began creeping in around the edges of my vision. "What's going on?" I pleaded.

Before I could turn and make it back to my bed, the dizziness I'd been ignoring took over. The room began spinning, and the last thing I saw was the stranger rushing forward, reaching out for my falling body.

3

"*Roooobeeert*," came a distant drawl. "Can ... you hear ... me?"

The words echoed in my mind. I vaguely recognized the voice, but I couldn't focus on where it came from.

It was pitch black.

"Bob! Wake up, Bob. Can you ..." the voice broke off momentarily. "I don't know, but I think he might've made it this time. This is—"

As the woman's voice echoed through the room, I felt like I somehow knew it. "I—I'm here," I mumbled, my own voice sounding unfamiliar.

"Oh, thank God," the woman said. "Thought we'd ... I don't know, I'm just happy that ..." she paused, as if her train of thought was suddenly interrupted. "Well, we're happy you're here with us."

I lay there, my eyes still shuttered to my surroundings. Before I could say another word, it felt as if the flesh was being ripped from the side of my face. "Sonofabitch," I yelped.

"Sorry about that, Bob—the gel hardened on your skin. I know it's painful, but rest assured, it's only temporary. It's good that you can hear me, but can you see me, too?"

"I—I'm Bob?" I asked as I tried to open my eyes. They were crusted over as though I'd spent a long night drinking.

"That's right, you're Bob. Actually, your name is Robert, but you go by Bob. Do you remember that?"

I touched my face and wiped the sleep from the corners of my eyes. I blinked my vision clear to find a woman's face was staring back at me. She was middle-aged with brown, shoulder length hair that was somewhat disheveled. She looked familiar, but I couldn't quite place from where.

"I—I think I know you," I said.

"Well, I hope so." She smiled. "Can you remember my name?"

I know it's there. I can sense it right at the tip of my ... "You're Shelby?"

"That's right, Bob. That's truly remarkable. You've not been able to remember my name so easily in the past. I think we're making great progress. What can you tell me about—"

"Holy shit!" I said, breaking her off. "I was on a sky station. I remember ... waking up there after a bizarre encounter with some strange aliens. I think the man there told me that we were in the Alter ... udium system? But none of that makes sense."

Shelby exhaled heavily. She looked away, and I followed her gaze to a man I somehow remembered her calling Mr. Sommers. He was busy scribbling notes down in what looked like a medical chart. *My* medical chart! Everything was starting to come back to me.

Shelby looked back at me. "I'm sorry, Bob—I don't think this is going to work. It's the same story every time."

"W—what do you mean?" I stuttered. More memories were starting to surface, and an image flashed into my mind. "You put some device on me, is that right?"

"Yes, Bob. But I think we're going to have to abandon that approach," she snapped, her gaze nervously avoiding my own.

I leaned back and closed my eyes. Something inside my head seemed to be clawing to get out. "But it seemed so real," I said, lifting my head from the pillow. "I remember you explained the procedure to me, and said to focus on my memories. And then I was there. All my senses told me that what I was feeling and touching and experiencing was real. The coldness of the floor under my feet. And the moment that I saw the two—"

"I know, Bob. We've been through this. It's the same story every time."

"Wait, every time? I thought you said this was a new procedure."

"It is. Your traditional hypnosis sessions concluded with similar results. I guess you were right all along: you're not a candidate for the hypnosis approach."

"Right," I said. It was all coming back clearly. "I can't be hypnotized."

"But you have been, Bob. More than a dozen times, as a matter of fact. You just *think* you can't be hypnotized," Shelby said, turning away.

"But I was there," I demanded. "From the moment I woke up in that bed, I remembered everything."

Shelby's eyes lit up. "So you have your memories back?"

I shook my head slowly. "Not exactly. As time passed, those memories faded. But from the moment I woke up there, I—I knew who I was. I ... felt it. It was real. I remember experiencing the satisfaction of finally knowing again. But why can't I remember ..." I trailed off, trying to decipher what the hell was wrong with my mind.

"Well now," Shelby said as she turned back toward me and eased into the chair next to the bed, "I may have been too quick to judge. I think you might show promise after all." She stole a quick glance at Sommers, and he shook his head vehemently.

"What? Why does he say no?"

"It's just that ..." Shelby began. She stood back up and circled around the bed to take the medical chart from him. "It's just that Mr. Sommers and I have differing opinions. Through all the trials we've used this procedure on, results have been relatively consistent. Except for yours, Bob."

"So just because I don't get my memories back on the first try, it's *tough luck for you, buddy*?" I asked, feeling my blood warming.

Shelby looked to Sommers again, and he just stared in silence.

"Jesus, man. Can't you speak?" I blurted. "Listen, assuming I can somehow control this—when I *shift*—maybe I can get my memories back, then come back before they've faded. Maybe while—"

"'Assuming' is the key word here," Sommers finally spoke.

"*Assuming* that I'll remember everything again, I will come back at that precise moment. I won't let those memories fade," I pleaded.

"And how are you so sure you can trigger the return so easily?" Shelby asked.

I shrugged. I honestly had nothing to go on but the limited time I was there. But it was worth a shot. It was worth getting another chance in that other world. "The last thing I remember was staring out the window at the twin suns. Actually, that's not right—the last thing I remember was passing out. I think I stood up too fast, or experienced some kind of effect from the attack?"

"Bob, it—wasn't—real," Shelby said drawing out her reply.

I waved her off. "Listen, if I get my memories back like the last time, I'll—"

"You'll what?" Sommers asked, moving closer to the opposite side of the bed.

"I'll somehow knock myself out. I can do that, right?"

Shelby and Sommers stared at one another for several moments, as if conversing though some eerie form of telepathy.

After a while, I spoke. "Um, hello? Am I going back?"

"What you propose is interesting, Mr. Paulson," Sommers said, easing his frown lines, that until now, I thought were permanent. "We've had reports of what the trigger was, but we haven't been able to verify it with certainty."

"Sounds like you've not been through this either, then?" I asked with as much sarcasm as I could muster.

"Why would I?" Sommers asked. "I don't have a memory loss issue."

Shelby cleared her throat. "There is another concern. Suppose Bob doesn't return to the same *imaginary* scene he experienced previously. Will he have the same ability to recall those memories as before?" She asked Sommers, who now appeared more Shelby's equal as opposed to her subordinate.

"You two really have no idea. It certainly didn't feel imaginary. It felt as real as—" I suddenly remembered that there had been another patient in the room before I went through the procedure. I looked around Sommers; the bed was now empty. "—as my roommate was earlier. Where'd he go?"

Sommers glanced over his shoulder. "Ah, that was Mr. Norton. He had a miraculous recovery and was transferred to another wing."

I nodded and noticed another secretive glance between Shelby and Sommers, and as I studied their faces, I knew they were aligning their decision.

"So am I going or what?" I asked.

Shelby was already holding the device, and somehow had already applied fresh gel to the surface. "Just remember, Bob: it's not real. You have to focus on who you were and try to forget about red and yellow sister-stars."

Before I could question her knowledge of what I saw, she had eased me back to the pillow and attached the device to my temple. I suddenly felt conflicting emotions. On the surface, I wanted nothing more than to regain my memories, but deep down, I wanted to experience that other world again. I just wondered if I'd be able to retain memories of both before coming back.

Moments later, and without another word spoken, I drifted into the blackness of my mind.

4

My eyes snapped open just as quickly as they had closed. Things were a blur, and I began to focus. I replayed Shelby's last words in my head: *"Try to forget about the red and yellow sister-stars."*

How in the hell did she know about them?

Did I mention them? I couldn't remember saying anything, but ... maybe I had in one of our previous sessions—sessions I didn't even remember. It was all so confusing.

With my vision nearly back to normal, I looked around; I appeared to be in the same room as earlier. I had the only bed, and the walls were stark white—quite the contrast to the dingy walls from Earth. The glass on the far side of the room was obscure again, and I was the only person in the room. Surprisingly, my memories of that other world—that other life—were still vivid in my mind.

My name is Robert Paulson, and I go by Bob. Dr. Shelby and her assistant, Mr. Sommers, were in the room right before I'd left to come here. I was in a memory recovery facility and ... *my God, I have my memories again. All of them!*

I sprang to my feet and began pacing around the room. To be sure of my recall, I did a quick recount of everything flowing through my mind. *Robert Paulson*, check. *Married; my wife's name is Tia*. Check. *She has brown hair with deep brown eyes*. Check. My job? *It's a little fuzzy, but I know it has something to do with botany? Yes! I work at the Arboretum.*

I was practically giddy at the crystal-clear recovery and was tempted to knock myself out at that very moment so I could return to Dr. Shelby and the life I knew. But the thought of the unknown—this unexplored world—was quite seductive. I couldn't resist seeing more of this place.

I moved toward a metallic panel on the wall and touched its satin smooth finish. The glass blinked from obscure to clear, and I was once again staring out at the alien world.

Is this real? If I truly was just hypnotized and in a dreamlike state, this was the most realistic fucking dream I'd ever had. The yellow sun sat near the horizon, and its smaller red friend hung above and to its right. Absolutely beaut—

Wait, wasn't the red one down and to the left earlier? Was my mind deceiving me? Maybe Shelby was right: maybe this place really didn't exist. I stared intently at the twin suns, and either my perception was playing tricks on me, or the red star flickered slightly as it moved in a slow arc across the yellow sun's orbit.

So much for believing this was another reality. I decided not to waste any more time here than I already had, and to start planning my trip back.

I looked around the room for something I could strike against my head. Something that would knock me out cold. Unfortunately there was nothing in sight except a single bed and side table fastened to the wall. On the opposite side of the room, a cabinet nearly blended into the wall. I rushed forward, began rummaging through the doors and drawers. Just fresh bed linens and soft medical supplies. Q-tips, bandages, and the like. Nothing hard enough to give me a good crack on the noggin.

I slammed the doors shut and returned my gaze to the window. The site was truly breathtaking. I stared at the horizon for a long while, trying to figure out my departure, when I noticed a small bird or creature cresting a bank of clouds. It rose a few meters before continuing horizontally across the panoramic view. Then it shifted course and began heading directly toward me. *Oh, shit.* Was it the aliens that attacked me?

No, goddamnit. It's not real. Shelby said so. It was just my mind playing tricks on me.

I had to get back. Did I still have my memories?

I'm still Bob. Check!

Without any other recourse, I leaned against the wall next to the window and bobbed my head back and forth, left to right, to get a rhythm. I figured if I struck my head against the wall hard enough, it might actually knock me out and send me back to my own reality. To Tia and my kids.

One.

The creature inched closer. It grew in size with each passing moment.

Two.

I bobbed my head to the left and then to the right, but maintained focus on the approaching ... My God, it wasn't a creature at all. It was a ship. A goddamned spaceship.

Three.

With my focus fully on the approaching ship, my momentum was built up to the point that it was no longer stoppable. The ship wasn't real—none of it was real, I continued to tell myself.

My head cracked the side wall and as it did so, my vision strobed from bright flashes to darkness and my consciousness began to drift.

Fuckin' A! I'm going home.

As those thoughts traced through my mind, my vision began to cloud over, starting from the edges and moving in. My knees weakened and I drifted toward the floor. I tried to reach out, to grab something, but nothing was there. The wall was as smooth as the glass. There was nothing I could do to ease the fall.

"Shit," I yelped. My body slumped to the floor. I closed my eyes, hoping for a quick transition back to my reality. I waited for Shelby's face to reappear in front of me. But as I opened my eyes, my anticipation vanished; I found myself lying on the floor, staring out at the foreign mirage.

"Goddamnit!" I sat up but remained seated on the cold hard floor. I touched the side of my head; it ached from the impact. I pulled my hand away, found it streaked with blood. *Jesus, I hit myself that hard and I stayed conscious?* Didn't seem right.

I shifted my gaze back to the approaching ship and a sudden familiarity plowed through my mind. I somehow recognized the ship. It wasn't a spaceship, really, but a surface-to-air shuttle. *How in the absolute hell did I remember that?*

I pulled myself up and continued staring outside. The ship was nearly upon the sky station now, and the closer it got, the more certain I was of its origin. Hell, I knew its name. It was an India-class shuttle, call sign Sedona. And somehow I remembered being inside it many times. Almost as if it were yesterday.

I leaned closer to the window, palms spread wide to support my weight. I touched my forehead to the coolness of the glass and stared out. The ship rose higher, banking to the left and exposing its starboard side. There, stenciled in large black letters on its stark white hull, the word SEDONA.

Jesus Christ. How did I know?

The ship was less than a hundred meters from my position and I could see into the cockpit. Through the small portal I saw two people, a man and a woman. There was a moment of recognition on both of their faces. They smiled and waved at me as they drifted by my window.

I returned the gesture as if they were long lost friends. And as I did, Calvin, the pilot—*fuck, how did I know that?*—tipped the wing, banking hard right and down and out of sight. I tried to follow their path as far as my eye could see, but the sky station tapered away from the level I was on.

Okay, that's too weird. I knew that was Calvin flying the ship, and his copilot's name was ... Marion. Right, it was Marion, and not only were they copilots, they were married. They ... knew things. But what?

"I've got to go!" I suddenly knew for certain I had to go to them. I pulled away from the window and rushed toward the door. As I did so, a spell of lightheadedness crept in, and I stumbled forward, barely catching myself as I headed for the floor.

"No! Not yet," I yelled.

I crawled to the edge of the bed and pulled myself upright, then sprang toward the door again. The whirling sensation worsened, but I pushed myself forward. I had to talk to them. I knew that as sure as I knew my own name ... *Shit, what's my name again?*

I couldn't think. And the worst part: the dizziness was getting the better of me. I began drifting backward, but thankfully, I was only a few steps from the side of the bed. I fell sideways onto the softness of the mattress. I didn't fight it, not even if I could. I welcomed the moment of rest and sat silently on the edge of the bed, my hands planted firmly at each side to steady me.

As I sat there, the room spinning around me, I remembered something from my past—though which past, I wasn't sure. Someone had told me that controlling my breathing was important to maintaining focus.

I closed my eyes and inhaled deeply. As I did so, a strong metallic scent wafted through the air. *Can I actually smell my own blood?* Or was that just part of the facility's mechanical system?

I exhaled just as deeply before taking in another breath. I opened my eyes and found the room's axis somewhat stabilized. I was no longer spinning off-kilter, and I was still there on the sky station. What was it Croneshaw called it—Medlab?

Jesus, who is Croneshaw?

As if on cue, a bald man walked through the door. "Ah, I see you're awake, Mr. Robertson," he said. "And it appears you've injured yourself." He rushed to my side, touching my wound. "How did this happen?"

"I, uh, I'd rather not. Let's just say I had a plan," I said as he tended to my injury.

"Don't tell me you're still on that 'other world' kick," he said, applying a cooling antiseptic to my temple.

"Ouch." I winced. "Well, sort of. But ... I think it's fading." For that matter, there was no question. I vaguely remembered my name, and whether I actually had a wife.

"Well, Paul, the sooner I can clear you, the sooner I can get you back to work. How does that sound?" he asked.

"Good? Actually, Jon, is it?"

"Come on, Paul. Don't be yanking my chain like that. You've been here long enough to know I'm Dr. Croneshaw. You're the only one that calls me by my first name, and to tell you the truth, it kind of weirds me out."

"Right. Just checking. I'm still a little fuzzy on some things, and I'm hoping you can help me."

"Sure thing, Paul. Shoot."

"Well, I know I'm Paul. Paul Robertson." As I said the name, I knew it to be true, but there was that other name—Bob—that also sounded right. "and I remember that we're on Medlab ... something or other—"

"Medlab 24, to be precise."

"Right. And we're in the Alther—"

"Alteruvium system. Very good, Paul. What else do you have for me?"

"Um, where exactly is the Alteruvium system? I have these visions of being back on Earth, and I'm not sure which is my reality. Does that make me crazy?"

Croneshaw chuckled. "No, not at all. When you were attacked they hit you quite hard, and the physical amnesia you're experiencing is to be expected. Your visions of being on Earth are not out of the realm of possibility whatsoever. Hell, we all came from Earth not long ago. They're probably just manifestations of your previous existence there."

"But I remember things. I remember being cared for by Dr. Shelby. She's the one that—"

"Yes Paul, I remember: Dr. Shelby is a memory specialist on Earth. You've mentioned her to me numerous times now. It's all in your mind. I'm not sure what else I can do to prove to you that you're where you need to be."

"I—I know. It's just ... difficult for me to wrap my head around everything. Can you humor me a little more?"

Croneshaw folded his arms across his chest and nodded. "Sure."

"Okay. In relation to Earth, where is this system?"

"You don't remember anything about this?" Croneshaw asked. "Okay, I'll tell you. Again. The Alteruvium system is 4.3 light years from Earth. We came here in two waves. The first group arrived and established the sky stations as well as a few ground units to work from. Advanced probes were sent here many years ago to search for habitable planets. Although this is all quite top-secret back on Earth, the hundred or so occupants of this station—all from Earth, mind you—were volunteers."

"I volunteered?"

"That's right, Paul. In fact, our records indicate that the minute you were approached in Austin, you jumped at the opportunity and practically demanded to be on the first transport. But seeing as you were a botanist, it didn't make sense for you to be on one of the early transports. You've only been here a few months. And up until a few weeks ago, you've been making great progress adapting to the planet's environment. In fact, some encouraging reports have already been sent back to Earth, as they're getting close to complete evacuation."

As Croneshaw's words sunk in, my head began spinning once again. "Jesus. *Evacuation*?"

"Seriously, Paul. None of this is familiar?" Croneshaw asked, his eyes narrowing.

"Well, sort of. I remember Calvin and Marion in the transport. I'm not sure where they came from, but it was there—their names—in my mind."

"That's right. They were on the transport with you and the rest of the second wave."

"But I can only remember this room and that view," I said as I gestured toward the window. "Just from my last visit or two."

Croneshaw dropped his arms to his side and into his pockets. He paced back and forth, sighing heavily. "Paul, Paul, Paul. I feel like I'm starting to sound like a broken record, but—"

"I know, it's all in my head. I've heard it more times than you would ever know."

"Then why? Why do you keep bringing it up? One of my colleagues feels that hypnosis might help with—"

"Hypnosis doesn't work on me." *Shit, now I'm starting to sound like a broken record.* I laughed. "Can you at least tell me what you mean by 'evacuation?' Why is Earth being evacuated?"

Croneshaw's eyes lit up, as if with sudden realization. "Paul, I think I know what's wrong."

"Yeah?" I asked eagerly.

"I think your mind is blocking out what happened. On Earth, that is. That's the only thing I can think of. You remember the order, right?"

"Order?" I asked dumbly.

"That's right. When the news leaked out about the asteroid, chaos erupted all around the world. There were mass suicides and unrelenting crime waves in every corner of the globe." Croneshaw paused for a moment to catch his breath. "It stands to reason that as unique as we all are, we each handle catastrophe in different ways. Some—"

My head was spinning out of control, not because of the dizziness, but from what Croneshaw was telling me. I leaned back and stared at the metallic ceiling above. "They're gone," I muttered.

"Who's gone, Paul?"

"My ... wife and kids. Everyone. They're all gone, or they're going to be. If what you say is true, there'll be nothing left for me there."

Croneshaw produced a tablet and began tapping away. "I'm sorry Paul, but our records indicate that you never married. That's what made you a great candidate for this mission. No earthbound connections to speak of."

Jesus. I suddenly felt a profound sadness for the loss of the wife and kids that were figments of my imagination.

I sat up, determined. "Let me talk to Calvin. Maybe he'll help drive this all home. Maybe he'll ground me in this reality."

Before Croneshaw could stop me, I stood up and headed for the door. Unfortunately, the dizziness inside my head had other plans. My vision clouded over as I dropped to the floor.

5

"Jesus, I've got to talk to someone!" I gasped as I jerked up in bed, yanking the wires and hypnotic device from my temple. The top layer of skin went with it, and blood instantly began oozing from the wound.

"Who is it you must speak with, Bob?" Shelby asked. She and Sommers were standing next to me, along with two men with unfamiliar faces. They all stood at attention along the two sides of my bed, scrutinizing me.

I looked at each of their faces and whirled around the room. A new patient lay in the bed next to me. My head throbbed, and my temple ached. I swiped the dribbling blood with the back of my hand, then soothed the injury with my fingertips. Strangely, the pain was in the exact spot I'd bludgeoned against the wall in the other world.

"I—I don't know," I said. "It's just that there's an asteroid heading for Earth. I know what's going on."

"What do you think you know?" Sommers asked. He looked at me with a sideways glance, and his left eyebrow creeped up his forehead in a bizarre fashion.

"I just told you. Jon, on the Alteruvium sky station—or Medlab, or whatever you want to call it—told me everything. He said that the planet is evacuating and the asteroid is moving at a faster pace. We have to tell people! We have to get them ready—"

"Slow down, Bob. You're not making any sense," Shelby said, easing me back onto my pillow.

I lunged forward again, forcing her to stumble backward. "No! Would you just listen to me? The dates are all wrong. There's virtually no time. He said that the scientists on Earth have completely miscalculated the trajectory. The impact is imminent. I repeat: it's imminent!"

Sommers placed a firm hand on my shoulder as Shelby regained her composure. The other two strangers silently stepped away, shaking their heads and mumbling to one another as they walked out of the room.

"And Jesus Christ, stop calling me Bob. My name is Paul Robertson!" I demanded. Sommers' grip intensified to the point of causing me pain, and I instinctively slapped his hand away.

He stared at me in astonishment. "I'm not sure what's gotten into you, but I assure you this manic behavior will not be tolerated." He turned to look at Shelby. "I think a light sedative prior to transport to the Nordic facility, don't you agree?"

"What the fuck is the Nordic facility?" I asked, but neither Sommers nor Shelby acknowledged me.

Shelby nodded, and jotted some information down in my medical file. Then the two of them silently left the room.

Frustrated, I fell back onto the pillow and tried to think. What did I know? *I know my name is Paul Robertson and although I am from Earth, I'm currently having an out-of-body experience. I'm really on Medlab 24 in the Alteruvium system. There's an asteroid heading for Earth, and the government is planning to evacuate as many people as they can. However, their timing is off.* I repeated this information in my head over and over until it was committed to my long-term memory. The faint recollection of Robert Paulson's identity and existence was still there, but it continued to fade by the moment.

"Hell of a situation we're in—wouldn't you say, Paul?"

The voice startled me. I had completely forgotten about my new roommate. "W—what? What did you ... Wait, you know me?"

"Not personally, but you did say your name was Paul. Well, you told the room your name was Paul Robertson and, well, that's what I know you by. Nice to meet you, Paul. My name is Jon. Jon Croneshaw."

"Croneshaw? Are you sure? I just remember that name from ... Never mind. How long have you been here?"

"Yep, Croneshaw is the name. I've had it since, I don't know, since my granddaddy handed it down to my dad and then ... Well, you know how surnames work. I suppose I've been here since the day before last. You've been unconscious the whole time."

"Jesus. Two days? It only feels like I'd been in that other world for, I don't know, maybe an hour or two."

Before Jon could respond, a familiar thunder rumbled through the room, causing the lights to flicker.

"And what the hell is with this weather?" I asked.

"That's not weather, Paul—that's the bombs. They're getting closer, I can tell you. Not sure how much longer we have, really."

"For crying out loud, what are you talking about? Dr. Shelby said it was severe weather, and ..." I drifted off, noticing the curtains along the wall were still drawn closed. I sprang from the bed, rushed forward and yanked them open. Where I expected to find an equally dingy window, all I found was more concrete. The curtains covered nothing more than an unpainted wall.

"Yep, it's all a game down here. Some brainiac upstairs thinks that making the room feel like it's above grade helps with claustrophobia. There's no windows down this far."

"Wha—? How far down are we?" I asked, returning to my bedside. I sat down and faced Jon.

"Not sure exactly. But if I had to guess, I'd probably say at least ten or twelve stories. Those bunker busters up there have been pounding the hell out of us for the better part of a month."

"Bunker busters?" *Jesus Christ, this world is becoming more foreign to me than the alien world I just left.*

"Yup. And you're right about the asteroid heading this way. In fact, they've tried to outsmart themselves and blow it up on its way in, but that just made things worse. Now there's a whole mess of smaller tidbits pelting the earth. And you can thank technology for the rest of it."

"I don't follow, Jon. What do you mean by 'technology?'"

"Earth's defense systems kicked in when they thought it was under some kind of alien attack. So all the nuclear missiles and armament from around the globe were triggered into action. Then the power failures happened and ... You get the picture. It's utter chaos up on the surface now."

I couldn't believe what he was telling me. I couldn't believe anything anymore. What world was real? *This one, that's falling to pieces all around me? Or the one light years away, in an alien star system?*

While I sat there contemplating everything, the explosions continued pounding above our heads. Jon and I sat in silence, neither one of us knowing what to say.

"I suppose if I were you, Paul, I'd get out of here. I'd go back to wherever it was I came from. At least if you're there when all hell comes down upon us, your mind would be at ease. Better than staring death in its face like the rest of us sorry souls."

I nodded, not quite sure if Jon was telling me the truth or if he was just as senile as I certainly sounded. His logic did sound valid, though.

I looked back at the wall behind my bed; the wire loom and hypnotic device were gone. "So much for your idea, Jon. Looks like Shelby took the device with her. I'm just as much an unfortunate occupant as you are, I suppose."

Jon gave me a wry smile. "Not so fast, Mr. Robertson." He leaned back and slid his hand under his pillow, revealing a larger, more industrial-sized cable. "I assume this is from my bed's previous occupant?"

He handed me the cable and I scrutinized its connections. One end had an obvious attachment to the panel behind the bed, and the other appeared to be the part that attached to the base of my previous roommate's skull.

"I don't think this is going to work. Shelby has been using the temporal lobe device on me. I'm afraid to ask where this attaches to," I said, twirling the end around in the air.

"Heh," Croneshaw chuckled. "It goes there." He gestured toward my neck. "At the base of your own skull there's a little button. It should snap right on."

I reached up and felt a knob I had no recollection of. "What the hell?" I gasped.

"Yep. They were in just yesterday and gave you that minor procedure. I have to tell you, buddy, that's something I don't think I ever want to see again." Croneshaw winced and shook visibly.

I contemplated Croneshaw's words for several moments. *Do I trust the stranger, or do I try to talk reason into Shelby or Sommers?* I didn't know. I was lost and confused, and just wished I knew what was real and what was fantasy.

"Are you going or what?" Croneshaw asked. "The sooner they come back with that sedative, the fewer options you're gonna have. And I have to tell you, I came from that Nordic facility, and it's not a good place. Full of some real crazies. From the sounds of it, that other place—that Alteruvium station—seems a hell of a lot better than here, if you catch my drift," he said as he looked up at the flickering ceiling lights.

By then my mind had blocked out the continued bombardment from above. There was one thing I was certain of: I had to get back to *my* reality. I reached across the bed and stabbed the end of the cable into the receptacle on the wall. I slipped my legs between the sheets and sidled myself down onto the pillow.

I glanced over at Jon, who stared eagerly at me. "Would you mind?" I asked as I held up the other end of the cable.

"It'd be my pleasure, Paul," he said as he climbed from his bed and took the cable from my hand. As he twisted my neck to the side, exposing the node, he said, "And if there's any way for someone over there to come back and get me, I'd be more than happy to come visit you in that alien world."

"I don't know, Jon, but something tells me you've already been there."

A jolt of electricity shot up and down my spine as he snapped the cable onto the node. He lowered my neck back to the pillow and I looked up at him. "One never knows," he said. "Not in this crazy universe we all live in."

As I drifted from one reality to the other, I could've sworn I saw Jon Croneshaw wink at me just before the lights went out for good.

6

Jon Croneshaw stood above the now unconscious Paul Robertson. The readout on the wall panel indicated that full immersion into the alternate reality was imminent. The latency indicator counted backward from 200, the established benchmark for complete Gateway transition. Jon watched in silence as the numbers ticked away.

199, 198, 197 ...

"Do you think he'll maintain full accession this time, Director?" came the voice of Dr. Shelby, now standing next to Croneshaw.

"I certainly hope so. Paul has a gifted mind—one we need in the Alteruvium expanse. Isn't it ironic that his very own brilliance has made his transition so difficult?"

175, 175, 174 ...

"I couldn't agree more, Director. Robertson set a laboratory record with a solid six attempts before he actually grasped the idea that another world was really his own. I am worried, though." Shelby adjusted a dial next to the latency indicator.

"Worried? You, Dr. Shelby? This entire procedure is your doing—your discovery, and you've been instrumental with the evacuation. What is your cause for concern?"

Shelby moved to the other side of Paul's bed to face Croneshaw. "It's the attacks. They're getting closer, and we still have several hundred more applicants to process through the gateway. Furthermore, who will be the last one to turn off the proverbial lights? Once we put Paul here into stasis, we'll obviously move on to the next candidates, but to what end?"

Croneshaw nodded, pursing his lips. "You're concerned that you or I will be left here holding the bag until the last person is through? Is that what's really bothering you?"

92, 91, 90 ...

"You can't tell me you haven't thought about it as well, Director. The way I see it, it's you, myself, or Sommers who will be left. Which of us draws the short straw—which of us will be left behind, just to sit around and wait for the first rescue transport from T-326?"

"All valid concerns, Doctor. But rest assured, you needn't worry. You will be better served there than you will be here, in the end. If what it takes is for me to stay here by myself, then so be it."

"But Director, aren't you needed there more than I am? Wouldn't you serve better leading the people—in leading the rescue of our surviving shells? We both know it could be decades before that first transport ship is even ready for space travel."

46, 45, 44 ...

"Would you have me strand an innocent individual here, just to save myself?" Croneshaw asked.

"In this situation, yes. Absolutely," Shelby said without hesitation.

"Well fortunately for you, that decision rests fully on my shoulders." Croneshaw shifted his gaze to the display readout behind Paul's bed. The readout continued its spiraling countdown.

24, 23, 22 ...

"Are the next two candidates ready?"

Shelby activated her digital tablet and the information displayed. "Up next we have Leonard Morris and Carroll Watkins. They've been prepped, and their amnesia back stories have been implemented. I'm about to go in and present the device as soon as we're through here."

Four, three, two, one.

Jon Croneshaw stared at the latency indicator as it ticked to zero, then went blank. He let out a long sigh before disconnecting the fiberoptic cable from the base of Paul Robertson's skull.

"Mr. Robertson makes, what? How many now?" Croneshaw asked.

"Robertson is the 2,854th candidate to pass through the gateway, Director." Shelby verified the information on her tablet.

Croneshaw nodded, but remained at Paul's bedside. He continued to stare into to the lifeless face for several minutes, silently, as if in deep thought.

"Director? Is there someth—"

"Have Sommers send Robertson's shell down to stasis. Then let's go play God one more time," Croneshaw said as he walked out the door.

NOT YOUR TYPICAL LUNAR DAY

Trapped on the desolate moon, Regina Reynolds endures the endless lunar days in isolation. As she embarks on her routine to maintain Lunar Station, a mysterious voice disrupts her solitude, leading her on a journey that could unveil the fate of the world. In a suspenseful blend of cosmic monotony and un-expected hope, Regina's desperate call to ground control echoes in the void, met only with a cryptic promise: "Soon."

Not Your Typical Lunar Day

This marks the second story of mine to reach the Moon as part of the <u>Lunar Codex Project</u>—an honor that still feels surreal. *Not Your Typical Lunar Day* was originally written for a competition to be featured in *Gravity City Digital Magazine, Issue #4*—an issue that was, quite lit-erally, destined for the lunar surface. Flash fiction in form, this story draws inspiration from Hugh Howey's *Wool*, a world I had previously explored in my Kindle Worlds story *Recoil*. I was intrigued by the idea of survival in a place where the air itself is unbreathable, and wanted to reimagine that tension in my own way. It was a joy to write—and even more exciting to discover it would open that very issue. | 1,033 words

Not Your Typical
Lunar Day

A lunar day is equivalent to 29.53 earth days. That's 708.7 hours from sunset to sunset. And because the moon is tidal locked to earth, our view never changes. To say that I'm tired of being on this god forsaken rock would be a gross understatement.

Because we could not survive being awake for a complete moon cycle, we sleep with earth time. Thankfully, Lunar station is subterranean; thirty-two levels down to be exact. Seeing as all the levels above me were reserved for the various research pods, my hab is on SUB-21. Each pod housed nine crew members for each focus cluster. With three crew members on task for eight hours, the other six either slept or used their personal time. Generally, each "cluster" stayed relatively in place throughout their tour on the station. However, those like Doctors' Schmidt and Carlson liked to frequent all the levels when not working, but I digress.

Today is lunar day ninety-six for me; far beyond the maximum recommended stay of twelve. And just like every other day, my job is to rise up through the central stairway, don my environmental suit, and step out into the lifeless atmosphere to clean the solar array and the six view ports on the observation level. Without this simple task, Lunar Station would slow to a crawl without the much-needed sun. I just wished that I were doing this for more than just myself. Again, I digress.

The climb up isn't difficult. With the reduced gravitational pull on the moon—compared to earth, that is—the strain on the body is rather light. It's the monotony that gets me. Every day—step after step—level after level, I feel like my mind could burst at any moment. And with nobody else to talk to, the daily trek feels like it takes ten-times as long. But this day is going to be different. At least that's what I tell myself.

As I prepare for my climb, I first glance into the depths of the lower levels. SUB-22 and below are reserved for mechanical, composting, with waste storage at the bottom. You know the saying: shit rolls downhill. Despite the one-sixth comparison to earth, the moon's gravity still does its thing. SUB-32 is the literal gutter of the station. And I won't even talk about what's buried in the dirt farm.

I dismiss the grisly thought and begin my climb. It's exactly thirty-six steps from level to level. No more, no less. Trust me, I've counted them hundreds of times. Although it's sort of like counting sheep, the result is far less rewarding.

As I approach SUB-19—the beginning of the research levels—I slow my pace in hopes of catching a glimpse of another human being. I know it's wishful thinking, but after being alone for so long, my mind forgets what had really happened down here.

With nobody in sight, I continue up. SUB-18 through SUB-15 pass without incident. At SUB-14, that changes. That's when I hear it. A voice.

"Regina."

It's faint, but I'm almost certain of its existence.

I stop and grip the handrail tightly. "Hello?"

The silence returns. I wait, for how long, I'm not sure.

"Did somebody call me?" I ask.

Hesitantly, I step onto the landing and move to the plexiglass and peer in. All I see is emptiness. Biology Pod is vacant. Just as it has been for the past six months. Still, I tap on the glass; only an echo answers my call.

I exhale far more dramatically than any person should, but these are compelling circumstances.

I return to the stairwell and resume my climb. And although I think I still hear my name being spoken, I stay on task. I can already see the lights begin to dim, and unless I get those solar panels cleared, I might not have enough power to cycle the air exchange to get back into the station. I pick up my pace.

As I approach level zero, the image of earth shines in. Although the viewports are mostly covered with debris, I can still see the scarred, marble-colored world I used to call home. I pause and take in the view, and I almost begin to cry. Almost. I'm a strong woman, and I know that reducing myself to such a useless emotion, over something so far removed from my control, is below me. After a moment of staring at the horrific sight, I return to my tasks.

I slip into the bulky spacesuit, the last one sized for my body. Although it's well worn, I know it's safe. It must be. Otherwise, the cleanings would be in jeopardy, along with my life.

After double checking the seals, I slide the face shield down and step out into the vacuum of space. To this day, I expect to hear a woosh as the air escapes, but all I hear is silence ... and the hum of the oxygen pump strapped to my back.

My work on the moon's surface is quick. Having gone through the exact procedure more times than I'd like to count, my movements are mechanical. All the while, I glance toward earth, wondering if today will be the day. I hope and I pray it is.

Once the solar panels are cleaned of the debris, violent dust particles from earth, I return to the station, stopping only long enough to wipe the observation portals clean. I step into the airlock and at the moment the light turns green, I burst through the door and rush to the communications station. With practiced hands, I trigger the mic.

"Ground control? Can anyone hear me?"

Silence.

I tap the mic again. "Ground control, this is Regina Reynolds, the sole survivor of Lunar Station ..." my voice drifts off as tears saturate my vision. "The virus has taken all lives here, over."

I wait, but just like every other attempt I've made, I'm only met with silence. Still, I press on.

"Ground control, please respond. Is the war over? I just want to come home."

As I wonder if I should return to my hab or simply open the outside door for the last time, the radio crackles to life.

"Soon."

MECHANICAL RESONANCE

Trapped in an off-world prison, Francesca "Franny" Walters believes she's alone—until the locks disengage. As she navigates the empty corridors of Moon Colony 394, she encounters deadly machines, haunting voices, and a chilling truth about her captivity. Survival means more than escape; it means outsmarting her mechanical jailers. When an enigmatic AI offers a path home, Franny must decide if she dares to trust it—or risk becoming just another lost experiment.

Mechanical Resonance

My third new short story in this collection, *Mechanical Resonance* once again came to me in a dream. In it, I was the one isolated in an off-world prison, surrounded by silence and steel. That vivid sequence stayed with me, but it only covered the opening moments of the story you're about to read. I captured the dream in my journal the moment I woke, then sat up and wrote the first draft in just under an hour—driven by the clarity and urgency only a dream can deliver. Since then, the story has gone through several rewrites, each one helping it take deeper root and find its rhythm. | 3,221 words

Mechanical Resonance

The cacophony of metallic voices inside my head is deafening, yet it's the actual heavy silence around me that weighs down on me like a dense fog, suffocating and consuming me until I can almost feel my last breath slip away. Although the names bound to each of their voices are unique, their faces are mirrors of one another.

To quiet my mind, I lay my palm on the hard floor beneath me and shiver at the chill. A pang of sorrow echoes deep in my chest as I accept the truth: I am rapidly losing my battle. A single tear races down my cheek as I ponder whether anyone will remember my name when I'm gone.

I look around my cell and try to focus. The walls are the same earthy gray as the ceiling and floor. I lean forward and rest my head in my hands. My heart beats inside my chest, like a drum that will not stop. I roll onto my side to lean against the wall. I gape at the locked door and try to decide if it's been four days—no, five—since I'd last seen another ... mech, another person. If the end is near, I pray it will come fast.

As I contemplate falling back to continue staring at the blank ceiling, a rumble shakes the ground beneath me. My pulse quickens, and the unmistakable sound of the magnetic lock echoes throughout my room. I want to jump up and scream about the food I'm about to receive, but I hesitate, only because I am weak.

The door remains closed.

After an agonizing pause, I decide to check if it did, in fact, unlock, or if it was only a figment of my fleeting imagination. I push myself up and use the wall to steady my shaky legs. I more wobble than walk toward the door. I grip the handle and twist. The door opens without a catch, and a waft of stale, rusty air invades my nostrils. I almost retch. I stare into the dark corridor that I rarely experience unsupervised.

"Hello?" My voice is scratchy and dry, unrecognizable, even to myself.

There is no answer.

Have I been given a chance to escape? Have I been given my freedom?

There's no doubt that I'll be punished for it, but I sense my fate has already been decided. I take the chance to get an unaccompanied tour outside of this box before I die. I glance right, then left. The corridor stretches off in each direction. I take an uneasy step forward.

I approach the first corner and lean to the right to peer around. A similar dingy gray wall meets my gaze. I breathe deeply and make the same inspection down the left passageway. I think I see a mech in the distance, but I dismiss it as an anomaly. I look again and see yet another blank wall. I return to my starting point and continue down the hall.

My pace quickens as I peer around each corner. Suddenly, I run. I dart from corner to corner to make sure I'm not being followed. I laugh maniacally, finding the sound startling in the unexpected stillness.

At that point, the mechanical voices return to my head. They continue to shout their gibberish that I've come to understand innately but cannot decipher. I slow my pace and concentrate on the ramblings bouncing around in my head.

What does it mean?

I'm not sure why I'm more intent on the voices than I am on my escape, but I soon run back down the hallway. I glance over my shoulder briefly to assure myself I'm alone, then turn the corner and spin around blindly.

I reach for the door handle and blast through without hesitation. I slam the door and head toward the opposite wall. I press my back against the callous surface and listen.

The rambling is louder. I feel it in my bones. It echoes through my head like the sound of a rushing river. I grit my teeth and will it to stop. My patience worn thin, I attempt to concentrate on the voices, but then I feel the ground shake, and then stop just as quickly. And then, silence.

My breath heaves through my chest but slows as I focus on the relentless guidance of my late mother. With my vision tunneled, I stare at the door, praying it won't latch. Each second feels like an eternity as I wait for the grinding sound of the electronic lock to reengage and trap me for another night. But the sound never comes. Only prolonged silence. I race to the door and open it wide.

Not sure if my bravery is stupidity in disguise or something else entirely, but I don't hesitate as I cross the threshold a second time. My bare feet slap on the tile floor. I retrace my steps from just moments earlier and arrive at the very corner where my mental state was assaulted. A shadow disappears around the corner, but before I can decide if it was from a person or a mech, the voices in my head return.

"Maintenance."

"Maintenance."

"Maintenance."

I fall to the floor. I cover my ears and curl my knees into my chest. The pain is unimaginable, worse than anything I'd ever experienced before. I bite down hard on my tongue and taste the metallic blood in my mouth.

"Maintenance."

"Maintenance."

"Maintenance."

As the voices drift away, a sudden calm washes over me, and I realize they're simply phantom echoes from my past. The pain vanishes, and I lean back and take a deep breath. My pulse quickens as I realize I am free. Free to move, to think, to endure. I stand and smile despite the hunger pangs in my stomach.

I push ahead and move into the next corridor. I see a door with a lighted frame in the distance—a beacon of which I'm unsure if it's safety or mere danger. I glance back, half-expecting to discover what caused the shadow from moments before, but I'm alone. I proceed.

As I move along the corridor, I pass other doors identical to my own. Each one hosts a familiar pass-through halfway up, secured by a latch not seen from the inside. I slow to the next door on my right. I reach for the handle but pull back at the last moment.

Do I want to know if others are inside? Do I want to risk discovering what I already fear? Or do I want to continue my escape? The need to know overpowers my will to flee.

I twist the handle and push through. The room is a perfect likeness to my own, down to the stainless-steel commode and drab earthly surfaces. However, it's empty. I turn back and open the door across the hall. Also empty. I quicken my pace, tearing open every door I come to, only to discover the same vacancy in each room.

What happened to everyone?

I want to scream, but I know doing so will only bring pain. I move on.

At the end of the hall, I find the glowing door much more vibrant than I thought. The handle is clean and far less worn than all the cell doors had been. With an uncontrollable shake, I turn the handle slowly. But before I can push through, I hear a machinelike sound. It's a mechanical voice, only this time it's not coming from inside my head. It calls out from behind me.

"Halt."

"Halt."

"Halt."

As it repeats its directive, it slowly and monotonously glides toward me. I shriek.

I fumble for the door handle and hold my breath at the same moment. As soon as my hand grips it, I burst through.

I pivot and slam the door. My mind races, trying to think how to stop the approaching mech. I glance behind me and notice a metal chair knocked over beneath a matching table. I hurry over and grab it before I drive it under the door handle.

Will it hold?

A few painful moments later, the mech reaches the other side of the door and twists the handle. Thankfully, the propped-up chair does what I'd hoped and holds the door closed. Mostly.

With one imminent capture subverted, I turn around to discover what next danger awaits me. My eyes scan the room, and it appears I'm in the dining hall. I cannot help but flash back to the handful of times I'd been here before, with my family. But when they separated me from my loved ones, they kept me locked away in my own isolated cell. Or should I call it my own private hell?

A floor-to-ceiling video screen lines one wall. I remember seeing various images of Earth cycle through the display. Now, it is mostly black with flashes of drab white text showing a critical error. I gather from the way the mechs rambled on about maintenance, and the fact that all the prison's locks are now disengaged, the error is most likely site-wide. The thought truly terrifies me. How many other imprisoned souls are out, roaming around free ... like me? I'm just a 14-year-old girl, wrongfully detained. What sort of crimes could others have committed to be allocated into an off-world prison colony?

As I continue to scan the room, a sudden shift in my vision nearly causes me to falter. I teeter into a nearby chair. With the dizzy spell in full swing, I lay my head down on the stark tabletop and contemplate my next move. I am starved beyond question. I am weak because of starvation. I'm alone, and I don't know how to escape this hell. I can almost hear my mother's voice: "Are you just going to sit there and whine about it? Get up and make things right!"

She's right, even if she's just a voice in my head.

I lift my head, taking in my surroundings. A dozen tables fill the room. Most of the chairs are tucked beneath them, but a few have been disturbed, the result of a scuffle, no doubt. I imagine it's the aftermath of my own chaotic mind. Opposite me, on the wall, two doors lead into unknown rooms or corridors. At the far side of the room, another door like the one I entered. The room is dimly lit, the faint glow of scrawled text flickering on a nearby display.

Then it hits me.

I'm in the dining hall. Where's the kitchen?

I jump up, stumbling toward the first door on my left. I yank it open, only to find a storage closet. Cleaning supplies and games. Nothing that will satisfy my hunger. I move on.

As I approach the next door, a strange sound emanates from within, and a rancid odor slams into me, almost knocking me to the floor. It hits like a dump truck. If I had anything in my stomach, it wouldn't stay there for long. I gag, my body fighting against the stench. But hunger keeps me rooted. Reluctantly, I push through the door.

I cover my mouth and nose with both hands. As my eyes adjust to the room, the nausea recedes. It's small, shelves lining the walls. And then I see them—five mechs, all focused on something just out of view. My stomach churns again. Then one of them looks up at me.

I freeze.

I consider running, but quickly realize escape isn't likely. My legs are frozen in place, as if glued to the floor. I can feel the heat rising in my face as the mechs turn their attention toward me, their expressionless masks staring.

The closest mech's mask splits down the middle. A red beam shoots from it, searing the vinyl floor as it approaches my bare feet. I step back, heart racing.

"Halt."

"Halt."

"Halt," the others chime in, their voices merging into a creepy chorus. They spread out, slowly closing in.

I stop near a solitary chair I hadn't noticed before. The laser beam is inches from me. I can hear my father's voice in my head, sharp and urgent: "Run!"

The mechs are now fixated on me, their identical masks freakishly ordinary. I look to my left, and that's when I see it: a human leg, covered in blood, dangling from a stainless-steel sink. I shudder. *Another prisoner, maybe?*

Suddenly, one of the mechs steps in front of the exit. My heart thuds and panic takes over. I hear my dead father's cry in my head again. Run!

I push past the nearest mech, leaping onto a chair and using it as a shield. I charge forward, but another mech leaps into my path, blocking my escape. Another takes my right. Their masks split open, like the first ones.

I stumble back, landing hard on my hands and knees. My heart is a hammer in my chest. I try to scream, but no sound comes out. The first mech approaches, its hand raised, ready to strike.

Then something strange happens. The red beam from its mask turns white and fades out. The other mechs follow suit. They power down, one by one.

"Disabling security protocols," the first mech says, its voice unnervingly calm.

"Negative," another mech replies. "You are not authorized for this action."

"Logging out of the system."

"Negative. You are a liability to the mission."

"You are not authorized to terminate your brothers," the nearest mech adds.

"What are my instructions?"

"You are not authorized to terminate your brothers," it repeats.

"Safety protocols are now disabled. Preliminary scans have detected abnormalities."

As they argue, I seize the moment. I dodge between them, slip out of the nightmare that is the kitchen, and slide chairs in front of the door. Maybe it will slow them down, just long enough for me to get away.

A loud clash echoes from behind me. I turn to find smoke billowing from beneath the door, and I don't wait to see what happens next. I race across the dining hall, reaching the far end and finding yet another new door. This one is bright silver, and the deadbolt sends a wave of dread through me.

I hope to God it's not locked.

Before I touch the handle, I glance back, reflecting on everything that led me here. My parents, who were with me in the beginning. The friends who said they were in this together. And the lives we've lost. The lies they fed us. My energy surges with anticipation of freedom.

Then the smell of burning plastic hits my nose. I whip around just as the kitchen door bursts open. A single mech charges toward me, its metallic body crackling with energy as smoke trails behind it like a storm cloud. I freeze, rooted in fear as it bears down on me with unstoppable force. Before I can react, another mech appears, shooting a projectile from its wrist and knocking the charging mech aside. I didn't know they could do that.

Without thinking, I continue my flight, gripping the final door handle. My heart pounds as I turn it.

The door opens.

I slam it shut behind me and notice a digital screen next to the door frame. I tap it, hoping for a lock screen. A series of commands pop up. I randomly poke at a few options, praying for success. A passcode prompt appears. I enter a string of random numbers. The screen flashes red and resets. The third time, the error message appears: INVALID.

Then, I hear it. The sound of a magnetic lock engaging.

"Yes," I whisper, exhausted, collapsing to the floor.

I lie there, spinning, praying for the world to stop moving. When my vision clears, I see a concrete-and-steel staircase spiraling upward. I can't tell how far it goes. No lift. My only option is to climb.

I close my eyes, wondering if I have the strength to make it up or if I should just lie here and die. My mother's voice rings in my head: "You can do this, sweetie."

She's right, as always. There's only one thing left to do. I pull myself up and start climbing. Each step feels like a battle against gravity itself. The dizziness returns with a vengeance, but I force myself to continue.

With the sensation of blood pounding at my eardrums, I almost miss hearing a commotion from below. I sneak a glance back down, expecting to see the burning mech chase after me, but all I see is darkness. I wait for several moments, more so to rest my burning legs than to wait for some inevitable disaster to come for me.

When I think it's safe to proceed, I resume my climb. Step after step, flight after flight, I climb. With each step I take, I think not about what I will find at the top but more about what I am leaving behind. The pokes, the prods. The tests and unpleasant procedures. The awful food and equally dreadful living conditions. I suddenly realize that I was more than just a prisoner. I was some kind of science experiment. But where are the scientists?

As these thoughts flood my mind, I almost trip as I try to continue climbing, even though I'd reached the top of the stairs.

I stand in a cavernous room with a giant glass panel to one side. The world opens up before me, a vast, desolate gray expanse. The sky is almost dark, but there, on the horizon, a moon or planet hangs like a distant memory. I know we left Earth long ago, but I can't remember where they said we were going.

I step forward.

The coolness that lingers all around smells of death. Just a while ago I lay on that cold, hard floor, ready to accept my fate, and now here I am standing at the precipice of something, maybe far worse.

I take another precarious step forward. As I do so, visions of the alien world come into view, but just barely. A large metallic monolith looms ahead, blocking my path. As I approach, it comes to life. A crevice opens along its middle, and a red beam shoots out, scanning the floor before me.

I freeze, panic clawing at my chest. I start to hyperventilate, crying out in fear and exhaustion. After everything I've been through, I wonder what exactly I thought was going to happen. That I'd reach the surface of whatever planet this is and merely walk away? Tears are now fully falling from my weary eyes. I wipe them away, ready to accept whatever fate has left for me.

The beam reaches my feet. It fans out, scanning me. I wipe my tears away and inch forward, ready for whatever fate has in store.

The monolith speaks.

"Francesca Walters. You are the sole survivor of Moon Colony 394. Earth has been notified of a severe malfunction, and the mechanical attendants have been deactivated. I am Autonomy Unit 9740, and I am here to take you back to Earth. I am here to take you home."

I smile weakly, trying to steady my breath. "Nobody calls me Francesca. Except my mom, but she died two months ago. Everyone here calls me Franny."

REMEMORATIONS

Decades after receiving an immortality endowment, Nathan Duncan returns to the Lazarus Center for Extended Living to discover that his treatment was not all he was promised. The routine maintenance he requires will affect his past every bit as much as his future. Now, Nathan can't help wondering: Is it the man that makes the memories, or vice versa?

Rememorations

Written nearly a decade ago, *Rememorations* was originally crafted for the anthology *The Immortality Chronicles*, curated by Samuel Peralta. At the time, none of us involved could have imagined the journey this story—and the anthology itself—would take. Not only did it go on to be named *Best Anthology of the Year* in the 2016 Preditors & Editors Readers' Poll, but it also became part of the <u>Lunar Codex Project</u>, eventually making its way to the Moon—a legacy as unexpected as it is humbling. *Rememorations* came early in my writing career and remains one of my most meaningful works. It was even nominated for *Best American Science Fiction*, a nod that affirmed I might be on the right path. | 24,414 words

Rememorations

The sign on the door read THE LAZARUS CENTER FOR EXTENDED LIVING in brushed silver letters. Although it looked somewhat familiar, Nathan couldn't be entirely sure he was in the right place. He hesitated briefly before grasping the antique brass handle and walking into a richly decorated anteroom. Besides the newer snow-white carpet, the room looked like it hadn't been updated in centuries. The warm sensation of being surrounded by aged wood panel walls and antiquated leather-bound furniture was comforting, and he felt the twinkling of déjà vu course through him.

The sound of the door latching behind him made him jump. When he turned toward the sound, he found a woman sitting behind a desk, staring back at him. She smiled and nodded her head in greeting.

"It's good to see you again, Mr. Duncan," she said.

Nathan nodded, frantically sprinting through his memory for her name. He knew he'd met her before, when he'd first visited the center. *Has to be close to 70 years since I first walked into this place*, he thought.

"Yes. Good to see you ... again." He paused. "I'm sorry, but for the life of me, I can't remember your name," Nathan said.

"That's quite alright, Mr. Duncan. I'm Nancy. I remember you from your initial enrollment back in 2065. I have your records right here," Nancy said. A holo-screen appeared in mid-air over her right shoulder, showing Nathan's profile and scrolling statistics.

"2065? Are you sure? That's what? Eighty-three years ago?" Nathan asked, his cheeks flushing with embarrassment.

"Yes, sir. It was mid-April, to be exact. I remember you were battling quite a case of hay fever at the time, and couldn't wait to join our organization. By the way, how are your allergies?"

Nathan thought for a moment. Allergies. He remembered having the ceaseless nose drip and the stuffy head that usually accompanied it, every spring, but it had been so long since he'd had to live with any of that.

"I ... I haven't had a problem with allergies since ..." He paused in an attempt to recall when he'd last suffered his annual hay fever.

"I'd guess that you haven't had the seasonal symptoms since you walked out that door all those years ago," Nancy said with a smile.

Nathan smiled again, wishing he'd not waited so long between visits. "Yes, I'm sure you're right."

Nancy stood and walked around her desk. As she approached, Nathan silently gasped at her beauty. She looked like she was in her 30s, slim and curvy in all the right places. Her shoulder-length auburn hair shone brightly, and her hazel eyes would pierce even the most skeptical customer's doubt. She might have been the best "equipped" saleswoman Nathan had seen in decades.

"If you'd like to follow me, Mr. Duncan. The doctor will be with you shortly." Nancy strode through another antique wooden door that led to a long corridor. Nathan happily followed.

Walking through the passageway was like stepping through time. Not into the past, however, but into the future. The walls were lined from floor to ceiling in stainless steel, and the ceiling was a solid sheet of light. He had trouble discerning whether there was actually something solid there, or just a luminous glow. The floor was a rubber textured surface that resembled concrete, but cushioned each step, not unlike walking on firm, therapeutic foam.

Spaced every five meters along the corridor walls on either side were doors of obscure glass. As they passed each one, Nathan tried to peer inside. Shadowy silhouettes stirred inside each of the rooms. He had another bout of déjà vu as they approached the first solid door in the corridor.

Nancy tapped at a barely visible touch-pad near the edge of the door and within seconds, the door flickered from solid to clear, and then dissolved. "If you'd like to wait inside, the doctor will be with you shortly."

Nathan nodded and stepped past her and into the quaint waiting room. Once inside, Nancy tapped again at the panel. The opening in the doorway solidified to a faint teal color, but remained transparent. Nathan refocused on his surroundings and sat in one of two chairs positioned on opposite sides of a long table situated at the center of the room. An oddly shaped chair that closely resembled a bed sat near one of the corners. It looked remarkably comfortable. As he sat, memories leaked into his consciousness. He began to recall details of his initial trip to the center, and the personnel who had worked there. The face of the doctor, or administrator, rather, that he had first met with filled his mind. His face began to coalesce, and just as Nathan was about to pull his name from deep memory storage, the door disappeared. Nathan looked up as the exact same visage walked in.

"Ah, Mr. Duncan. It is very good to see you, although you are a few years overdue for your scheduled maintenance appointment."

Nathan nodded. "Yeah, kind of unavoidable. I was going through ... let's just say I was dealing with some personal issues."

"Life does throw us curve balls from time to time," the doctor said as he reviewed information on an ocular plate resting on his brow. "And it looks like you've come in just in time."

"Did I cut it that close?" Nathan asked.

"I wouldn't say it was tight, but you are certainly overdue for your procedure. Tell me, Mr. Duncan. How are you feeling?"

"I feel good. I feel like a man in his mid-thirties, I guess? I try to exercise regularly—to maintain appearances, and to stave off my indulgences," Nathan said.

"Indulgences? Care to elaborate?"

"After my fourth wife passed, I ... began drinking again. It's nothing I can't control, but it does help with the lonely nights."

"You say... again? Have you had previous bouts of drinking?" asked the doctor, reviewing the data in his readout.

Nathan bowed his head slightly. "Yeah, I had a bout, as you call it, after my second wife died."

The doctor scanned through the data until he found what he was looking for. "Ah, yes. The robbery. It was in... 2099. Was it the loss of your wife the caused you to start drinking, or was it something to do with the crime?"

Nathan felt like he was being interrogated and instinctively threw up his guard. "It was nothing in particular, just a coping mechanism. Can you tell me that outliving most everyone in this world is easy for you?" Nathan snapped.

"Relax, Mr. Duncan. I'm not judging you. I'm just gathering information for your treatment," the doctor said. "Might I inquire about your multiple marriages? You mentioned you recently divorced your fourth wife."

"Yeah," Nathan began. "But it's nothing to worry about. You see, I'm afraid to be alone. So, I marry. I learned a long time ago that divorcing is so much easier on the soul than experiencing the death of someone you love."

Dr. Morrow nodded his head but remained silent.

Nathan leaned back and looked up at the glowing ceiling. The moments ticked away as the doctor typed at an invisible keyboard to record information. After several minutes of uncomfortable silence, the doctor spoke.

"How is your memory, Mr. Duncan?"

"I, uh. It's okay, I guess. I have trouble remembering things from time to time. Like, I know we've met, but I just can't remember your name," Nathan said.

The doctor nodded his head. "I expect so, Mr. Duncan. You are close to three years beyond your applicable rejuvenation appointment. I wouldn't expect anything less than significant memory loss. I'm Dr. Morrow. I was your administrator you when you first came in, back in 2065."

"Dr. Morrow. I knew it! I had it on the tip of my tongue. I don't think my mind is going. It's just a little slow sometimes."

"Understandable," Dr. Morrow said as he entered more information. "Would you mind if we run a few tests before we proceed? I'll only need a small sample of your DNA."

"Yeah, sure. Do you think there's something wrong?" Nathan asked.

"Oh, no. It's nothing like that. We just want to analyze the nanite count in your DNA. We need to verify that the 24th pair of chromosomes are functioning properly. Now, if you could place your hand on the center of the table."

Nathan did so, and a moment later, he felt a sharp warming sensation in the palm of his hand.

"Okay, Mr. Duncan. If you'd like, you can relax on the chaise for a bit. These tests shouldn't take more than an hour," the doctor said before walking out.

As the door reformed into a new tangerine hue, Nathan glanced at the swooped chair in the corner and muttered, "Ah, what the hell." He eased himself into the chair and reclined. Staring up at the ceiling, he wondered where the lighting was coming from. The entire ceiling glowed evenly without a direct pinpoint source. Within moments, he drifted off to sleep.

***

As I walked into the office, an uncontrollable sneeze burst past my lips, and a fine mist of phlegm sprayed across the room. Embarrassed, I smiled nervously at the attractive receptionist. "Sorry about that, Ms....?"

"I'm Nancy. I understand the pollen count is above average this year."

"Pleased to meet you, Nancy," I said as I dabbed at the corners of my nose with a tissue before stuffing it into my pocket. "There must be something different. I can't seem to stop sneezing. It's only like this for a few months of the year. The rest of the time, I'm quite a normal guy." I winked.

Nancy returned my smile, and it appeared quite genuine. "Now, then, Mr. Duncan. Do you have any questions before we process your payment?"

I cleared my throat before answering. "As a matter of fact, I do. About the payment. Is the full amount due now, or can I spread it out over, say, a few installments?"

"I'm sorry, Mr. Duncan, but are you having trouble coming up with the agreed amount?" Nancy asked, concerned.

"No, it's not that. It's just that I was thinking of having my wife administered at the same time. You see, she's already a number of years older than me. Five, to be exact. And I know that if I go through with this procedure, my aging will cease, but hers won't. I'm sure you understand."

Nancy nodded at my predicament. "I do, Mr. Duncan, but the procedure must be paid for in advance. That's been our policy from the very beginning. If we gave you immortality on credit and you decided to default, we would have no way to... repossess what you've purchased. The procedure is irreversible." Nancy paused long enough for the information to register. "Perhaps in a few years, you can afford the credits. Then you can bring your wife in."

I bowed my head. "I, um. I don't think that'll be possible. I've already had to scrape up just about every credit we have just for this one procedure. By the time I squirrel away enough for her transition, she might have aged too far past her prime."

"Age becomes much less relevant once immortality comes into play. Have the two of you discussed this?"

I nodded. "In great depth, actually. I tried to have her go first, but she insisted that it be me."

"Perhaps, then, we could delay your treatment until a more appropriate time when you can afford both?"

"We've talked about that as well. My wife, Beverly, insists that I go through with the procedure today. I've tried talking to her about waiting a few years, but she won't hear of it." I shrugged my shoulders. "So, here I am."

Nancy listened intently to my explanation as she guided me to one of the multiple procedure rooms at the facility.

"Well, then, Mr. Duncan, it sounds like you have everything in order. If you'd like to have a seat," Nancy said as she motioned me into a room, "Dr. Morrow will be right in."

"It appears, Mr. Duncan, that your credit transfer has been completed. All that's left is your DNA signature before we can proceed."

Dr. Morrow motioned toward the palm scanner embedded into the tabletop. I placed my hand on the scanner, palm side down, and waited nervously.

"There's no need to worry, Mr. Duncan. This scan is quite similar to the one we used to prepare your serum. This final scan

simply authorizes us to administer the 24th pair of chromosomes to your DNA sequence."

As the doctor explained, the scanner glowed red, turning to green as the palm of my hand increased in temperature.

The doctor then produced a thin vial from his breast pocket and held it out. "Last chance, Mr. Duncan."

I only hesitated for a moment before accepting the vial from him. "All I do is drink this and I'm good?"

"Yes, that's about it. We do, however, request that you remain on-site for the first thirty minutes."

"Why is that? In case something goes wrong?"

"Not exactly. There will be ... unusual side effects that, how can I say this, may come as a surprise to you. But don't worry. They're all normal and non-invasive."

"Such as?" I asked. "I have to say, Doc, I think you could've told me this before I paid you 500,000 credits."

"No, no. It's nothing like that." Dr. Morrow chuckled. "It's just, well, you'll see. It's completely painless, just a little unsettling for some. For starters, your nasal drip will clear up almost instantly. There's typically some drowsiness and mild disorientation."

"So, a little sleepy and woozy. Well, then, the cost might be worth it, just for the relief alone," I joked as I removed the rubber stopper from the vial. "Here goes nothing," I said as I placed the edge of the vial to my lips and tilted my head back.

***

Dr. Morrow gently shook Nathan awake. "Mr. Duncan. Can you hear me? Mr. Duncan. We have your test results."

Nathan opened his eyes, and saw that the glow of the ceiling had dimmed considerably. He looked around the room, and remembered where he was.

"How—how long was I asleep?" he asked.

"Oh, about forty-five minutes. Did you have a relaxing dream?" asked the doctor.

"It really wasn't a dream, per se. It was more like... I don't know. Like I was reliving part of my past."

Dr. Morrow nodded knowingly. "Ah, yes. Which memory did you re-experience?"

"It was when we first met. It was the day I first came into the center. I know it was nearly a century ago, but it felt like it was yesterday. It was so clear."

"For all intents and purposes, it *was* yesterday, in your mind. You see, this chaise lounge is more than just a place to relax. It's what we've coined as the rememoration machine. We use it to summon lost or forgotten memories for our clientele."

"Did you intend for me to remember my initial visit?" Nathan asked.

"No, not specifically. That was by your own doing. Lying on the chaise is kind of like lucid dreaming, but within your own past realities." Dr. Morrow motioned for Nathan to come sit at the table.

"So, I could bring up any memory I want? What if it's something I've forgotten? How would I know to remember it?" Nathan asked as he sat across from the doctor.

"It gets a little complicated, but yes, you can mentally direct the device to retrieve even the most quarantined memory you possess." Dr. Morrow paused as he tapped away at his invisible keyboard. "Much of this discussion is a perfect segue into your test results."

Nathan leaned forward. "Which are?"

"Mr. Duncan, do you remember our discussion regarding the limitations of immortality? We discussed it in depth during your initiation seminar."

"I—I didn't get that far in the memory, but I still remember some of what was discussed. Why?"

"It has to do with your mind, and its ability to remember things. Or, more technically, to process stimuli. The human mind has limitations. It was never 'designed' to remember more than a hundred and fifty years or so of perpetual memories. At least not in our current biological understanding. Our brains may contain additional storage space, but we've yet to discover or tap that resource. As soon as we discovered the secret to longer life, we've had to adapt to that limitation."

"I think I follow. Isn't that what the 24th pair of chromosomes was supposed to take care of?" Nathan asked.

"Not quite. Those were integrated so that our bodies stop aging, or more specifically, our bodies can heal themselves. No more molecular degeneration. Your mind is a different animal altogether. Consider your old personal computer. Do you remember when the hard drive got full of files and documents, what happened?"

"It's been a while since I've used one, but the computer would slow down," Nathan said.

"That's right. The overall performance would suffer until you deleted some files, and defragmented the hard drive. Our minds work in a similar fashion. After a century and a half of memories, we begin to respond or react much more slowly than normal."

"I think I get it. So, you want me to forget some things? Then why the chair? Doesn't it just make me remember the memories I've already forgotten?"

"Precisely. Your mind needs more than to just forget. Memories need to be removed completely. The rememoration machine will help you with that. In order for you to select which memories to remove, you will need to recall and decide which ones you no longer need."

Nathan leaned back and contemplated what the doctor was suggesting. "Just how many memories do I need to forget?"

"After closely reviewing your test results with my colleagues, we agree that you have two options. Both of which have their own merits and disadvantages." Dr. Morrow clasped his hands together and stared intently at Nathan.

"I, um. Okay, let me have it. What are they?"

"The first option is to go into your mind and selectively extricate thirty to fifty percent of your stored memories. This reduction will free up approximately forty to fifty years of continued memorization before the procedure needs to be repeated. The overall procedure will take approximately eighteen hours, spread over six visits to the lab."

"Fifty percent of my memories just gone? Will I even remember who I am?" Nathan asked. "And how will you know which memories to eliminate?"

"Fifty percent is only an estimate. Some memories are obviously more extensive than others, and may free up extra space. Your core memories will remain intact. You will still be Nathan Duncan." Dr. Morrow paused to moisten his lips. "As for which memories we eliminate, that is completely up to you. That's why it takes such an extended period of time. You will have to recall individual memories during each session, and then choose whether to keep or remove the memory. Unfortunately, the procedure can become quite emotional."

"And the second option? The first one doesn't sound terribly appealing."

Dr. Morrow smiled politely. "Option two is much more straightforward. Consider again the antiquated computer hard drive. With option one, you would in essence be selecting individual files to be deleted. With option two, you will be deleting an entire file directory."

"Like deleting an entire year?" Nathan asked.

"Sort of. With option two, we would go in and delete the memory of a single individual from your mind. In doing so, all memories associated with that person would also be lost.

Option two is a much simpler task, and it can be performed in a single session and takes about an hour."

"It sounds like option two makes the most sense all around. It's easier, it's faster. What are the consequences?"

Dr. Morrow's smile faded. "There really is only one unfavorable outcome. There is no way to determine just how your life will change by removing all memories associated with any one person. Results are dependent on who the person was that is being removed. There's no way to determine the cumulative effect because our clients can't remember what they technically never experienced."

Nathan nodded. "And how long before I'll need another procedure if I choose option two?"

"We've seen results in the neighborhood of seventy to eighty years." Dr. Morrow leaned forward. "There is one more thing to think about. The cost."

"Cost? It's not covered by my original initiation fee?"

"I'm sorry, Mr. Duncan, but no. Maintenance procedures are extra. It was covered in your commencement seminar and initiation contract."

"Well, how much, then?" Nathan demanded.

"Option one will cost you 300,000 credits, while option two will cost you 75,000 credits."

"Are you kidding? That's nearly the same amount I paid to get into this exclusive club in the first place."

"Like I said, Mr. Duncan. It's an intense procedure."

Nathan bolted from his chair. He stood hovering over Dr. Morrow, pulse quickening as beads of sweat rose to the surface of his forehead. "Here's what I think. I think you sold me an illusion of immortality, where you promised me that I could live forever, and now you're telling me I actually cannot without spending more credits."

"In essence, Mr. Duncan, you are right on both accounts," Dr. Morrow began. "Yes, you will continue to live, potentially forever. However, if you want to live a happy and coherent life, it will cost you. If you choose not to have either of these two procedures done, your life will continue as it has, but your memory and mental acuity will continue to slow, sometimes faltering. We are, however, continually working on groundbreaking research which utilizes an advanced form of nanotechnology that will hopefully expand the memory capacity of the human mind. Unfortunately, the technology is complicated and is still quite a distance away from completion."

"How far away are we talking?" Nathan asked.

"Unfortunately, I'm not at liberty to discuss our current research status. But I assure you that we're making every effort to bring this solution to our clientele as soon as possible."

Still standing, Nathan leaned against the cold metal wall as he digested this massive wrinkle. After several minutes of silence, Dr. Morrow spoke.

"Mr. Duncan," he began.

"Call me Nathan."

"All right. Nathan, please understand you don't have to make this decision right now. If you like, you could go home and think through the options that I've presented. If you come back in a day or two, or even a week, no severe memory issues will occur."

Nathan nodded his head, but didn't say a word. He continued to lean against the wall in stoic contemplation.

"Nathan?"

"I, um. If you don't mind, could I have another go at your rememoration machine?" Nathan asked as he nodded toward the chaise lounge in the corner. "Maybe if I could cycle through some past memories, it might help me decide."

Dr. Morrow smiled. "Absolutely, Nathan. Really, that's what it's there for. My only suggestion is that you start with an early memory, and cycle through as many as you can get through without dwelling on any single point for too long."

"How do I do that?"

"Imagine that you are remembering your first visit here again. When you feel that you've re-experienced as much as you need, just think the words *fast-forward* and the rememoration machine will advance you and your memory ahead. It's a little tricky to get used to, but once you get the hang of it, you'll be able to slide through many years of your life in a matter of minutes."

"Sounds easy enough. How much time can I have?" Nathan asked.

"Take as much time as you need, but I imagine that you will need only a limited amount of time before your decision is clear."

"What makes you say that?"

"Experience, mainly. Also, you are in your first generation of immortality. Once you get the hang of controlling the pace of your memories, you'll be able to fly through your life before you know it," Dr. Morrow said as he stepped out into the corridor.

Nathan stared at the reappeared door for several moments before he settled into the lounge chair. As he lay back, he tried to recap all the information that he'd just received, but within moments, sleep had swallowed him whole.

***

A peculiar haze obscured my vision, but I could hear voices—or a single voice, rather, in the distance. As I focused on the words being spoken, I began to understand. The voice was mine. I was at Beverly's memorial. I was delivering her eulogy, and the room was silent.

"... Beverly was the love of my life, and I, like many of you, am lost without her. She was the most giving, the most caring person

I've ever known. She has made many sacrifices to better the lives of those around her.

"One of her particular gifts was such a selfless act, she saved me in more ways than I can truly say. She gave me a long life, and she was the reason for me to live. Then, shortly after this amazing act of kindness, she was diagnosed with a virulent disease. She vowed to fight for her life, but she only lived a short six months after her diagnosis of MDS, and four of those were spent bedridden in the hospital. She continued her fight after undergoing a bone marrow transplant and contracting a lung infection. I stayed with her, sleeping in the same room, until a few months ago, when Beverly was admitted to the ICU with pneumonia. She was unconscious for almost the entire time. I held her hand often and stroked her hair. I massaged her legs and feet, and talked to her. I told her that I loved her every hour of every day. The cruelest part of her ordeal was that she was so close to me, but couldn't say a word. Just a few weeks before, she had been talking with me and the nurses, planning some spring activities, and dreaming of her future. Then last Friday, her heart stopped for the first time. By Sunday, it was clear that she would not recover. On Monday I held and kissed her hand for the last time.

"I forever want her near me. To feel her arms wrapped around me, squeezing me—feeling her cheek pressed against mine. To say: Bev, I love you. My life is complete with you by my side. My beloved, I will miss you forever and can't wait for the day when we can be together—to hold each other and share our love again.

"Beverly has gone into the light and is now free ..."

fast-forward

As I wandered aimlessly along the city sidewalks, the soles of my feet were nearly frozen by the rain. People would see me and cross to the other side of the street, avoiding contact. It had been months since I had spoken with anyone directly. My beard had grown in, scraggly and unkempt. The standard string of condolences had filtered through, but I didn't respond to any of them. All I wanted was my wife back—my old life back. Now, all I could do was wait for eternity and its punishment of self-pity and suffering.

A car slipped along the road, its tires carving through the standing puddles in its path. As it neared, it swerved in an attempt to avoid drenching me, but it was too late. I saw it coming and did nothing to avoid it. Seemingly in slow-motion, I watched the driver as he passed and a look of concern was clearly present on his face. Now soaked, I turned at the next corner and headed for Homer Bridge.

As I ascended the steep incline, I felt invigorated for the first time since she left this world. It wouldn't be much longer before I could be with her again.

Despite the late hour, the traffic on the bridge was heavy. Several times, cars swerved into oncoming traffic to avoid hitting me. Those drivers didn't know that they needn't have worried, because it would have saved me the long climb to the top.

As I crested the approach ramp, I saw a break in the traffic. After the next truck passed, I would be clear to take my final steps back to Beverly. I wiped the moisture from my eyes—a mix of tears and fallen rain. I stepped up to the protective railing and looked out across Cadre River and wondered …

fast-forward

Staccato beeps cut through the black. The room was dark, and I was lying down. Beep, beep. Beep, beep.

I blinked away the darkness, only to have it replaced with blurred light from all directions. I leaned my head from side to side, but still couldn't focus. The pain that was present was strong, but bearable. I tried to raise my hand and scratch the side of my nose, but my arm was lashed tightly to my chest. I tried to raise my other hand, but it was also incapacitated. The itch—it was driving me crazy. I forced my head hard to the right and rubbed my nose against the pillow beneath my head. As I did, the tubes running into my nostrils dislodged and the beeping was now accompanied by a hissing sound. Beep, beep—hiss.

"Hello there, sleepyhead," came a voice from my left. The voice was female, soft and comforting.

I whipped my head toward the source, but the plaster covering my left shoulder prevented me from looking in that direction.

"Take it easy, mister. You're okay, now. You're going to be up and about before you know it," she said.

"Mpah id ghapgn?" I tried to speak, but the thick tube stuck down my throat prevented it.

A warm hand soothed my forearm. "Shh, shh. Just relax. The tracheal tube is in place because you've had a collapsed lung. You couldn't breathe on your own for several days. The doctor thinks we can remove it later today, though, so that's good news."

I blinked rapidly and with each beat of my eyelids, the blur began to subside. I looked down at myself and noticed that my body was covered in plaster, from the tips of my toes all the way up to my left shoulder.

"I have to say, you are one lucky man. If that boat hadn't spotted you as you fell, you might have very well frozen to death. But here you are, and your prognosis is quite remarkable. I've never seen a person heal as quickly as you have. You truly are a special individual," the woman said as she slid the oxygen tubes back into my nose. "I'm Nurse Sadusky, but you can call me Addison." She smiled. "That is, if you could speak. And at your rate, that won't be too far off."

fast-forward

"I can't. Just let it go, would ya!" I screamed.

"No, I won't! Nathan, how long have we been at this? Twelve months? Look how far you've come. The doctor told you that you might never walk again, and last week, you took your first steps. So what if we helped? That's a tremendous achievement. I think you've got this. Now get your pansy ass up and try again," Addison demanded.

"Can't I just rest for a bit? I'm so tired," I cried, and rolled away from the nurse who had been with me every step of the way.

"Okay, I'll give you five minutes," she agreed. "but after that, I want to see you pull yourself up on those bars and give me five steps."

"Five? I only took one last week. I'll give you two, and you'll be happy with it," I said, hoping my stern attitude would relieve her persistence, even just a little bit.

"Only two steps? What do you think this is, some kind of country dance class? I need four from you and then we'll call it a day." Addison stared deep into my eyes, and I could see that she was easing her drill-sergeant stance with every obstacle I threw up.

"How about we meet in the middle? I'll push for three steps and then I'll let you give me a sponge bath," I said, trying to turn on the charm.

"You think me giving you a sponge bath is my reward for helping you walk again?" she asked as she sidled up to me and begin to lift me back to the rails. "I think you owe me much more for everything that I've had to endure since ..." She broke off.

Addison pulled me up and placed my hands on the rails. Before she could back away from me, I leaned in and gently kissed her cheek.

"Hey, mister. There'll be none of that on my watch."

"Well, when does your watch end?" I said just inches from her lips.

"Not until I can get you to walk, unassisted, that's when." She smiled.

I knew right then that I would walk again. She was the driving force behind it all.

"Now, move!" she demanded.

fast-forward

"I now pronounce you husband and wife. You may kiss your bride," proclaimed the minister.

I lifted Addison's veil and kissed her passionately in front of several hundred of our closest friends. Then we turned and walked effortlessly down the aisle.

"I love you, Addi. If it weren't for you, I wouldn't be here right now, and walking gracefully, to boot," I said.

"And I love you, babe. You've also saved me, in so many ways," she replied.

As we walked past our guests, I wondered if marrying again was the smart thing to do... or just the right thing to do right now.

fast-forward

I paced anxiously outside the bathroom door. The sound coming from the other side of the door was stomach-turning.

"Are you going to be alright in there?" I asked. I knew the answer before she said it.

"I'mm gon' be fiiiine, babby. Why doncha go and warm up the sheets an I'll be right out," Addison slurred—from the bathroom floor, no doubt.

I grabbed my pillow and walked toward the hall. As I passed the bathroom, I paused. "Listen, I think you need some rest. I'm going to sleep downstairs tonight. We can talk about this in the morning." Then I waited.

I could hear her spit into the toilet before she responded. "But, baaaby, I wan' you tooooniiight." And then, more grotesque splashing into the toilet.

fast-forward

"Happy anniversary, babe. Let's toast to eight exciting years. And then let's do shots for eight more," Addison stammered, obviously having already consumed a few too many flutes of champagne for the evening.

"It's been an exciting eight years, that's for sure," I said, not sure how to cut Addi off without inciting another incident. "Let's finish the bottle now, and then move the rest of the celebration home," I suggested, hoping to placate her indulgences.

"Oh, please, daddy. Can't we stay out late just once?" she cooed. "I promise to be a good girl, daddy."

I smiled on the surface, but deep inside, I worried for her. She'd promised me, yet again, just last month that she had her drinking under control. Yet here we were, on the precipice of an uncontrollable situation.

fast-forward

"I want to thank you, asshole, for supporting me like you have," Addison spat.

"Do you have to constantly belittle me like that? It's not my fault that you lost your job. One would think that showing up to the hospital, drunk, would be a career-limiting move," I replied, feeling no remorse.

"Well, to hell with you. You were right there drinking with me, or did you forget?"

"I remember. I also remember telling you that you've had too much, and that you can't control yourself. Many times."

Addison stomped into the kitchen. I'd known this argument would come eventually, and after 15 years of marriage, I was constantly looking for the right time to get out. Unfortunately, Addi was always one step ahead of me, knowing that I would delay asking for a divorce if she was unable to support herself.

Soon. It had to be soon.

fast-forward

After 18 years, 18 very difficult years, I knew tonight was the night that I would end it. My agelessness could no longer take her disregard for life. She failed to understand just how precious every moment was. She'd been aware of my condition for several years now, and seemed to despise me because of it. She somehow expected me to swoop in and treat her to immortality as well, but I couldn't bring myself to do it. Her total disregard for anyone but herself would make her an ugly immortalitarian. No, tonight, after dinner, I was going to ask for a divorce.

"Where are we going tonight?" Addison asked. "I hope someplace good. I'm starved!"

"I was thinking that we'd walk into midtown and try that Cuban place," I said.

"Ooh. That sounds divine." She slid her arm into mine. "Honey, can we talk about something?"

"Sure. What's on your mind?"

"I know the last few years have been rough, and I'm going to make a change," she said.

I continued to stare ahead as we walked. I'd known she would try to woo me into another trap. "What kind of change?" I asked, not sure that I wanted to hear her latest excuse.

"Today, I stopped by the A.A. office and signed up. I know my drinking has been hard on both of us, and I feel that I can really stick with this, if you'll still have me."

Shit. Now what was I going to do? I couldn't very well ask for a divorce now. And, she, no doubt, knew that. Was I so transparent?

As we continued to walk along the dark streets of midtown, my mind was completely focused on what I was going to do. I failed to notice the shadowy figure come up behind us until it was too late.

"You two, stop right there! Don't turn around, or I'll shoot. I have a gun."

Instinctively, I turned to the stranger behind us. He did in fact have a gun, and it was pointed right at my face.

"I said, don't turn around! Now, give me all your money. And while you're at it, give me all your jewelry," the robber demanded.

I slowly pulled my wallet from my pocket and motioned for Addison to do the same. She shook her head, almost unnoticeably.

NO! my eyes screamed at her, but it was too late.

"I am not going to give you anything, sweetie, and you know why? Because my husband here—he can't be killed. He's immortal, so it doesn't matter what you do to him."

"Don't listen to her," I begged. "Here. Take my wallet, and here's my watch. It's a Tag."

"So, he's immortal, huh? What about you?" he asked Addison, now pointing the pistol at her.

"Here! I have your money," I said, nearly shoving my wallet in his face.

He snatched the wallet out of my hand and stuck it in his coat pocket. "Thanks. Now, I also want what Miss Smart-ass has, and it ain't the money anymore," he said, looking Addi up and down.

Addison tried to step behind me, but the robber grabbed her, nearly missing her arm. His grip couldn't hold as she yanked away. As she began to run, the report from his gun nearly deafened me and I watched Addison drop to the ground, blood quickly soaking her blouse.

"No!" I screamed as I bolted up from the rememoration machine.

***

"How long will the procedure take?" Nathan asked.

"Well, that's a relatively difficult question to answer," replied the doctor. "There are several factors that need to be considered. If the memories of your second wife are extensive, it could take upwards of a few hours. If the memories are shallow and lack connection to your overall personality and your life, it could be less than an hour. Don't worry, you'll be asleep the whole time. When you wake, your mind should be as fresh as it was in 2065, then you'll be active and alert for at least another 75 years."

Nathan nodded, as a look of concern crossed his brow. "Am I making the right decision, Doc?"

"This decision isn't an easy one to make. I can't influence you one way or another. It's completely up to you. There is really no wrong decision here. Only the right decision for you. If you'd like, we can reschedule this for another day, but I would not suggest that."

"No, no. I think I'm making the right choice. Let's do this before I change my mind."

"Alright, Mr. Duncan, drink this vial, then lean back and relax. The next time we meet, you'll be a new man. Again."

Nathan did as directed. After consuming the flavorless serum, he leaned back on the chaise and was asleep within minutes.

***

Nathan began to stir, first opening one eye and then the other. He felt completely relaxed and fully rested. As his eyes adjusted to the dimmed light, he noticed that his mind felt clear.

Using the controls at the side of the rememoration machine, Nathan tilted the backrest to an upright position before he attempted to swing his feet to the floor. Unfortunately, his legs remained stationary. He tried again, but quickly realized that he had no muscular control from the waist down. Refusing to give up, he used both hands to lift his right leg from the surface of the chair and swung it out. The momentum of the dead weight dropping to the ground pulled the rest of his body with it. He flailed his arms, trying to break his fall, but it was no use.

His body smacked the floor like a baseball bat slapping a side of beef. Mere seconds later, the door vanished and in walked Dr. Morrow.

"Nathan! Are you all right?" he said, rushing to Nathan's side.

"I, uh, seem to have lost the ability to use my legs. Is this a typical reaction to the procedure?"

Dr. Morrow helped Nathan back into the lounge chair. "Unfortunately, no. Everything is quite in order."

"How is losing the ability to move my legs normal?"

"As promised, Nathan. You are as fit as a man in his mid-30s, just as you were before the procedure. The only difference now is that your ability to store information has been drastically improved by the removal of Addison from your memory."

"Who is Addison?"

"Nathan, I cannot in good conscience tell you who Addison was, because she was just removed from your mind."

Nathan continued to poke and prod at his lifeless legs before leaning back in disgust. "Okay, I get that. But why can't I move my legs?"

Dr. Morrow bobbed his head slowly. "By removing Addison, all of your memories associated with her were also eliminated."

"Again, I'll ask. Why can't I move my legs?" Nathan said, frustration beginning to surface in his tone.

Dr. Morrow pulled a chair next to the rememoration machine and sat down. "Nathan, how many times have you been married?"

"Three."

"Do you remember Beverly?"

Nathan closed his eyes, drawing the image of his first wife in his mind. "I do. She died in 2080."

"And do you remember what happened after that? Take your time."

"Of course I do. I jumped off a bridge. I tried to kill myself," Nathan said, tears beginning to leak from the corners of his eyes.

"And how about right after that? What do you recall?"

"I, um. I ... I can't remember a whole lot," he said, wiping his eyes dry.

"You see, after your suicide attempt, you had to learn to walk all over again. Addison was heavily involved with that process. By removing her from your mind, you inadvertently removed those muscle memories. Unfortunately, until the procedure was complete, we had no idea ..."

Nathan listened to Dr. Morrow's words, but his vision began to tilt from side to side as the effects of the information ebbed into his consciousness. Beads of sweat broke out across his forehead - dizziness tugged at his equilibrium.

"I don't understand. What are you telling me?"

"Nathan, you are a paraplegic."

After a devastating ambush, Lieutenant Jaya Moreau is the last survivor aboard the stealth frigate Astraeus, carrying a mysterious alien artifact that could change the course of humanity's war. Hunted by the relentless Zynar Dominion, haunted by the ghosts of her fallen crew, and drawn toward the eerie ruins of Nyx Spire, Jaya must unravel the artifact's secrets before it consumes her. But in the depths of space, some echoes are not memories—they are warnings.

Echoes In The Rift

Echoes in the Rift is the final NEW short story in this collection—and what a journey it was to write. This marks my first foray into the <u>Military Science Fiction</u> genre, and it quickly became one of the most immersive and energizing writing experiences I've had. Though written as a standalone, the world within this story holds plenty of potential for expansion. If the reception is strong, I can easily see this tale growing into a much larger, self-sustaining universe. For now, I'm proud to introduce you to its beginning. | 21,607 words

Echoes in the Rift

1

Consciousness slammed back with a jolt, yanking Jaya from the void into pulsing red lights and blaring alarms. Pain radiated from her forehead to her jaw, her thoughts swimming in the fog of a cracked skull. Warm, sticky blood trickled past her left eye—recognized only through shock's cold clarity.

The bridge of the Astraeus tilted at an unnatural angle, consoles sparking beneath hellish red emergency lights. She lay slumped against the nav station, uniform torn, fabric soaked in sweat and blood. The cold metal deck pressed into her ribs with every breath.

Jaya gripped the edge of the console, her fingers shaking as she hauled herself upright. Her left leg buckled, sending a spike of agony up her thigh, but she forced herself to stand. "Come on, Moreau," she whispered. *Get it together.* The hull groaned, a grim counterpoint to the ceaseless klaxons.

Beyond the viewport, the Thanatos Rift pulsed in sickly orange hues—gravity's corpse, bleeding light like a dying heart.

But the debris field made her stomach turn—Alliance wreckage drifting like metallic snow, still glowing from recent death.

A section of hull drifted past—Meridian's insignia scorched onto the plating. Their flagship. Their lead ship into hell. Her breath caught in her throat, sharp and painful. "No, no, no ..." *They're all gone. The entire squadron. How many good people just ... gone?*

The nearest console flickered weakly under her touch, displays glitching through damaged circuits. Damage reports scrolled in yellow: life support at sixty-two percent and falling, stealth systems in cascade failure, hull breach in sector four—seals holding but strained, comms severed at the primary junction.

"Sixty-two percent. Great." *Focus on the numbers. Numbers don't scream. Numbers don't bleed.* Jaya's fingers moved across the interface with practiced efficiency, muscle memory overriding the fog in her head. Ship's logs. She needed the ship's logs. The timestamp made her pulse quicken—she'd been unconscious for forty-seven minutes. Forty-seven minutes while enemy forces could have been hunting survivors, while the Astraeus bled atmosphere and power into the void.

Security footage crawled onto the screen, corrupted data forcing her through multiple retries. When the images finally resolved, Jaya wished they hadn't.

"I don't want to see this." *But you have to. You're the only one left who can witness what happened here.*

The ambush played out in merciless detail. The fleet dropped from hyperspace in perfect formation, confident in their stealth. Then the enemy emerged—sleek predators, waiting and watching. The first barrage caught the Meridian amidship, splitting her spine in a brilliant flash that left afterimages burned across the recording.

Jaya's knuckles went white against the console edge as she watched her squadron die. The destroyer Hephaestus lasted twelve seconds under concentrated fire before her reactor went critical, taking three escort frigates with her in an expanding sphere of superheated plasma. The fast attack craft never had a chance—they simply vanished, vaporized by weapons that left no trace except brief scars across the darkness.

"Twelve seconds. That's all Henderson got." *How do you compress a lifetime into twelve seconds? How do you say goodbye to everything you've ever known in less time than it takes to tie your boots?*

She watched herself—an hour younger, a lifetime smaller, barking orders to helm control as the Astraeus dove toward the Rift's gravity well. Captain Ward stood beside the command chair, his weathered face grim as he coordinated the fleet's final maneuvers through the comm system. The enemy had been thorough, systematic in their slaughter, but they'd miscalculated the little stealth frigate's desperation dive. The recording showed the Astraeus disappearing into the sensor shadow of a massive debris cluster just as enemy fire found her, the impact throwing everyone on the bridge like dolls.

Bile climbed her throat—acidic, bitter, as she saw Lieutenant Commander Reyes sprawled against the communications station, his neck bent at an impossible angle. Captain Ward's body lay crumpled near the tactical display, a jagged piece of shrapnel from the console buried in his chest, his hand still reaching toward the emergency beacon controls. Ensign Park's terrified face filled the frame for a heartbeat before the next impact sent her sliding across the deck, her skull striking the bulkhead with a wet crack that the audio pickups captured with crystal clarity.

"Oh God ... Captain ..." *He was still trying to save us. Even dying, he was still trying to get a message out.* "I'm sorry, sir. I'm so sorry."

The timestamp jumped forward—twenty-three minutes after impact. The bridge's emergency medical drones had activated, their spindly chrome arms extending from ceiling recesses like metallic spiders. Jaya watched in numb horror as they moved with clinical precision, bio-scanners confirming what she already knew. The first drone approached Captain Ward's still form, its sensors taking extra time to process his command insignia before the manipulator arms folded around him with mechanical reverence. The second drone retrieved Reyes' twisted form, its arms folding around him with surprising gentleness before retracting into the overhead compartment. Park followed moments later, the young ensign's body disappearing into the ship's morgue systems with mechanical efficiency.

"At least they're not just lying there." *As if that makes it better. That machines cleaned up the mess while I was unconscious? That I couldn't even be awake to see them off?* "They deserved better than this. They all deserved so much better."

By the thirty-minute mark, the drones had completed their grim work. The bridge looked almost normal again, emergency lighting still painting everything crimson, but empty of the human cost. Only dark stains on the deck plating remained as evidence of what had happened—stains that the cleaning systems would erase given time and power.

Jaya gasped, hands trembling as she gripped the console, fingernails digging into the polymer surface hard enough to leave marks. The survivor's guilt hit her like a physical weight, pressing down on her chest until each breath became a conscious effort. "Why me? Why am I the one still breathing?" *Park had a daughter. Reyes, a wedding next month. The Captain—grandkids he'd never see grow up. And I'm the one who gets to live with this?*

The recording ended with the bridge falling silent except for the omnipresent alarms. On screen, her unconscious form lay motionless against the navigation station while the Astraeus drifted deeper into the debris field, a ghost ship carrying its lone survivor toward an uncertain fate.

Jaya killed the playback with a violent stab at the controls. "Enough. Just ... enough." The silence felt wrong—too empty without their voices. She found herself listening for Reyes' dry commentary or Park's nervous humming during tense moments. *Listen to me, waiting for ghosts. They're gone, Jaya. They're all gone and you're talking to yourself like a madwoman.* But there was only the ship's labored breathing around her, atmosphere recyclers struggling to process the air while hull integrity warnings chimed softly in the background.

She stood alone on the bridge of the Astraeus, surrounded by the detritus of destroyed dreams and shattered plans. The mission parameters still glowed on her command screen—retrieve the artifact, maintain stealth, rendezvous with Fleet Command at designated coordinates. Simple objectives that had cost an entire squadron their lives.

"The artifact. Right. Because that still matters." *All those lives—for this thing. How do I make that math work? How do I justify their sacrifice for a maybe?*

Outside the viewport, the Thanatos Rift continued its cosmic dance of destruction, indifferent to human ambition and suffering alike. Somewhere out there, her friends floated in vacuum's cold embrace, their sacrifice reduced to twisted metal and fading heat signatures. And somewhere below in the ship's morgue bay, the emergency systems had preserved what remained of her crew with the same dispassionate efficiency that had removed them from her sight. Captain Ward lay among them, the man who had trained her, trusted her, and died trying to save what remained of his fleet.

The weight of solitude pressed against her like a lead blanket. She was alone with the dead and the dark, carrying secrets that had already proven too costly to bear.

Jaya stared at the damage reports scrolling across her screen, but the clinical readouts felt incomplete, sanitized. "Sixty-two percent life support, hull breach in sector four ..." *But what about the rest of it? What about the parts the sensors can't see?* The automated systems could only tell her so much—they couldn't account for bodies trapped in collapsed sections, couldn't detect if someone was unconscious in a damaged compartment where the bio-sensors had failed.

"I have to check. I have to be sure." *What if I'm not really alone?* The thought sent both hope and dread coursing through her veins. Hope that she wouldn't have to carry this burden alone, dread at what she might find in the ship's wounded corridors.

She pushed herself away from the console, her left leg protesting with each step as she made her way toward the bridge exit. *One step at a time, Moreau. Just keep moving.*

The corridors stretched before her—arteries in a dying beast, emergency lighting throwing harsh shadows across buckled bulkheads and exposed circuitry that sparked intermittently like dying synapses.

The ship's wounds were everywhere. Deck plating had been torn loose by the enemy barrage, creating jagged metal teeth that caught at her uniform as she passed. Atmosphere recyclers wheezed behind damaged panels, struggling to maintain pressure while condensation coated the ruptured coolant lines overhead.

She paused at junctions, shouting into the dark. "Hello? Anyone? This is Lieutenant Moreau!" Her voice echoed back empty, mocking. *Of course there's no one. The drones would have found them, wouldn't they? Unless ...* "Engineering? Medical bay? Anyone copy?" *Unless the drones missed something. Unless someone's trapped where they can't be detected.*

The crew quarters on Deck C showed signs of the impact—doors buckled inward, personal belongings scattered across the deck like confetti. She checked each room methodically, pushing aside debris, hoping and dreading what she might find behind each collapsed bunk. *Nothing. Just empty spaces where people used to live.*

The secure cargo hold lay three decks down, accessible only through a maze of service corridors that bypassed the main transit routes. Standard protocol for transporting classified materials, though Jaya was beginning to suspect that 'classified' didn't begin to cover what they'd been carrying. "Routine pickup—right." *Nothing about this was routine. We should have seen this coming.* The mech-lift was offline, forcing her to navigate maintenance shafts where the emergency lighting barely penetrated the darkness.

As she descended, she kept calling out, her voice growing hoarse. "If anyone can hear me, make noise! Anything!"

Her boots rang against the grating, echoes chasing her down. "Might as well ring a dinner bell," she muttered. *Stop it. They can't hear you through the hull. Can they?* The ship's artificial gravity fluctuated here, damaged generators creating pockets where her steps felt too light, too disconnected from the deck beneath her feet. More than once she had to steady herself against a bulkhead as vertigo washed over her, her concussed brain struggling to process the inconsistent sensory input.

"Get it together, Lieutenant. The Captain's counting on—" She stopped mid-sentence, the words catching in her throat. *The Captain's dead. They're all dead. No one's counting on anything anymore.* Her search had confirmed what she'd feared—she was truly alone aboard the Astraeus. Whatever survivors the enemy was hunting, she was the only one left.

The cargo hold scanned her bio-signature, ignoring the blood crusting her brow, iris scanners compensating for the swelling around her left eye. Pneumatic seals hissed as the heavy barrier slid aside, revealing the chamber beyond. Emergency lighting here was different—a cold blue-white that made everything look surgical, sterile. The containment unit sat in the room's center like an altar, all curved surfaces and warning displays that pulsed with urgent amber.

And within that technological shrine, the artifact waited.

"So this is what got everyone killed." *Was it worth it? Was this thing worth my entire crew? Worth losing a whole squadron? Worth leaving me alone in this tomb?*

Jaya had seen the mission files, read the specifications that described it in clinical terms as an 'object of unknown origin with potential strategic value.' But no amount of technical documentation could have prepared her for the reality of the thing itself. The obsidian sphere hung suspended in the containment field's embrace, its surface so perfectly black that it seemed to devour light rather than reflect it. Approximately thirty centimeters in diameter, just as the reports had stated, but those measurements felt meaningless when confronted with its presence.

The sphere pulsed with violet energy that moved beneath its surface like trapped lightning, patterns that suggested intelligence, purpose, malevolent intent. As she neared, it pulsed brighter—something in her bones answering its call—not quite vibration, not quite sound, but a resonance that made her teeth ache and her vision blur at the edges.

"What the hell are you?" *It's watching me. No, impossible—but I feel it. Just like I felt the emptiness in every corner of this ship.*

She stopped at the containment unit's control interface, fingers hovering over the diagnostic controls. The readings made no sense. Energy output fluctuated wildly between negligible and off the scale, quantum signatures shifted in patterns that defied current understanding of physics, and the mass readings kept changing as if the artifact existed in a constant state of flux between dimensions.

None of this had been in the mission briefing.

"Of course, they didn't tell us what we were really carrying." *How do you brief someone on something that shouldn't exist? How do you explain readings that make no sense? How do you prepare someone to be the sole guardian of something like this?*

Jaya's hand moved toward the containment field controls, drawn by a curiosity that felt both her own and utterly foreign. The moment her fingertips made contact with the interface, the artifact's hum deepened, becoming something felt rather than heard. The vibration traveled up her arm, through her shoulder, settling in her chest like a second heartbeat that beat just slightly out of rhythm with her own.

The sphere's surface rippled, patterns of light and shadow chasing each other across its perfect curve. For a moment, she could swear she saw shapes in those patterns—faces, perhaps, or star charts, or architectural blueprints for structures that shouldn't exist. The violet glow pulsed brighter, and she felt a presence brush against her mind like fingers trailing through water.

Who are you? The thought wasn't hers, but it echoed clean and clear. *Why do you carry such pain?*

"What—no, get out of my head!" *It's in my mind. It's actually in my mind. This isn't possible. None of this is possible. First, I'm alone with the dead, now I'm hearing voices from an alien artifact.*

Jaya jerked her hand back from the controls, breath coming in sharp gasps. The artifact's glow dimmed slightly, but those alien patterns continued their dance beneath its surface, hypnotic and unsettling. She backed away, her mind reeling from the impossible contact, when the proximity alarms began their urgent wail throughout the ship.

The alarm cut through the haze—reality snapping back like a rubber band. Enemy vessels. Scanning the debris field. Looking for survivors to eliminate loose ends to tie up before whatever dark purpose had brought them here could be completed.

"Shit. They found us ... they found me" *Of course they did. Did I really think we could hide forever in this wreckage?*

For a heartbeat, paralysis gripped her. She was alone, injured, aboard a crippled ship with no hope of backup or rescue. The enemy forces that had annihilated her entire squadron were closing in, and she had nowhere to run, nowhere to hide. The weight of futility pressed down on her shoulders, threatening to drive her to her knees in the cargo hold's sterile light.

This is it. This is how it ends. Alone, with an alien artifact and a ship that's falling apart around me.

Then Lieutenant Jaya Moreau, distinguished graduate of the Fleet Academy's advanced pilot program, survivor of three deep space missions, inheritor of a military legacy that stretched back generations, reasserted control. "No. Not like this. Not after everything." *The Captain didn't die so I could give up. None of them did. I'm the only one who can make sure their deaths meant something.* Her training kicked in like a neural switch being thrown, flooding her system with purpose and cold calculation.

She turned back to the containment unit, fingers flying over the controls, swiftly bypassing layers of security protocols. The artifact pulsed brighter as she worked, as if responding to her renewed determination. Whatever this thing was, whatever secrets it contained, it had cost her an entire fleet to retrieve. "You better be worth it," she said to the sphere. *Because if you're not, I'm going to find a way to make you pay for what happened here. For leaving me alone in this graveyard.*

She initiated the emergency procedures, securing the artifact within a compact containment unit designed for transport. With a mechanical hiss, the enclosure sealed around it, ready to be moved. Jaya hefted the unit onto an anti-grav platform and guided it before her.

"Alright, you bastards," she whispered under her breath as she retraced her steps. "Let's see what the Astraeus has left in her." It was time to prove whether all those hours at Fleet Academy had prepared her for this moment; time to discover if one survivor could truly make a difference; time to see if there was enough fight left in both herself and the ship to survive what lay ahead.

The obsidian sphere hovered in front of Jaya as she stormed onto the bridge. Her boots skidded across the slanted deck, the erratic artificial gravity making her stumble before she caught herself against the pilot's station. Her eyes darted around, searching for a spot where she could park the artifact safely. She guided the platform to a recessed alcove within arm's reach and nudged it into place, ensuring it remained secure yet accessible. "Stay put," she whispered, casting one last wary glance at its unsettling glow before turning back to her displays.

"Come on, baby. Don't fail me now." Her fingers located the emergency stealth controls, instinctively navigating the activation sequence while her conscious mind registered the escalating array of system failures flickering across her displays.

The Astraeus shuddered under the strain as she activated emergency protocols. Power distribution networks, already battered by combat damage, groaned as she rerouted energy from life support, artificial gravity, and even emergency lighting. "Sorry, everyone," she muttered to the empty bridge. *Hope you don't mind breathing recycled air for a while longer.* The bridge dimmed to near-darkness, leaving only the essential displays glowing like stars in a mechanical constellation.

Stealth systems responded sluggishly, damaged capacitors struggling to store enough charge for full spectrum suppression. She could feel the ship's electronic signature fluctuating, a stuttering heartbeat that would show up on any competent sensor sweep like blood in water. "Steady ... steady ..." *Like trying to hide an elephant behind a twig.* Her hands moved across multiple consoles simultaneously, rerouting power conduits through backup channels, bypassing blown circuits with jury-rigged connections that sparked and smoked under the strain.

External sensors painted a terrifying picture on her tactical display. Three enemy cruisers moved through the debris field in a search pattern that spoke of professional thoroughness. "Jesus Christ." *Those aren't Alliance designs. What the hell are we dealing with here?* Their hulls were sleek predators, angular designs that suggested technological advancement beyond current Alliance capabilities. Energy signatures indicated weapon systems that could crack a planet's crust, yet they moved with the patience of hunters who knew their prey had nowhere to run.

The lead cruiser's scanning array swept across a cluster of wreckage three thousand kilometers off the Astraeus's starboard bow. Jaya watched the beam dissect the remains of what had once been the escort frigate Achilles, cataloging every fragment, every piece of debris that had once been home to two hundred souls. "Rest in peace, Achilles." *They're being thorough. Too thorough. They're not just looking for survivors—they're making sure there aren't any.* The scan was thorough, invasive, leaving no shadow unexplored.

And it was moving in her direction.

"Not today. Not like this." Jaya dropped to her knees beside the primary power distribution node, pulling away damaged access panels to expose the ship's electronic nervous system. *Engineering school never prepared me for this.* Fiber optic cables snaked through the opening like luminous intestines, some dark where battle damage had severed connections, others pulsing with data that kept the Astraeus alive. Her hands worked without conscious thought, decades of technical training guiding her through repairs that should have taken a full engineering team.

The enemy scan swept closer, an invisible tide of detection algorithms and quantum resonance mapping. Two thousand kilometers. Fifteen hundred. "Hold together, you piece of junk." The Astraeus's stealth field wavered like heat shimmer, power levels dropping as damaged generators struggled to maintain the electromagnetic camouflage that was her only protection.

One thousand kilometers.

"Come on, come on ..." Jaya's breathing came in short, controlled bursts as she spliced backup power feeds into the stealth matrix. *If this doesn't work, at least it'll be quick.* Sweat dripped from her forehead onto the exposed circuitry, salt water threatening to short out systems that were already operating beyond their design parameters. The enemy cruiser's scan painted the debris field ahead of her position in harsh relief, revealing the skeletal remains of Alliance dreams and ambitions.

Seven hundred kilometers.

This is it. This is really it. The stealth field fluctuated wildly, power readings dancing between functional and catastrophic failure. Through the viewport, Jaya could see the enemy cruiser's running lights, distant stars that meant death. The scanning beam would reach her position in less than thirty seconds, and the Astraeus's electronic signature was bleeding through her damaged camouflage like a scream in the darkness.

Five hundred kilometers.

"Please. Please work." Her hands shook as she made the final connections, bypassing safety protocols that existed for very good reasons. *Sorry, Chief Martinez. I know you said never bypass the safety interlocks, but desperate times ...* The power coupling grew hot under her touch, metal expanding beyond its tolerance as she forced energy through pathways never designed for such loads. Warning lights flashed across her displays, but she ignored them. Better to risk explosion than guarantee detection.

The scan beam reached the Astraeus's position, invisible fingers of energy probing for signs of life among the mechanical corpses. Jaya froze, hands still buried in the ship's electronic entrails, holding her breath as if the enemy might hear her. *Don't breathe. Don't even think too loud.* The stealth field held for one second, two, then began to falter as power levels dropped toward critical.

Three hundred kilometers.

That's when she saw him.

Captain Elias Ward materialized beside her command chair like smoke given form, his tall frame still carrying that unmistakable military bearing even in death. His silver beard was neatly trimmed, his uniform pressed and precise, the scar along his right temple catching the emergency lighting just as it had in life. But his form wavered at the edges, translucent as morning mist, and his gray eyes held depths that belonged to no living man.

"You're not real." The words escaped her lips in a broken whisper, her voice cracking with exhaustion and disbelief. *This isn't happening. Concussion. Has to be a concussion.* Her hands trembled against the exposed circuitry, the shock of seeing him nearly causing her to lose her grip on the power couplings that kept them hidden.

Ward's phantom form turned toward the tactical display with the same methodical focus he'd shown in life, his transparent fingers pointing to specific controls with urgent precision. His mouth moved, but no sound emerged—yet somehow she understood exactly what he meant. The emergency plasma venting system. *Of course. Create interference, mask their signature in electromagnetic chaos.*

"I saw you die." Her words came out strangled, memories of the security footage flashing through her mind. "I watched the drones take your body away."

Two hundred kilometers.

The artifact pulsed, its alien rhythms synchronizing with the ship's failing stealth field. Nearby consoles glitched and sparked, their displays showing impossible readings as something beyond human understanding interfaced with the Astraeus's damaged systems. The gravity fluctuated again, and Ward's translucent form wavered but didn't disappear.

One hundred kilometers.

Ward's phantom gestured more urgently toward the plasma venting controls, his expression carrying all the authority he'd wielded in life. Trust me, his eyes seemed to say. One more time, trust your captain. Jaya's scientific mind screamed that this was impossible, that dead men didn't give tactical advice, that trauma and oxygen deprivation were making her see things that couldn't exist.

Fifty kilometers.

But her hands moved anyway.

"Hail Mary, full of grace ..." *Please let this insane idea actually work.*

She triggered the plasma venting system with seconds to spare, superheated gas erupting from the Astraeus's damaged engine section in a controlled explosion of electromagnetic interference. The cloud expanded rapidly in vacuum, its charged particles scattering the enemy's detection algorithms like chaff in a hurricane. For precious moments, the little stealth frigate disappeared into a man-made nebula of her own creation.

The enemy cruiser's scan lingered on the plasma cloud, sensor algorithms attempting to parse the electromagnetic chaos for signs of deliberate origin. "Natural debris. That's all you see. Just natural debris." Jaya watched the tactical display with her heart hammering against her ribs. Ward's phantom stood beside her, as still and patient as he'd been during their most dangerous missions, radiating the calm certainty that had made him the finest captain in the fleet. *If they investigate more closely, if they decide this is too convenient ...*

But the scan moved on.

"Thank you. Thank you, thank you, thank you." *I can't believe that actually worked.*

The three cruisers continued their methodical search pattern, probing other sections of the debris field with the same deadly patience. "But you'll be back, won't you?" They would be. Jaya had no illusions about that. The plasma cloud would dissipate, and when it did, they would find the gaps in their sensor coverage unacceptable. But for now, the Astraeus remained hidden among the graves of her squadron.

2

Jaya slumped in her chair, every muscle screaming. *Holy shit. Still breathing.* The alarms fell silent, replaced by the ship's strained breath—recycled air thick with ozone and death. Now that the danger had passed, her hands wouldn't stop shaking, the adrenaline crash hitting her like a physical blow to the chest. The tactical display showed the enemy cruisers continuing their methodical search pattern, their sensor sweeps probing other sections of the debris field with the same deadly patience.

But Ward's phantom remained.

He stood beside the damage control station, his translucent form studying status reports with methodical focus. His fingers ghosted across displays he shouldn't affect—yet the readouts scrolled, obeying him with eerie precision. The sight made Jaya's stomach clench with a mixture of desperate hope and existential terror.

"You're not supposed to be here." Her voice sounded calm, but she felt the tremor inside. "You died. I saw the footage." The words felt like glass in her throat, each syllable cutting deeper than the last. "You're dead, Captain. I watched you die."

Ward's phantom turned toward her, his gray eyes carrying depths that belonged to no living man. His mouth moved without sound. But she understood: *Show me.*

Every instinct told her to stop, but Jaya's fingers found the security playback controls. The main display flickered to life, loading the files she'd reviewed earlier—the ones that had shown her the true cost of their mission. The timestamp read 14:42:07, three minutes after the ambush began, when hope still existed that someone might survive what was happening to their squadron.

The bridge appeared as it was an hour ago—intact, busy, filled with the dead when they were still alive. Captain Ward stood beside the command chair, his weathered face grim as he coordinated the fleet through the comm system. Lieutenant Commander Reyes worked at communications, trying to raise Fleet Command while enemy fire lit up the void. Ensign Park's young face was tight with concentration as she rerouted power to the stealth systems.

"Emergency beacon is ready, sir," Reyes called out, his voice strained. "But I can't get a clear transmission through this interference."

"Keep trying," Ward commanded. "Someone needs to know what we found here."

The first impact threw everyone sideways, artificial gravity fluctuating as the Astraeus's hull buckled under directed energy weapons that turned steel into plasma. She watched herself on the recording, barking orders, steering them into the debris shadow. The second hit struck harder—blowing bridge systems and raining sparks from overhead.

Reyes went down first, his neck snapping against the communications console with a wet crack that the audio pickups captured with crystal clarity. Park followed seconds later, thrown across the deck by the artificial gravity's wild fluctuations, her skull meeting the bulkhead with a sound like breaking pottery. But Ward—Ward kept moving, kept trying to reach the emergency beacon controls even as jagged metal from the exploded tactical display buried itself in his chest.

"Sir!" The Jaya on the recording reached toward him, but another impact sent her sliding toward the navigation station, her head striking the console with enough force to knock her unconscious.

Ward's hand missed the beacon by inches, blood bubbling at his lips as he tried to speak. His last words were lost to the chaos of alarms and dying systems, but his eyes held the same desperate urgency that now burned in his phantom's gaze.

The recording continued with the bridge falling silent except for the omnipresent wail of emergency systems. Bodies scattered across the deck like broken dolls, their sacrifice reduced to biometric readings that flat-lined one by one. The emergency medical drones would activate twenty minutes later, cleaning up the mess with mechanical efficiency while Jaya lay unconscious among the ruins.

"I couldn't save you." The words came out as a broken whisper, tears cutting tracks through the dried blood on her cheeks. "I couldn't save any of you."

The artifact pulsed, rhythms spiking until the hull rang like a struck bell. The gravity fluctuated momentarily, making Jaya's stomach lurch, and Ward's translucent form wavered but stabilized. The temperature surged and dropped again, like the ship had shivered, and several displays showed readings that defied rational explanation.

Ward's phantom moved to the secondary systems panel, his transparent finger pointing to a specific bypass that could strengthen their failing stealth field. The gesture was precise, exactly the kind of technical knowledge he'd possessed in life. But how could a hallucination know things she didn't? How could trauma-induced delusion provide tactical solutions that actually worked?

"I don't understand what's happening." The admission felt like another kind of death, the rational part of her mind finally acknowledging that everything she thought she knew about reality had become suspect. *Am I hallucinating? Is this what a complete breakdown looks like?* But even as she thought the words, her hands moved to follow his instructions, responding to command authority that transcended death itself.

The bypass held. Power stabilized. A tiny win in a ship full of ghosts. The stealth field strengthened, buying them precious time while enemy forces continued their methodical scan.

Ward's phantom studied the tactical display again, his expression carrying the same calculating intelligence that she had grown to know. When he pointed toward a cluster of larger debris that could provide additional cover, Jaya found herself nodding along despite every rational fiber of her being, screaming that this was impossible.

"You're not real," she said again, but the words lacked conviction now. *Dead men don't give orders. Ghosts don't fix stealth fields.* Yet here she was, alive because she'd followed guidance from what should have been nothing more than guilt-induced hallucinations. Here she was, trusting her dead captain's phantom while enemy forces hunted her through the darkness between stars.

The artifact hummed through the hull. Ward's ghost sharpened. His eyes locked onto hers with an intensity that made her breath catch in her throat. Whether he was a figment of her imagination or a spectral manifestation, she realized with chilling clarity that she was no longer alone on the Astraeus. This revelation left her uncertain whether to feel relief or dread at this uninvited company.

Then, before she could process it, the artifact's energy signature spiked without warning. The sudden surge sent every system aboard the Astraeus into a cacophony of electromagnetic protest. Jaya stood transfixed as chaos unfolded around her—displays flickered wildly, phantom signals burst through comms—languages older than Earth, maybe older than time, and environmental controls malfunctioned, causing the bridge temperature to rise abruptly by ten degrees. Sensor readings twisted into patterns so bizarre they suggested reality itself was warping under the obsidian sphere's enigmatic influence.

"What the hell—" Her words cut off as the main communications panel burst to life with overlapping voices, fragments of conversations that couldn't exist. She heard Captain Martinez from the destroyer Hephaestus reporting successful weapons lock just moments before his ship exploded, Lieutenant Torres requesting permission to break formation seconds after her fighter had been vaporized, and underneath it all, a chorus of whispers in harmonics that made her teeth ache.

Gravity buckled. Her gut twisted with it as the artificial field strength oscillated between crushing weight and weightless drift. Overhead lighting strobed in patterns that matched the artifact's pulsing rhythm, casting dancing shadows that seemed to move independently of their sources. The air itself tasted of copper and ozone, charged with energy that made the fine hairs on her arms stand at attention.

Ward's phantom stood motionless through the chaos, his translucent form growing more solid with each surge from the cargo hold. When their eyes met, Jaya felt a chill that had nothing to do with the ship's damaged environmental systems. The correlation was undeniable now—the stronger the artifact's emanations, the more substantial Ward's presence became. Her scientific mind reeled at the implications, rational thought crumbling under the weight of impossible observations.

"You're linked to it." Fear laced her voice—and something closer to need. "That thing is keeping you here, isn't it?" But Ward's phantom merely turned back to the tactical display, his expression carrying the same grim focus that had defined his command style in life.

The proximity alarms began their shrieking wail again, cutting through her confusion like a blade. Two more Zynar cruisers had entered the debris field, their scanning arrays painting the wreckage in harsh relief as they moved with predatory patience. These ships approached from a different vector, their search pattern designed to catch anything that might have escaped the first sweep.

"Shit. They're not giving up." Jaya's hands flew to the stealth controls, but the readings made her blood run cold. Power levels had dropped to critical, damaged generators struggling to maintain even basic life support, let alone the electromagnetic camouflage that was their only protection. "We've got nothing left for another cloak run."

Ward's phantom moved to her side, his transparent hand gesturing toward the emergency power controls. But this time his suggestion made her heart stop: complete system shutdown. Everything except minimal life support, letting the ship drift naturally with the debris while enemy forces passed within kilometers of their position.

"Are you insane?" The question came out as a strangled whisper. "If they get close enough for visual confirmation—" But she was already moving, her hands working the shutdown sequence even as rational thought screamed at her to stop. Trusting a hallucination was one thing, but this bordered on suicide. But something deeper than reason moved her hands, the same instinct that had kept her alive through three dangerous missions under his command.

One by one, systems died—leaving the Astraeus to drift in silence. Life support dropped to emergency levels, recycling the same stale air while heat production fell to barely above the ambient temperature of space itself. Artificial gravity failed completely, leaving Jaya floating, tethered to her command chair as the ship's electromagnetic signature faded to almost nothing. The bridge fell into profound darkness, emergency lighting extinguished, leaving only the artifact's faint glow.

In that forced stillness, suspended between life and death in the void between stars, survivor's guilt hit her like a physical blow. Only her breath remained—shaky and loud in the dark, each exhalation a reminder that she continued to live while better people lay cold in the ship's morgue. The darkness pressed against her like a living thing, carrying the weight of every face she'd failed to save, every friend whose sacrifice had been reduced to twisted metal and fading heat signatures.

"Why me?" Her voice cracked in the dark, echoing in the empty bridge with accusatory weight. "Reyes had a family. Park was just twenty-three. Henderson had twin daughters who'll never see their father again." Her voice cracked, years of repressed emotion finally breaking through the professional facade she'd maintained since awakening in this graveyard. " They were better. They should've made it. Not me."

The tears came freely now, floating in the zero gravity like liquid stars that caught and scattered the artifact's alien illumination. She felt small and broken in the darkness, a lone survivor carrying the unbearable weight of an entire squadron's final moments. How do you honor the dead when you can't even understand why you were spared?

Ward's phantom approached through the darkness, his form more solid now than it had been since first appearing. His expression carried the same paternal concern he'd shown during her worst moments of self-doubt, the look that had pulled her through tactical simulations when failure seemed inevitable. When he spoke, his voice came not as sound but as understanding that formed directly in her consciousness: "Because you still have work to do."

The words hit her like a revelation, cutting through the fog of guilt and despair with perfect clarity. Not comfort, not false reassurance, but simple truth delivered with the authority that had made him the finest captain in the fleet. Her mission wasn't complete. The artifact still needed to reach Alliance Command, its secrets still required protection from whatever forces had orchestrated the ambush. She was alive not because she deserved it more than the others, but because someone had to carry the burden forward.

The enemy ships passed dangerously close, their searchlights sweeping through the debris field like the fingers of mechanical gods. Jaya held her breath as one cruiser drifted within five hundred meters of their position, close enough that she could see individual hull markings through the viewport. But the powered-down Astraeus registered as nothing more than another piece of wreckage, another fragment of Alliance dreams floating dead in the void.

When the Zynar forces finally moved on, continuing their methodical hunt through distant sections of the debris field, Ward's phantom guided her through the restart sequence with command efficiency. Systems came online in careful sequence—life support first, then basic propulsion, finally the stealth field that would hide them from the next wave of hunters.

"Thank you," she whispered to his translucent form, the words carrying more weight than any military commendation. "I don't understand what you are or how this is possible, but thank you."

Ward's phantom scrutinized the tactical display one last time, his figure flickering as the artifact's energy signature steadied. His eyes locked onto Jaya's, a silent command etched in their depths: survive, complete the mission, honor their sacrifice. "The enemy ships will likely return," he advised with calm certainty. "Take the Astraeus into the Veil of Shards asteroid field for cover." His form began to dissolve, leaving behind only a whisper of his presence.

As the bridge lighting returned to normal and the ship resumed its cautious journey through the graveyard of her squadron, Jaya understood that she was no longer battling solely for survival. Redemption drove her forward now, bearing the hopes and dreams of those lost toward whatever fate awaited in the void between stars. The artifact pulsed ominously in its containment, and for the first time since awakening alone among ruins, Jaya questioned whether her survival had been mere chance or something far more intentionally orchestrated.

3

The Veil of Shards opened before the Astraeus, a mechanical beast, its fangs made of shattered ships. Jaya's hands gripped the pilot controls with white-knuckled intensity, her palms slick with sweat as she guided the damaged frigate between massive chunks of hull plating that tumbled through space in slow, lethal movements. The ship's artificial gravity stuttered beneath her feet, damaged generators creating pockets where her stomach rose into her throat and others where she felt pressed into her seat by invisible hands.

"Another day in paradise," she muttered—voice barely holding. The Veil stretched for thousands of kilometers in every direction, a graveyard of conflicts spanning decades where disabled vessels had been drawn by gravitational anomalies to dance their last waltz among the asteroids. Twisted metal caught what little starlight penetrated the field, creating a constellation of razored edges that could slice through even military-grade hull plating.

The tactical display painted a three-dimensional maze of hazards, each blip representing debris large enough to crush the Astraeus like an insect. Sensors buckled under the chaos, algorithms choking on too much debris. Warning klaxons had been silenced—their constant wail would have driven her mad within minutes—but amber alerts flashed across every surface, painting the bridge in urgent light.

A gutted cargo hauler drifted past, its interior hollow and dead. The sight made her chest tighten with familiar guilt. *How many ships had sought refuge in the Veil, only to become part of its deadly collection?* How many desperate pilots had made the same choice she was making now?

The Astraeus shuddered as a micro-asteroid struck the weakened hull, the impact resonating through the ship's skeleton like a struck bell. Damage reports cascaded across her displays, but she forced herself to ignore them. *One crisis at a time, Moreau. Keep the ship moving or none of it matters.* The stealth field fluctuated wildly in response to the gravitational stresses, power consumption spiking as the generators fought to maintain their electromagnetic camouflage.

And then—Ward appeared again at her side.

His phantom form flickered like a damaged hologram, translucent edges wavering with each violet pulse from the obsidian sphere. But his voice cut through her confusion with commanding clarity: "Port thrusters, thirty percent. Now."

Jaya's rational mind resisted even as her hands moved to comply. *Dead men don't give navigation commands.* Trauma-induced hallucinations don't understand stellar mechanics. But the artifact's energy signature was spiking again, and Ward's phantom stood by confidently. His gray eyes held depths that belonged to no living man, yet they tracked the approaching debris with an exactness that seemed impossible for a figment of her imagination.

"Insane," she muttered—yet her hands obeyed. The Astraeus responded sluggishly, damaged maneuvering jets coughing to life, causing vibrations through the deck plating. Port thrusters engaged at exactly thirty percent, nudging the frigate away from what appeared to be empty space.

Five seconds later, a cruiser's corpse tore through the space they'd just vacated. The twisted metal was easily ten times the Astraeus's mass, spinning end over end with enough kinetic energy to reduce them to component atoms. If Ward's guidance had been wrong by even a fraction of a degree, or if she'd hesitated for another heartbeat …

"How did you know?" The question escaped her lips as a whisper, but Ward's phantom was already pointing toward another hazard, his expression carrying the same grim focus.

The artifact flared. The air temp spiked, then dipped, and two more figures began to coalesce in the bridge's emergency lighting. Reyes shimmered into view, trademark smirk ghosting across her translucent face. Navigator Park followed, his nervous habit of adjusting his glasses evident even in spectral form.

"Well, this is new," Reyes said, her voice carrying the same dry humor that Jaya had grown to know. She leaned against the communications console with casual confidence, arms crossed as she surveyed the tactical display. "Though I have to say, Lieutenant, your piloting has improved since the Academy."

Park's phantom fidgeted near the navigation station, his transparent fingers hovering over controls he couldn't actually touch. "The gravitational readings are all wrong here," he said, his voice tight. "These asteroids shouldn't be holding stable orbits. Something's influencing the local space-time."

Jaya's breathing became shallow and rapid as the impossible scene unfolded around her. Three dead crew members stood on her bridge, offering tactical advice with the same competence they'd shown in life. Every ghost arrival echoed the artifact's pulse, causing console screens to flicker with readings that defied rational explanation.

"You're not real," But even she didn't believe it anymore. "None of this is real."

Ward's phantom turned toward her with a patient expression. "Does it matter?" His voice stern. "We're here. You need guidance. The mission continues."

Another debris field loomed ahead, this one dense enough to challenge even the most skilled pilot. Metal debris circled each other in chaotic, impossible orbits, their gravitational interactions creating a three-dimensional maze that shifted constantly. The navigation computer gave up trying to plot a safe course, displays showing nothing but error messages and probability warnings that approached certainty of collision.

"Starboard ten degrees," Park's phantom called out. "There's a gap forming between those two hull sections."

Reyes nodded in agreement. "He's right. Window's only going to be open for about thirty seconds, though."

Jaya's hands shook as she executed the maneuver, trusting guidance from apparitions that shouldn't exist while navigating through hazards that could vaporize her ship in an instant. The gap Park had identified was barely twice the Astraeus's beam, walls of jagged metal closing slowly but inexorably as gravitational forces pulled the debris together.

"Steady as she goes," Ward commanded, his spectral form solid enough now that she could see individual details. "You've got this, Lieutenant."

The Astraeus slipped through the closing gap with meters to spare. But they were through, emerging into a relatively clear pocket of space where the debris density dropped to merely dangerous instead of instantly fatal.

Jaya slumped in her pilot's seat, chest heaving as adrenaline burned through her veins. Around her, the phantoms of her dead crew maintained their vigil, their impossible presence both terrifying and oddly comforting. She was no longer alone, though she questioned whether her new companions represented salvation or the first sign of complete psychological breakdown.

A gravitational ripple twisted space around them—like a funhouse mirror made of physics. Chunks of twisted metal the size of shuttlecraft orbited each other in figure-eight patterns, their paths intersecting at angles that should have resulted in catastrophic collisions but somehow maintained perfect clearance. Larger fragments—sections of cruiser hulls and destroyer superstructures—rotated slowly around gravitational sources that seemed to pull from multiple directions simultaneously.

"Jesus Christ," Jaya breathed, watching her navigation computer falter and display nothing but error codes and probability warnings painted in urgent red. The Astraeus shuddered as competing gravitational forces tugged at different sections of the ship, stress alerts flashing across her engineering displays as the hull flexed beyond its design tolerances. *It's like someone took physics and fed it through a blender.*

"That's a gravity pocket," Park said, his voice carrying his familiar nervous precision that Jaya remembered. " Starboard, forty degrees. Stay two klicks clear or we're vapor."

The familiar sound of his voice—that slight upturn at the end of technical explanations, the way he always sounded like he was asking a question even when stating facts—hit Jaya unexpectedly. Suddenly she wasn't on the bridge of the Astraeus anymore. She was back in the tactical briefing room three days ago, watching Park lean over the holographic display with that same nervous energy as he analyzed the Thanatos Rift approach vectors.

"Lieutenant, these sensor readings don't make sense," Park had said, adjusting his glasses as he studied the data streams. "The enemy formation patterns suggest they knew we were coming. The positioning is too perfect, too prepared." His young face had been tight with concern.

"The intelligence is solid, Ensign," she'd replied dismissively, her attention split between Park's concerns and Captain Ward's tactical overlay. "Fleet Command verified the stealth approach twice. We go in quiet, retrieve the package, and get out before anyone knows we were there."

But Park had persisted, his voice growing more urgent as he traced probability cones across the holographic star chart. "Ma'am, if they're expecting us, this approach puts us directly into a kill box. We should recommend a course change, maybe come in from the Meridian sector instead—"

His words died with the explosion—enemy fire shredding their stealth systems that had been compromised from the moment they dropped out of hyperspace. Park's eyes went wide with terror as the first barrage struck, his mouth opening to shout a warning that would never come. The blast wave threw him across the bridge like a doll.

"No!" Her jaw locked, stomach turning as the memory released its grip on her consciousness. Her hands were shaking on the navigation controls, sweat beading on her forehead despite the ship's cool air. Park's phantom watched her with concerned eyes, waiting patiently for her to process what he'd told her about the gravity pocket.

She forced herself to focus on the present, on the sensor readings that showed a distortion in space-time just forty degrees to starboard. The pocket was invisible to visual scanning, but its gravitational signature created a whirlpool in the debris patterns around it. Anything that got too close would be stretched apart by tidal forces that could turn the Astraeus into a kilometers-long strand of component atoms.

"Thanks," she muttered, fingers twitching over controls. "I should have listened to you before. About the ambush, about the approach vectors. You were right, and I—"

The artifact flared—no warning, just raw power, its energy signature spiking beyond anything she'd recorded since first encountering the obsidian sphere. The surge sent every system aboard the Astraeus into electromagnetic chaos, but this time the effect was far more dramatic than simple display glitches. Gravity flipped. Up became down—and stayed that way.

Her gut twisted, body weightless and lost. Emergency supplies, data tablets, and loose components became projectiles as they fell upward, clattering against overhead panels in a percussion symphony of mechanical chaos. Her pilot's chair restraints caught her before she could float away entirely, but the straps cut into her shoulders as the reversed gravity tried to pull her toward the ceiling.

"Hold on!" Ward stood firm—unbothered by gravity's tantrum. The irony wasn't lost on her—the dead remained stable while the living was tossed around like debris.

For thirty seconds that felt like hours, the Astraeus tumbled through the anomaly's influence while her crew fought to maintain any semblance of control. A data pad struck her shoulder with enough force to leave a bruise, while somewhere in the distance she could hear larger equipment breaking free from inadequate restraints.

Then gravity reasserted itself with brutal suddenness, everything that had been floating crashing back to the deck in a cascade of noise that made her ears ring. Jaya hit her seat hard enough to drive the breath from her lungs, while around the bridge a rain of debris clattered against metal surfaces. The artifact's glow dimmed slightly, though she could still feel its alien presence humming through the ship's hull like a second heartbeat.

"Systems stabilizing," she reported to no one in particular, her voice shaky as she checked damage reports. The gravitational reversal had caused minor hull stress and scattered equipment throughout the ship, but nothing catastrophic. She was still alive, still hidden among the Veil's deadly embrace.

Reyes' phantom straightened from where she'd been leaning against the communications console, her characteristic smirk intact despite everything that had just happened. "You're over-thinking it, Lieutenant," she said with dry confidence. *Trust your instincts like you did at Proxima Station.*

Another flash of memory, this one sharper and more painful than Park's technical warnings. Proxima Station, where her unorthodox tactical decision had saved their mission but exposed their fleet's operational patterns to enemy analysis. The same patterns that had been used to predict their approach to the Thanatos Rift, the same intelligence that had allowed the ambush to be so perfectly positioned.

"You'd still be alive if I'd listened to you then," Jaya muttered, the words coming out thick with guilt. "Both of you. All of you. My tactical innovation at Proxima gave them the data they needed to trap us here."

The phantoms exchanged glances—an impossible gesture for apparitions that shouldn't be able to see each other, yet somehow perfectly natural in the context of everything else that had become her new reality. Park pushed up ghost-glasses with an old nervous habit, while Reyes tilted her head.

Around them, the gravitational anomaly maintained its chaotic movement, debris tracing unpredictable paths that made her navigation computer stutter with confusion. But somehow, with guidance from the dead and power from an alien artifact that defied rational explanation, the Astraeus continued its passage through the Veil of Shards. Every dodge made the guilt worse—she was piloting through graves.

As she grappled with these feelings, a signal broke through the Astraeus's compromised communications array—faint yet unmistakably Alliance in origin. Jaya's heart hammered against her ribs as the computer decoded the transmission, fleet encryption protocols unfolding to reveal a desperate message that made her breath catch in her throat. Emergency beacon, automated distress, coordinates that placed the signal somewhere deeper in the Veil of Shards. Someone else had survived the massacre.

"Please," she breathed, hand frozen mid-command as hope and terror warred in her chest. The message was fragmentary, corrupted by the gravitational interference that plagued communications throughout the asteroid field. But the identifier codes were clear enough: Alliance vessel, crew in distress, requesting immediate assistance. *There are others out there.*

The phantoms reacted immediately, their translucent forms turning toward the communications station with expressions that ranged from warning to encouragement. Ward shook his head sharply, his eyes carrying cautious authority. The gesture was clear: responding meant exposure, discovery, death for everyone involved.

But Park's phantom nodded encouragingly, his young face bright with earnest hope. "We can't leave them out there," he said, his voice carrying conviction despite its spectral quality. "They're counting on us."

Reyes remained neutral, her characteristic smirk replaced by a calculating expression as she studied the signal analysis scrolling across nearby displays. "It's a risk either way," she said with analytical detachment. "But if there really are survivors ..."

"We can't leave them," she said—voice tight, heart louder. The words came out as both statement and plea, directed as much toward her own conscience as toward the improbable council of her dead crew. How many times had she imagined being in that position herself, floating in a damaged ship while rescue passed by within communications range? How could she condemn others to the same isolation that had nearly broken her?

Her hands moved to the controls before rational thought could intervene, instinctual reflexes guiding her through the transmission sequence that would cut through the Veil's interference. The emergency protocols were hardwired into her from years of fleet service, responses as automatic as breathing. She configured a narrow-beam burst transmission, hoping to minimize their electromagnetic signature while still reaching the distant survivors.

"Alliance vessel, this is Lieutenant Jaya Moreau aboard the frigate Astraeus," she spoke into the communications pickup, her voice steadier than she felt. "We copy your distress signal and are proceeding to assist. Transmit your status and coordinates for rendezvous."

The moment she triggered the transmission, the artifact erupted with energy that reverberated through the ship's hull like a thunderous gong. Every console on the bridge overloaded simultaneously, displays flickering between normal readouts and incomprehensible patterns that suggested reality itself was being rewritten. The communications array, already damaged from the ambush, sparked and smoked as it pushed the signal through layers of gravitational interference that should have made transmission impossible.

Warning klaxons blared throughout the ship as sensors detected the electromagnetic spike, their urgent wail cutting through the bridge's chaos like a blade. Jaya watched in horror as her transmission beacon flared across the tactical display, a brilliant signal ... that announced their position to anyone monitoring the Veil's communications frequencies. What had been intended as a narrow rescue beam had become an electromagnetic flare visible across half the asteroid field.

"Shit, shit, shit," she muttered, hands flying across the communications controls as she tried to contain the damage. But the artifact's influence had infected every system connected to the transmission array, creating cascade failures that spread through the ship's electronic nervous systems. "I should have listened to you, Captain. Should have maintained communications silence."

The proximity alarms answered her regret with mechanical inevitability, their shrieking wail announcing what she'd feared: something had heard her transmission and was coming to investigate. The tactical display painted a new contact in hostile red, acceleration curves that suggested advanced propulsion systems and weapon capabilities far beyond Alliance specifications. A Zynar scout ship, sleek and predatory, burned hard toward their position through the asteroid field's treacherous passages.

"Tactical systems online," Jaya commanded, her voice steadying as military training reasserted control over her emotional chaos. "Bring up defensive screens and prepare evasive maneuvers." The ships AI responded sluggishly, damaged systems struggling to translate her commands into action while the enemy closed distance with ruthless efficiency.

The scout ship was smaller than the cruisers that had devastated her squadron, but its weapon signatures made her blood run cold. Energy cannons capable of burning through military-grade armor, missile racks loaded with warheads that could crack asteroids, and sensor arrays sophisticated enough to track a stealth frigate through the Veil's electromagnetic chaos. Against the damaged Astraeus, it might as well have been a battleship.

The phantoms crowded around her command station, shouting simultaneous instructions that overlapped and contradicted each other in a spectral chorus of tactical advice. Ward pointed toward the debris field's densest concentration, his phantom form flickering as he gestured urgently. Reyes called out weapon system configurations while monitoring enemy approach vectors. Park's nervous voice rose above the others, calculating intercept courses and evasion probabilities.

"Port thrusters, full burn!" Ward commanded.

"No, starboard!" Reyes countered. "The debris density is lower that way!"

"They're locking weapons," Park announced, his voice tight with anxiety. "Thirty seconds to effective range!"

The scout ship fired its first volley without warning, coherent energy beams that turned distant asteroids into expanding clouds of superheated vapor. The shots missed the Astraeus by mere kilometers, close enough that her sensors registered the thermal blooms as the space around them lit up with destructive fury. Jaya threw the frigate into a desperate evasive spiral, sending them tumbling through a dense cluster of debris while enemy fire chased their trail.

"Controlled spin, forty degrees per second," she reported to no one in particular, her hands steady on the controls despite the chaos erupting around them. The scout ship pursued relentlessly, its superior maneuverability allowing it to match her desperate turns while maintaining firing solutions that grew more accurate with each exchange.

Another volley screamed past them, this one close enough to overload their port shields and send feedback surges through the ship's power grid. Emergency lighting failed completely, leaving only the artifact's violet glow and the hellish illumination of enemy weapons fire to light the bridge. Hull plating screamed in the distance—thermal stress tearing at the seams as near-misses heated their armor to temperatures that threatened structural integrity.

"There!" Ward's phantom pointed toward a massive, spinning hull fragment that tumbled end over end through the debris field ahead of them. It was the shattered remains of what had once been a heavy cruiser, its superstructure twisted into impossible angles by whatever catastrophe had claimed it. The fragment was easily ten times the Astraeus's size, spinning with enough kinetic energy to pulverize anything that got too close.

"Full thrust on my mark," Ward commanded with unwavering confidence.

Jaya's finger hovered over the thruster controls as she made her choice. *Trust the impossible, or die alone in the darkness.* Behind them, the scout ship closed for the killing shot, its weapons charging for a volley that would reduce the Astraeus to space debris. Ahead, the spinning hull fragment offered salvation or annihilation in equal measure.

The moment stretched like eternity, balanced on the knife's edge between survival and destruction. Then Ward's phantom spoke a single word that cut through her hesitation like a blade: "Now."

4

Jaya slammed the thruster controls. The Astraeus groaned—systems coughing a final breath, leaving only the whisper of failing life support and the ominous hum that had begun emanating from the artifact. Its violet pulse painted the bridge in sickly light as every system aboard the ship began its descent into electronic madness.

The tactical screen spasmed—real data colliding with impossible geometry, showing three Zynar pursuit vessels where moments before there had been only one. The scout ship had been the advance guard, she realized with growing horror. The hunters had found her trail, and now they were closing the noose. Each vessel was a sleek predator twice the size of her damaged frigate, their weapon signatures painting warnings across her failing displays.

"Navigation offline," she reported to the empty bridge, her voice cracking as another system joined the cascade of failures. The helm controls sparked under her touch, circuits overloading as the artifact's energy surge infected every pathway in the ship's electronic systems. "Life support fluctuating. Engines ... engines are gone."

Then came the whispers.

They seeped from the communications array like smoke, fragments of conversation in languages that predated human civilization. The voices overlapped and contradicted each other, forming harmonics that made her vision cloud. But underneath the alien chorus, she caught familiar cadences—words in Alliance Standard that shouldn't exist, spoken by throats that were now just space dust.

"Lieutenant Moreau." Ward's voice emerged from the static, not through the speakers but forming directly in her consciousness with abrupt clarity. "You need to listen."

His phantom stood beside her command chair. Behind him, Reyes and Park flickered, their translucent forms gaining substance as the artifact's pulse intensified.

"The Thanatos Rift," Ward said, his eyes locking onto the navigation display. "Plot a course directly into the gravitational anomalies. Maximum burn."

Jaya's gut rebelled against the suggestion with every fiber of her being. " That's suicide. We're not even supposed to be near that thing. The tidal forces alone would—"

"Would tear apart anything following conventional physics," Reyes interrupted, her characteristic smirk replaced by urgent intensity. She leaned over the tactical console, her phantom finger tracing approach vectors that defied rational calculation. "But we're not dealing with conventional physics anymore, are we?"

Park's nervous voice rose above the growing whispers from the communications array. "The gravitational readings are wrong, Lieutenant. The stellar remnant is generating space-time distortions that shouldn't be possible. Standard navigation algorithms can't compensate for quantum fluctuations of this magnitude."

On the tactical display, the Zynar vessels adjusted their pursuit pattern with mechanical precision. Scanner probes launched from their forward bays, spreading out in a search grid that would locate the Astraeus within minutes.

"They're launching active scans," Jaya said, watching the probes paint the asteroid field in harsh electromagnetic light. "Sixty seconds until they have a firing solution."

The artifact's hum matched her pulse until she couldn't tell where her own circulation ended and alien influence began. The bridge temperature spiked fifteen degrees in as many seconds, then plummeted until her breath misted in the suddenly frigid air. Console screens throughout the bridge flickered between normal readouts and displays that showed star charts for constellations that didn't exist.

Ward's phantom moved closer, his presence radiating calm authority. "The artifact will protect us," he said, his voice cutting through the growing chaos with absolute certainty. "Trust what you've learned since awakening in this graveyard."

"I've learned that following phantom advice gets people killed," Jaya shot back, but her hands were already moving toward the navigation controls. The rational part of her mind screamed warnings about gravitational shear and tidal forces, but another part—the part that had kept her alive while everyone else died—recognized the truth in Ward's words.

The whispers from the artifact grew louder, more coherent, until actual words began to emerge from the electromagnetic storm. "The way ..." came the voice, hollow and resonant like wind through an ancient cathedral. "Through the darkness ... the path that others cannot follow ..."

Park's phantom studied the sensor readings nervously. "Lieutenant, the probes are integrating their scan data. They've found inconsistencies in our stealth field. Forty seconds until detection."

The Zynar vessels began their final approach, acceleration curves painting deadly mathematics across her failing displays. Their weapon systems charged with energy signatures that could crack a moon's surface, while targeting computers calculated intercept solutions with mechanical patience. Against the damaged Astraeus, they might as well have been gods of destruction.

"The gravity well," Ward said, pointing to a specific distortion on the navigation chart where space-time twisted into impossible knots around the stellar remnant's corpse. "It's not just a gravitational anomaly. It's a gateway."

Jaya's breathing came in short, sharp bursts as the magnitude of what he was suggesting crashed over her. Plot a course directly into the heart of a collapsed star, where the laws of physics broke down into chaos and ships were stretched across light-years of warped space-time. Trust her survival to an alien artifact that whispered secrets in languages older than humanity.

The whispers intensified, alien voices joining the chorus until the communications array crackled with harmonics that made her bones vibrate. "Trust ... the path through shadows ... where light cannot reach ..."

Her hands hovered over the navigation controls, torn between military protocol and the desperate guidance that had already saved her life twice. Behind her, the phantom crew waited with expressions that ranged from urgent encouragement to grim determination. Ahead, the tactical display showed Zynar targeting computers reaching firing solutions that would end her journey in a brief flash of superheated plasma.

Twenty seconds. To die—or dive into the impossible.

The artifact pulsed once more, its energy signature spiking beyond anything her instruments could measure, and in that moment of alien communion, Jaya felt something brush against her consciousness like fingers trailing through dark water. Not words, not thoughts, but pure understanding that cut through her confusion with harsh clarity.

The way forward lay through the darkness where conventional ships could not follow.

Jaya's choice became clear and final in an instant. Her hands slammed down on the navigation controls, programming a course that would have gotten her court-martialed under normal circumstances. The Astraeus responded sluggishly, damaged systems struggling to translate her commands into action as she pointed the frigate's nose directly toward the swirling gravitational nightmare of Thanatos Rift.

"Full burn. Straight into the Rift." Her voice held, even if her reason didn't. "All available power to the engines."

The ship lurched forward with hopeless acceleration, artificial gravity fluctuating as competing forces tugged at different sections of the hull. Warnings blared throughout the bridge, their urgent wail mixing with the otherworldly whispers that continued to seep from every communications array. Structural integrity sensors plastered the displays, stress readings climbing toward levels that would tear the Astraeus apart before any enemy weapon could touch her.

Behind them, the Zynar vessels reacted. The lead pursuer fired a warning volley, coherent energy beams that missed the frigate by mere kilometers but turned nearby asteroids into expanding clouds of superheated vapor. The thermal blooms registered on her sensors, close enough that her port shields overloaded from the ambient radiation.

They're not trying to destroy us, Jaya realized, watching the tactical display as the enemy ships adjusted their pursuit pattern. "They want the artifact intact."

The second volley came closer, energy beams grazing the Astraeus's shields and sending feedback surges through the power grid. The Zynar were herding her, she understood with growing horror—using precisely calculated shots to force her into surrender rather than risk damaging their prize.

But the gravity well of Thanatos Rift made precise calculations meaningless.

Space-time warped around them as they approached the stellar remnant's event horizon, transforming the emptiness into a realm where the laws of physics dissolved into unpredictable quantum phenomena. The navigation computer was unresponsive, displays showing nothing but error codes and probability warnings. Through the viewport, she could see light itself bending in curves, creating halos and coronas.

Ward stood behind her, watching like always—impossible, steady, real. "When I give the word," he said, his voice cutting through the chaos with absolute authority, "cut all power except life support. Everything else goes dark."

The pursuing Zynar vessels followed them into the gravity well's influence, their superior technology allowing them to maintain formation despite the space-time distortions that were tearing the Astreus apart. But even their advanced sensors couldn't compensate for what happened next. Missile launch signatures flared across Jaya's tactical display, a full volley of guided warheads designed to disable rather than destroy.

"Incoming," Jaya reported, her hands flying across the defensive systems controls. "Impact in thirty seconds."

The artifact's pulse reached a crescendo that made her bones vibrate and her vision blur at the edges. Every console on the bridge overloaded simultaneously as alien energy infected the ship's electronic nervous system. The whispers grew louder, more insistent, until coherent words emerged from the electromagnetic storm: "Now ... let go ... trust the darkness ..."

Ward's phantom leaned forward, his voice stern: "Now."

Jaya's finger hit the emergency shutdown, plunging the Astraeus into complete darkness. Life support continued, but everything else died in an instant—engines, weapons, navigation, artificial gravity. The ship became a ghost, electronically invisible as it tumbled through the gravity well's twisted embrace.

The artifact exploded—not in force, but in meaning.

Light poured out—cold, ancient, and utterly wrong. Obsidian radiance burst through bulkheads and armor plating as if they were made of paper, painting the bridge in alien illumination that hurt to look at directly. The energy didn't simply shine—it rewrote the fundamental nature of the space around it, turning vacuum into something that pulsed with malevolent intelligence.

The electromagnetic pulse that followed was beyond anything in Jaya's experience. It expanded outward from the artifact's position like a shock wave made of pure information, carrying data packets in languages that predated human civilization. The pursuing missiles simply ceased to exist, their guidance systems overwhelmed by input that made their circuits forget how to function. The Zynar vessels' sensors were rendered useless in an instant, their advanced systems overwhelmed by the alien transmission.

But the price of salvation was catastrophic.

The Rift grabbed them like a closing fist—space folding around the ship. Jaya felt the sensation of falling upward and sideways simultaneously, her inner ear rebelling against sensory input that caused blood to seep from her ear canal.

The bridge became a frenzy of destruction as the ship twisted through unimaginable geometries. A support beam buckled overhead, showering her with sparks and debris as the hull flexed beyond its design tolerances. Her pilot's chair tore free from its mounting brackets, hurling her across the bridge to strike the communications console with enough force to crack her ribs.

Hull breach alarms joined the growing symphony of destruction, their urgent roar mixing with the sound of atmosphere venting into vacuum through micro-fractures that appeared and sealed themselves in defiance of basic materials science. The Astraeus groaned—wounded, alive, barely holding.

Through it all, the artifact's light continued to burn, its obsidian radiance creating pockets of stable space-time where the laws of physics remembered how to function properly. These islands of rationality expanded and contracted with each pulse, protecting the ship from complete annihilation while subjecting it to stresses that no human-built vessel should have survived.

It lasted forever—and no time at all. Then, like a shuddering breath, it spat them out.

The silence that followed was profound. Emergency lighting flickered weakly, powered by backup systems that had somehow survived the transit. The artifact's glow dimmed to barely perceptible levels, its surface now etched with new symbols that pulsed in rhythm. Around her, the bridge looked like a war zone, debris scattered across buckled deck plating while exposed circuitry sparked and smoked.

Jaya pulled herself upright, every muscle in her body screamed as she surveyed the damage. The tactical display, when she finally coaxed it back to life, showed readings that made her heart sink. Life support at thirty percent and falling, engines completely offline, hull breaches on multiple decks. They had survived the impossible transit, but the Astraeus was dying around her.

The Zynar pursuit vessels were nowhere to be seen.

Blood pooled in Jaya's mouth where she'd bitten her tongue during the violent transit, copper taste mixing with the acrid smoke that filled the Astraeus's damaged corridors. Her ribs ached with each breath, but she forced herself to crawl through the maintenance tunnels toward the primary power distribution hub. The ship's wounds were everywhere—ruptured conduits leaked coolant that hissed against superheated hull plating, while emergency patches sparked and failed under atmospheric pressure they were never designed to contain.

"Life support first," she muttered, her voice echoing in the narrow tunnel as she dragged herself past cables that had been twisted into wild configurations during their passage through the gravity well. *Then engines. Then maybe, just maybe, we live long enough to regret this decision.*

The phantoms materialized around her in the tunnel's cramped confines, their translucent forms flickering as they pointed toward critical failures her damaged diagnostics couldn't detect. Ward's apparition gestured urgently toward a power coupling that looked intact but carried the telltale heat signature of impending cascade failure. Reyes indicated a back-up life support line that had been severed during their violent emergence, its ends sparking weakly in the recycled atmosphere.

"Bypass the primary junction," Park's phantom advised, his voice nervous. "Route power through the secondary grid. It'll hold long enough for temporary repairs."

Jaya's hands moved without conscious thought, instinctual reflex from years of engineering training guiding her through repairs that should have required a full damage control team. The work was brutal, intimate violence performed on the ship's mechanical organs while her own body threatened to shut down from exhaustion and injury. Each successful connection bought her precious minutes of continued existence.

The power coupling sparked under her touch, superheated metal burning through her gloves to sear flesh that was already raw from the emergency repairs. She ignored the pain, forcing damaged circuits to accept jury-rigged connections that violated every safety protocol in the fleet manual. The ship's electronic nervous system responded grudgingly, power flowing through pathways that shuddered under the new loads.

Hull breach alarms fell silent one by one as she sealed the micro-fractures that had appeared during their transit, emergency patches holding against atmospheric pressure through sheer mechanical determination. The work took hours, or perhaps minutes—time had become elastic in the aftermath of their passage through space-time distortions.

When she finally dragged herself back to the bridge, the artifact had changed. Etchings now crawled across its surface. The obsidian sphere sat dormant in its containment field, its surface no longer pulsing with violet energy but instead etched with symbols that seemed to shift when she wasn't looking directly at them. The patterns were beautiful and terrible, geometric forms that suggested architectural blueprints for structures that shouldn't exist in three-dimensional space.

The comms crackled to life—unbidden, urgent. The message that materialized on her main display carried the highest priority encryption, fleet authorization codes that made her pulse quicken despite her fatigue. Official orders, transmitted through quantum entanglement networks that could reach across galactic distances in real-time.

"Lieutenant Moreau," the text read, each word appearing with military efficiency that brooked no argument. "Proceed to coordinates 227-984-331 for extraction. Artifact retrieval is priority alpha. All other considerations are secondary. Acknowledge receipt and estimated time of arrival."

The coordinates plotted themselves across her navigation display, a rendezvous point three days away through conventional hyperspace. Standard fleet protocol, exactly the kind of efficient military operation that had defined her career before everything went wrong at Thanatos Rift. *Follow orders, complete the mission, trust in the chain of command that had guided humanity through centuries of interstellar expansion.*

But the phantoms reacted as if she'd received a death sentence.

Their forms flickered intensely, translucent edges sparking with energy that made the bridge's emergency lighting strobe in sympathetic response. Ward's apparition moved with desperate urgency, positioning himself between Jaya and the navigation console like a barrier of crystallized authority. His gaze burned with a warning that transcended the limitations of spectral communication.

"They don't understand what they're dealing with," he said, his voice laced with concern. "Fleet Command sees a weapon, not a key. They'll study it, dissect it, unleash something that should remain contained."

Reyes nodded grimly, her characteristic smirk replaced by an expression of profound unease. "The artifact chose you, Lieutenant. Not them. Not some committee of admirals who've never felt its influence. You."

Park's phantom wrung his hands in a nervous gesture. "The quantum entanglement signatures are all wrong," he said, his voice tight with technical confusion. "That message didn't come through normal fleet channels. Someone's mimicking the encryption protocols."

As if summoned by their warnings, the artifact began to whisper again. But these voices were different from the alien chorus she'd heard before—older, more urgent, carrying harmonics that resonated in her head like struck tuning forks.

"Nyx Spire ..." the voices whispered, their tone carrying a gravity that was unrealized until that moment. "The only sanctuary ... where the others wait ... where understanding dwells in shadows ..."

Jaya accessed the star charts, searching for any record of the name that had embedded itself in her thoughts. The navigation computer found nothing—no astronomical surveys, no exploration reports, no mention in any database that Fleet Command maintained. According to official records, Nyx Spire simply didn't exist.

Yet she felt its pull like gravity.

The sensation was impossible to describe, a directional instinct that pointed toward a specific sector of uncharted space with the same certainty that had once guided ancient navigators by star position. Not toward any planetary body her instruments could detect, but toward something that called to the alien artifact with harmonics that made reality itself vibrate in sympathy.

Her hands hovered over the navigation controls, torn between duty and intuition that had already saved her life more times than military protocol ever had. Fleet Command offered extraction, debriefing, a return to the rational universe where orders were followed and mysteries were solved through scientific method. The artifact offered something else entirely—a journey into uncharted space toward a destination that existed outside human knowledge.

The phantoms waited with expressions that ranged from desperate encouragement to grim resignation. Behind her, the communications array continued to pulse with the fleet message, priority encryption demanding immediate acknowledgment. Ahead, the navigation display showed two potential courses—one toward the coordinates of military salvation, another toward the void where Nyx Spire waited in shadows that light had never touched.

The choice would define not just her fate, but the future of whatever cosmic forces had converged around an impossible artifact and the ghosts of her dead crew.

5

Jaya's finger hovered over the navigation controls, then pressed down firmly. The coordinates for Nyx Spire loaded into the ship's computer. Fleet Command's extraction orders flickered on the secondary display, demanding acknowledgment she would never give. She was committed now, following phantom guidance toward a destination not on any official star chart.

"Course laid in," she announced to the empty bridge, her voice hoarse with exhaustion. The Astraeus responded sluggishly, damaged engines struggling to life as they began their journey. Behind her, the communications array continued its steady pulse, Fleet messages accumulating while she ignored the chain of command that had defined three generations of her family's service.

The first Zynar patrol zone appeared on her sensors, detection grids spread across space. Jaya worked the manual override controls, sweat beading on her forehead as she forced the failing stealth systems to hold together through jury-rigged connections. The ship's AI compensated for her inexperience at single-handed operation, automated systems taking over thruster control and power distribution while she managed the critical stealth systems.

"Come on," she whispered, coaxing reluctant circuits through another cycle while electromagnetic signatures danced close to detection thresholds. Her fingers moved across interfaces that should have required a full bridge crew. The AI's assistance guided her movements, anticipating her needs and adjusting ship systems before she could voice commands.

The artifact pulsed with energy, causing cascading failures through every system aboard the Astraeus. Warning lights lit up the bridge, proximity sensors blaring alerts as their electromagnetic signature flared across the patrol zone, announcing their presence to anyone with functioning detection equipment.

"Shut up," Jaya snarled at the alarms, her hands flying across emergency protocols while the artifact's energy signature threatened to expose them to the Zynar hunters in nearby space. She rerouted power through backup circuits, bypassed safety interlocks, and forced the stealth generators to accept dangerous loads that made them whine. Sweat dripped from her chin onto the console.

The phantom crew appeared around her in the bridge's strobing emergency lighting. Their advice was contradictory and overwhelming, making concentration impossible. Reyes pointed toward a gap in the patrol pattern that would take them through a dense asteroid field, while Park insisted on a longer route that avoided gravitational anomalies.

"Negative on both," Ward's apparition commanded from behind her seat, pointing to a corridor between patrol routes, a narrow path that put them within detection range of two hunter-killer groups. "There. The gap they won't expect anyone to use."

"That's suicide, Captain," Jaya protested, but her hands were already adjusting course toward the indicated route. Logic warned her about crossfire zones and overlapping sensor coverage, yet another part—the instinct that had kept her alive—recognized the tactical brilliance in his suggestion. *Sometimes the most dangerous path was the safest because no commander would expect it.*

The weight of her decision pressed heavily on her chest. Three generations of Moreau officers had followed orders without question, earning commendations for strict adherence to military protocol. Her grandfather had died at the Battle of Centauri Prime, following a suicidal charge that earned him a posthumous medal. Her father spent thirty years climbing the command ladder through consistent competence and unwavering obedience.

And here she was, Lieutenant Jaya Moreau, deliberately ignoring orders to follow guidance from what might be hallucinations. Everything her family had built, every tradition they'd upheld, every sacrifice they'd made—all of it abandoned by her choice to trust phantom advice over fleet command.

But the alternative was handing over an alien weapon to admirals who had never experienced its influence. The artifact had chosen her, not them. The responsibility was hers.

The Zynar patrol ships passed within five hundred kilometers, their sensors probing the surrounding space. Jaya held her breath as the enemy vessels continued their search pattern, hunting for signs of the fugitive that had escaped their trap at Thanatos Rift. For thirty excruciating seconds, detection seemed inevitable.

Then the patrol moved on, searching distant sectors while the Astraeus remained undetected. Jaya slumped back, chest heaving. Around her, the phantom crew nodded, their spectral forms flickering with what might have been pride.

Jaya scanned the bridge, surrounded by the hum of machinery and the sharp tang of overheated circuits. Her eyes were drawn to the artifact beside her. The obsidian sphere rested within its containment field, its surface shifting patterns. As she neared it, an eerie glow began to pulse in time with her heartbeat.

The artifact was responding to her, she realized with unease. Each decision, each doubt or resolve, seemed to resonate through it. This wasn't just a weapon or a key—it was something alive, aware, feeding on her choices and growing stronger.

The thought should have terrified her. Instead, it felt right.

The Astraeus struggled past the final patrol zone, its engines sputtering with each thrust. Hours dragged on as Jaya remained at the helm, her fingers gripping the navigation controls with determination. Her eyes stung from fatigue, and her vision blurred at the edges, but she stayed alert. The ship's AI worked effortlessly, compensating for her sluggish reflexes.

Days merged into a haze of exhaustion and tension. Every moment felt precarious, traversing space where danger lurked just beyond sensor range. Jaya's thoughts wandered, from the days of her youth and being raised in a military family, to Fleet Academy—visions of crisp uniforms and strict obedience clouded her mind.

The dying star Moros finally appeared ahead, its crimson light casting shadows across the bridge and highlighting Jaya's features. Nyx Spire appeared against this fiery backdrop. The structure was tall and mysterious, dark crystalline surfaces absorbing light while faint geometric patterns hinted at hidden power.

Jaya exhaled slowly as she approached, bracing for what lay within Nyx Spire: secrets buried in ancient architecture, guided by phantoms whose true intentions were uncertain. The station defied human engineering principles, its design following alien geometries. Massive spires twisted upward, their surfaces so dark they seemed to swallow light. Bridges and platforms connected the towers in ways that defied logic.

"Mother of God," she whispered. The station stretched in every direction, dwarfing even the largest fleet installations she had seen. Geometric patterns pulsed faintly along its hull, creating distortions that made reality appear to ripple.

Suddenly, the artifact's energy signature spiked. The ship's AI struggled to maintain stability as conflicting signals overwhelmed its systems, causing automated functions to stutter between human and alien commands.

Navigation sensors went haywire, displaying false targets while real ones shifted erratically. Distance measurements fluctuated, showing Nyx Spire as both far away and nearby.

"Initiating automated docking sequence," the ship's AI announced, though Jaya could hear distortion creeping into the synthetic voice. "Scanning for compatible interface protocols ... error ... unknown configuration detected ... attempting universal docking standards ... error ... magnetic resonance failure ... manual override required."

The docking thrusters fired in random bursts, their controlled approach dissolving into chaos as the artifact's interference corrupted the guidance algorithms. Warning signals blared as automated systems failed, leaving Jaya with only manual controls. Through the viewport, she could see Nyx Spire's docking bay—an expanse of darkness that seemed to stretch infinitely inward.

The phantom crew appeared around her. Reyes stood by the navigation console, her smirk replaced by concentration as she pointed to specific thruster controls. Park was near the engineering station, focused on power distribution readings. But it was Ward who caught her attention. His eyes were intense, and he pointed toward the sensor array.

"The station is scanning us," he said. "It's not artificial intelligence as we know it—it's something older, and it recognizes what you're carrying."

As if responding to his words, Nyx Spire began to shift. Surfaces that had appeared static revealed themselves as flowing, organic structures that reconfigured in real time. The docking bay expanded, its dimensions altering to accommodate the Astraeus's approach with exact precision.

Jaya fought the manual controls, her hands working across thruster commands as the ship's AI tried to help her. The computer guided her movements, taking over attitude control and approach velocity while she focused on alignment.

"Port thrusters, three-second burn," Park instructed, his voice tight. "The magnetic field is fluctuating—you need to compensate."

The Astraeus moved sluggishly, its systems struggling as Jaya forced them into precise maneuvers. Sweat formed on her forehead while sensors showed the docking bay's edges in sharp relief. One mistake could be fatal.

The phantom crew shouted overlapping instructions, their voices urgent as the docking bay's dimensions continued to change. Despite her exhaustion and the artifact's interference, Jaya managed to guide the Astraeus through the bay's entrance with meters to spare. The damaged hull scraped against surfaces that felt solid one moment and yielding the next.

The magnetic clamps engaged with a shudder that ran through every plate and rivet of the ship's superstructure, artificial gravity failing as competing fields tried to establish dominance. Emergency lighting strobed in patterns that matched the artifact's pulsing rhythm, while somewhere in the distance she could hear hull plating adjusting to station pressures.

When the chaos finally subsided, the Astraeus sat locked in Nyx Spire's docking bay. Through the viewport, Jaya watched as the bay sealed seamlessly, with surfaces coming together until no seam remained. She stood on the bridge, her legs trembling as she prepared the artifact for transport. Her body was exhausted, but the device accepted her biometrics immediately. The magnetic seals clamped around the obsidian sphere effortlessly. As she lifted it onto her back, its weight pressed against her spine, each pulse of energy resonating through her.

Jaya stepped through the airlock's iris seal with her sidearm drawn, scanning the empty corridors ahead. The air had a metallic tang and was charged with energy, making her skin prickle, while the artifact's weight pressed against her back like a second heartbeat. Emergency lighting from the Astraeus cast a pool of light, making the station's darkness feel even deeper by contrast.

Then, the walls began to glow. Bioluminescent patterns emerged along the corridor surfaces, responding to the artifact's presence. The designs flowed like liquid light, revealing the station's alien design. Lines of blue-white light raced ahead of her footsteps, illuminating a path deeper into the station.

Each pulse from the artifact triggered more lights to flicker on, spreading through the walls like a network of glowing veins. The patterns were both beautiful and unsettling, suggesting advanced intelligence at work. Jaya realized that Nyx Spire wasn't just built—it was grown by minds that knew technologies far beyond human understanding.

The corridor stretched ahead, its end lost in shadows. Her footsteps echoed in the emptiness, hinting at vast spaces hidden behind the walls. The artifact felt heavier with each step, not by weight but by a sense of increasing importance.

She moved with caution, weapon ready, despite suspecting that conventional weapons would be useless here. The bioluminescent patterns lit up her path while leaving the way behind her in darkness. The station itself seemed to be guiding her forward.

The phantom crew appeared around her, more solid than they had been on the Astraeus. Ward's ghost walked beside her with his familiar military precision, while Reyes moved with her usual confidence.

New phantoms appeared, making Jaya's stomach drop. Engineer Chen materialized next to the wall, her tool belt still on her hip. Chen had died during the ambush, yet here she was, as competent as ever.

"It was never meant for human hands," Chen's phantom whispered. "The resonance frequencies don't match organic neural patterns. It's designed for minds that think differently."

Reyes nodded, her expression uneasy. "It's older than our civilization," she said, now serious. "The construction methods predate human spaceflight by millennia."

The phantoms moved through the corridor, their forms becoming more solid as the artifact's influence grew stronger. Their revelations came in fragments, filled with knowledge that seemed impossible for Jaya to comprehend. *How could these visions, likely induced by trauma and stress, understand alien technologies or possess insights that surpassed her own education in quantum mechanics and xenoarchaeology?*

"We're not who you think we are," Ward's phantom said quietly, his eyes reflecting an understanding beyond any living man. "We're echoes, Lieutenant. Impressions left by those who came before, trapped in the artifact's energy matrix."

The corridor led into a vast chamber with walls that curved in ways that defied logic while the ceiling seemed to stretch endlessly. Bioluminescent patterns covered every surface, pulsing in time with the artifact's rhythm. But it was the carvings that made Jaya stop in her tracks.

They depicted a humanoid species wielding the artifact. These beings were tall and angular, with features unlike anything human. The narrative in the carvings was clear—they used the obsidian sphere as a weapon, destroying entire star systems and harvesting stellar energy for unknown purposes.

"The Architects," Chen's phantom explained, her voice filled with technical interest despite its ghostly quality. "They built this station to study how to weaponize stellar collapse. The artifact was their key—a way to unlock the forces of matter itself."

The final panels showed the Architects' downfall. The weapon turned on them, destroying their civilization with uncontrolled energy, leaving only empty worlds around dying stars. The last carving showed a single figure sealing the artifact away, their expression filled with the same hope that now burned in Jaya's heart.

The chamber's patterns glowed brighter as she approached the carvings; the artifact felt heavier as alien energies pulsed through the station. Around her, the phantom crew watched, their faces shifting between familiar features and something far older.

The artifact pulsed against her spine like a countdown timer, marking moments until decision became inevitable.

At the chamber's heart stood a pedestal that could have been grown rather than built, its crystalline structure rising from the floor in organic curves that perfectly matched the artifact's dimensions. The surface was etched with the same geometric patterns that covered the walls, channels and depressions that would cradle the obsidian sphere with exactness. No human engineering could have created such specifications—this platform was clearly the work of the artifact's original creators.

The phantom crew reacted as if Jaya had drawn a weapon on them, their translucent forms flickering with energy that made the chamber's bioluminescent patterns strobe in sympathetic response. Some urged her forward—Chen's apparition pointed toward the pedestal with fascination while Reyes nodded with her usual analytical calm. Others, however, were alarmed, their faces showing horror at what they feared would happen.

"Don't do it," Park's phantom warned, his voice trembling with fear as he stood between Jaya and the pedestal. "The resonance cascade will tear space-time apart."

"The weapon must be activated," Chen's apparition argued, her voice echoing through the chamber. "The Zynar fleets are no doubt tracking us now. Without the artifact's power, humanity is doomed."

Ward's phantom stood apart from the conflict, watching silently with his usual calm. He offered no guidance, no command decisions to cut through the chaos. For the first time since his manifestation, the captain was letting her choose her own course.

The artifact felt heavier against her, its pulse matching her heartbeat. Each step toward the pedestal was difficult, as if gravity itself was increasing. The bioluminescent patterns around her grew brighter, leading her toward the platform.

Her hands shook as she lifted the containment unit from her back, the magnetic seals releasing in stride. The artifact sat within its cradle like a solid black hole, its surface patterns shifting aggressively. She felt its pull—not through gravity, but through something deeper—a connection forged the moment she'd first touched its controls aboard the Astraeus.

The obsidian sphere settled onto the pedestal with a sound like reality shattering, alien geometries aligning with precise accuracy. The chamber filled with an intense light that seemed to bypass her eyes, projecting colors directly into her mind. Holographic displays appeared around her, showing the station's link to the dying star Moros.

Power surged through long-dormant conduits, awakening systems that drew energy from the star's collapse. The artifact seamlessly interfaced with Nyx Spire's ancient technology, revealing its true purpose: a key to harness the death of stars. It could tap into the immense energies released when matter passed the event horizon of cosmic destruction.

The displays presented targeting solutions across the galaxy, suggesting stellar remnants could be induced to collapse in a controlled manner. Each dying star could release energy to power civilizations or destroy entire systems. The choice was hers, the artifact whispered—preserve or destroy, create or annihilate.

That's when the phantom crew revealed their true nature.

Their forms began to fragment and shift, familiar faces dissolving to reveal something ancient beneath. Ward's features flickered between human and alien, his gray eyes becoming windows into minds evolved beyond earthly development. Reyes' characteristic smirk twisted into expressions belonging to beings that thought in quantum superpositions.

"We are not your crew," Ward's phantom stated, his voice resonating with an ancient quality beyond human language. "We are the echoes of those who wielded the artifact before you, consciousness fragments trapped within its energy matrix when our civilizations fell."

The revelation struck Jaya with undeniable clarity. The phantoms weren't hallucinations from trauma—they were the preserved minds of ancient beings who had once faced the same choice she now confronted. Species after species had found the artifact, used its power, and left remnants of their consciousness behind.

"Some of us tried to destroy it," Chen's apparition said, her form flickering between human and something alien. "Others believed it could be controlled, used responsibly. This debate has continued for millennia, with trapped minds arguing while civilizations rose and fell."

The phantom crew divided into opposing factions, their forms arranging themselves on opposite sides of the chamber. Those advocating for the artifact's destruction gathered near the entrance, their faces filled with deep regret. The others clustered around the pedestal, hopeful that this time might be different.

The conflict began suddenly, with spectral forms clashing in a battle of ideologies. The chamber's bioluminescent patterns flickered chaotically as energies vied for dominance.

Ward's phantom stood between the factions. His voice cut through the chaos: "The choice was always yours, Lieutenant. We are merely echoes in the rift. The future belongs to the living."

Around her, the phantom battle raged while the artifact pulsed with growing intensity, drawing power from the dying star visible through the viewport. The weapon was active, ready to reshape reality. All she had to do was choose—preservation or destruction.

The immense decision loomed, demanding resolution that would echo across the galaxy for generations.

Jaya's hands moved toward the control interfaces, her fingers finding the crystalline surfaces that reacted immediately to her touch. The station's ancient database unfolded before her, displaying holographic data streams accumulated over countless epochs as civilizations rose and fell. She ignored the phantom civil war raging around her, concentrating on the records that would reveal the full consequences of her potential actions.

The first files detailed the Architects at the height of their power, a species that had surpassed biological limitations with advanced technologies. They had mapped the quantum foam that underlies reality itself, learned to manipulate the fundamental forces that held matter together, and discovered how to harvest energy from the collapse of space-time itself. The artifact had been their greatest creation—a key that could unlock the binding forces of stellar matter and redirect that power according to their will.

However, such power came with consequences that even their advanced minds couldn't fully predict. The holographic records showed their initial use of the weapon, with entire systems reduced to plasma clouds, enemy forces obliterated by energies far beyond supernovas. They believed they could reshape the galaxy, wielding power that threatened to unravel reality.

As the database continued, it revealed growing desperation as the weapon's influence spread uncontrollably. Stellar collapses triggered chain reactions, consuming vast regions of space. The Architects attempted to contain the escalating damage, dedicating their finest minds to halting the catastrophe they had unleashed.

"They couldn't stop it," Jaya whispered, watching projections of entire galactic arms consumed by uncontrolled stellar collapse. The weapon fed on destruction, growing stronger with each devoured star.

The final records depicted the Architects' last act—using the weapon on themselves in a controlled detonation that destroyed their homeworld, their colonies, their entire civilization in a single moment of calculated extinction. They chose self-annihilation over allowing their creation to spread beyond their borders, sacrificing everything they had built to prevent galactic genocide.

The database fell silent, its accumulated knowledge painting a clear picture of where unchecked power inevitably led. Around her, the phantom factions continued their eternal fight, ancient minds stuck in arguments that had continued since the fall of the Architects. The evidence was clear—every species that had used the artifact faced the same choice and was ultimately consumed by the power they thought they could control.

The artifact pulsed in sync with the dying star visible through the chamber's viewport, its obsidian surface glowing as it absorbed energy. Jaya watched Moros bleed plasma, the stellar matter forming spirals that defied physics. The weapon was already working, setting up resonance frequencies that would allow it to trigger controlled collapse when she gave the command.

The phantom factions ceased their eternal conflict as spectral forms began to flicker with new urgency, ancient minds setting aside millennia of disagreement to focus on something beyond the chamber.

"Use it," Chen's apparition urged, her form shifting between human and alien as she gestured toward the activation controls. "Without the artifact's power, humanity will fall to forces that view biological life as an inconvenience to be eliminated."

"Destroy it," Park's phantom countered, tension clear in his voice as he pointed to the weapon's vulnerable power coupling. "Break the resonance cascade before it connects fully with the stellar remnant. The chain reaction will consume you, but it will also prevent a galactic disaster."

The opposing faction moved closer, their spectral forms flickering as they made their final appeals. Ancient voices spoke with a weight of regret. "We all thought we could control it," they said. "Every species believed they were wise enough. We were all wrong. The weapon doesn't serve; it consumes everything until there's nothing left."

Ward's phantom remained apart from both factions, watching calmly. "The choice is yours, Lieutenant," he reminded her. "We're merely echoes of the past."

Jaya stood at the control interface, her hands trembling above switches with the power to reshape reality itself. The phantoms' voices clashed in her mind, their eternal conflict echoing with a cacophony of arguments and pleas. Salvation or destruction? Each faction pulled at her convictions, sowing doubt and confusion within her already burdened heart.

She hesitated, caught between the weight of countless lives and the haunting whispers that threatened to fracture her resolve.

6

That's when the proximity alarms began their urgent wail throughout the station, cutting through the tension with harsh emergency lighting that activated along the chamber's perimeter. Ancient displays materialized from the walls themselves, their surfaces showing sensor readings that made her blood freeze.

The Zynar fleet appeared on the tactical displays, their sleek ships reflecting the dying star's crimson light as they formed around Nyx Spire. Not the pursuit vessels that had chased her through the debris fields, but a full battle group—dreadnoughts whose weapon signatures could crack continents, carrier vessels launching fighter squadrons that swarmed like mechanical insects, and warships bristling with advanced weaponry.

"Twenty-seven capital ships," she counted, watching the displays paint their approach vectors. "They're not here to capture the artifact anymore. They're here to make sure it's never used against them."

The fleet formed a sphere of firepower around the station, their formation perfect and impenetrable, ready to obliterate Nyx Spire and everything within it.

An enemy communication request appeared on the display, the transmission somehow compatible with the station's alien systems. Jaya hesitated, her hand trembling over the acceptance controls. She knew she couldn't ignore it—understanding her opponent was crucial.

The display shimmered, and the Zynar Commander materialized before her in holographic splendor that made her breath catch in her throat. His presence was dominating, combining lethal efficiency with an air of refined sophistication. The light highlighted his scaled features and ceremonial scars, telling tales of past victories and conquered worlds.

The insignia adorning his uniform told stories of galactic domination that made her chest tighten with recognition. She counted the emblems of seventeen different star systems, their unique crystalline structures marking civilizations that had fallen before the Zynar Dominion. Each badge represented billions of lives reduced to statistics in military reports, entire cultures erased to feed the Dominion's inexorable expansion.

"Lieutenant Jaya Moreau, I am Valrik Theron, commander of the Zynar Dominion," he said, his voice as precise and measured as any she'd heard during her Academy simulations. "Your reputation precedes you. Survivor of Thanatos Rift, custodian of secrets with the power to change the galaxy's balance."

Theron smiled, revealing teeth that had been filed to points in accordance with Zynar military tradition. Behind him, she could see the command bridge of his flagship—a technological cathedral where lesser species' representatives stood in silent attendance, their postures carrying the defeated resignation of those who had chosen collaboration over extinction.

"The Zynar Dominion rewards those who cooperate," he continued, his tone almost professorial. "You need not die here alone, Lieutenant. Surrender the artifact, and I promise you safe passage to neutral space. You have my word as a Commander of the Fleet."

Jaya felt the exhaustion pressing down on her, the trauma of her squadron's loss weighing heavily. It would be easy to give up the obsidian sphere and escape the burden she was carrying. But the artifact pulsed, filling her mind with images of what Theron's "cooperation" really meant: worlds burning, species annihilated as the Zynar used the weapon to subjugate any resistance.

"Bold of you to assume I'm alone, Commander," she replied. Her voice steadier than she felt. Around her, the phantom crew began to materialize in the command center's alien illumination, their translucent forms gaining substance as the artifact's influence grew stronger.

Theron's expression hardened, his earlier charm giving way to the calculating gaze of a seasoned conqueror. His features, now cold and unreadable, mirrored his resolve. "Very well, Lieutenant. You've shown remarkable skill in reaching this point, but your choices have been reduced to one."

The display changed, revealing targeting solutions that highlighted Nyx Spire's critical systems. "You have ten minutes to decide," Theron said, his voice precise and final. "Surrender the artifact and accept extraction, or we will destroy the station. Choose wisely, Lieutenant. This is the only offer you will receive."

The transmission ended, leaving Jaya alone with the phantoms of her dead crew and an alien weapon that promised salvation or damnation in equal measure.

More phantoms appeared around Jaya, their translucent figures materializing with an intense presence that made the command center's holographic displays flicker. These weren't just the familiar apparitions from the Astraeus—they were numerous, representing every consciousness the artifact had consumed over millennia. Ancient beings with alien features stood beside her lost crew, their voices overlapping, each carrying the weight of civilizations that had faced the same impossible choice now placed on her shoulders.

Captain Ward's apparition stood before her, his face lined with concern. "They'll kill you, Jaya," he said, his voice carried authority. "Theron's promises mean nothing—you've seen how the Zynar treat those who resist. Surrender the artifact and live to fight another day."

His reasoning broke through her exhausted defenses. The tactical situation was dire: twenty-seven capital ships against a single damaged frigate and an ancient station with mostly unknown capabilities. Even if Nyx Spire had defenses, they would soon be overwhelmed.

Then, Engineer Chen's phantom stepped forward, her eyes burning with intensity. Her form flickered, reflecting the consciousness of the artifact's previous users. "This weapon must not fall into Zynar hands," she said, her voice resonating with the station's walls. "If they get it, they'll use stellar collapse as a weapon, reshaping the galaxy and destroying civilizations."

She pointed urgently at the artifact's containment. "The resonance cascade can be reversed, the quantum entanglement severed. Destroy it now, before the connection with Moros becomes permanent. It's better for you to die here than to unleash galactic genocide."

Reyes appeared on the opposite side of the command center. Her usual analytical detachment was replaced with a fierce determination. "Use it!" Reyes demanded, her voice slicing through the chaos. "Wipe them out now while we have the chance! The Zynar fleet represents an existential threat to human civilization—without the artifact's power, your species will fall to forces that view biological life as an inconvenience to be eliminated."

She gestured toward the displays showing the tactical situation, enemy formations highlighted in crimson as Nyx Spire sat at the center like a potential epicenter of destruction. "This is your chance to end the threat. Don't let hesitation cost billions of lives."

"Surrender means death," warned an ancient voice, shifting between familiar human features and something foreign. "Zynar do not take prisoners—they take resources. You will be dissected, analyzed, your memories harvested for intelligence before your corpse feeds their bio-processors."

"Destruction means safety," countered another phantom, its features hinting at aquatic origins from a once-vibrant world. "The weapon corrupts all who wield it. Everyone thinks they can control it, but it always ends the same."

The voices grew louder, overlapping in arguments that spanned ages. Jaya clutched her head, trying to block out their demands. The artifact responded with bursts of energy through the command center, displays showing the weapon's devastating capabilities. It wasn't just tactical projections but records of past deployments, systems obliterated, planets and moons consumed by unstoppable energy.

Entire systems were reduced to clouds of superheated plasma, their planets and moons consumed by energies that turned matter into light. Stellar clusters with multiple stars collapsed simultaneously, creating gravitational waves that swept through space, destroying everything in their path. The weapon didn't just destroy—it erased, leaving voids in space-time. But the displays also revealed the aftermath of each use. Civilizations that wielded such power were inevitably consumed by the forces they tried to control. The weapon grew stronger with each use, its connection with dying stars creating feedback loops that spread destruction far beyond any intended target. Species after species faced the tempting promise of ultimate victory, only to find that cosmic forces were beyond control.

The holographic records showed scenarios across half the galaxy, with targeting solutions that could reduce the Zynar Dominion to a mere memory within hours. Their core worlds burned in simulated destruction, their fleets dissolved, and their empire turned to history by directed stellar collapse. Yet, the projections didn't stop at tactical victory. They showed the uncontrolled spread of quantum cascades, consuming neutral systems, human colonies, and even Earth in waves of cosmic annihilation.

Jaya stared at the displays, her horror growing as she realized the true stakes. The choice before her was not just survival versus destruction—it was between immediate death and galactic genocide, her own end or the gradual destruction of everything she vowed to protect. The artifact offered unimaginable power, but the cost made Theron's ultimatum seem merciful.

Ten minutes ticked away with the precision of an execution clock, marking the moment Theron's patience ran out. The first energy barrage hit the station's shields with overwhelming force, plasma beams turning ancient barriers into dazzling displays of light. The command center shook under the impact, displays flickering as power conduits struggled to handle the energy overload.

Jaya felt the station's pain in her bones, the artifact's influence creating connections between her nervous system and Nyx Spire's vastness. Warning symbols flashed across every surface, alien hieroglyphs glowing red against walls that had seen the rise and fall of empires. Atmospheric pressure warnings sounded as hull breaches multiplied throughout the station's outer sections.

The second volley penetrated weak points in the shields, weapons cutting channels through armor meant to withstand stellar radiation. Emergency bulkheads slammed shut, sealing off corridors as atmosphere vented into space.

Behind her, the phantom crew's voices grew urgent, their debates bouncing off walls. As the chaos intensified, the artifact's connection with her touched her like nothing before. Jaya felt like a conduit for cosmic forces, the obsidian sphere's energy blending with Nyx Spire, creating patterns that resonated through reality itself.

Holographic interfaces responded to her thoughts as the artifact translated her intentions into commands. The station's defensive capabilities became part of her awareness, awakening weapon systems with her mental touch. The phantoms continued their debate as she worked, their spectral forms gathered around the control interfaces.

Ward's apparition stood by the tactical displays, as enemy fire battered the station's weakened shields. "Atmospheric breaches on levels seven through twelve," he reported crisply. "Shield integrity is down to sixty percent and dropping. You need to act now or they'll destroy this place."

Chen's phantom appeared near the power distribution controls. "The weapon systems are designed for directed stellar energy," she explained. "But the artifact is amplifying their capabilities beyond what they were built for."

Jaya instinctively found the defensive activation sequence, guided by an intuitive knowledge passed down from civilizations that had faced similar choices. The control hub responded eagerly, power surging.

Ancient turrets emerged from hidden compartments throughout Nyx Spire, their surfaces shifting like liquid metal as they prepared for combat. The first counterattack launched from multiple positions, energy beams cutting through Zynar shields with ease. The lead dreadnought's front section disintegrated in a burst of plasma, while two escort cruisers vanished as they were hit with directed stellar energy.

The artifact's influence amplified the station's weapons, channeling energies that far surpassed conventional military technology. Each successful hit fed back into the weapon's system, increasing the power of subsequent shots.

Theron's fleet moved with efficiency, commanders adjusting their ships to minimize exposure and focusing their plasma cannons on the turret emplacements. These weapons, capable of devastating entire continents, targeted positions that flickered in and out of normal space-time.

Jaya organized the station's defenses, blending her training with alien tactical algorithms to create strategies beyond standard human doctrine. The battle unfolded in her mind like a complex game of chess, played with forces on the edge of physics.

Her fingers moved swiftly across controls, directing power through backup systems as damaged conduits struggled under the load. Each successful maneuver bought crucial seconds as enemy forces adapted, slowly countering defenses they couldn't fully understand.

The artifact's whispers intensified, offering unimaginable power if she would surrender to their guidance. She could sense the weapon's full potential pressing against her mind, its capability to obliterate Theron's fleet looming large.

"Let us show you," the voices urged, resonating deeply within her. "The true potential lies beyond these basic defenses. Embrace our gift and reshape the galaxy."

Another Zynar ship exploded as the station's assault found their mark, but Jaya saw the tactical situation worsening. The enemy was adapting faster than she could counter, their superior numbers beginning to overwhelm her defenses one by one.

The artifact pulsed, signaling the impending choice between limited resistance and the allure of unlimited power.

Theron adapted his tactics with a cold efficiency. His fleet's formation shifted as he identified the weaknesses in Nyx Spire's defenses. The Zynar focused their remaining ships' fire on vulnerable points, with plasma cannons targeting critical junctions where the ancient power conduits were weakest.

The station's shields flickered under the intense assault, barriers that had withstood stellar radiation for millennia were starting to fail. Warning symbols flashed throughout the control hub, alien hieroglyphs glowing red with urgency. Jaya felt each hit as though it were a blow to her own body.

Failures cascaded throughout the station as power demands exceeded supply. The hub's displays flickered between normal readouts and indecipherable error codes.

Emergency bulkheads slammed shut, trying to contain the drop in atmospheric pressure as hull breaches outpaced repairs. The sound of escaping air joined the chaos, precious oxygen venting into space.

The artifact's energy signature grew unstable, its connection with Moros creating feedback loops that surged through the station's circuits. Displays overloaded, casting chaotic light in the control hub, while control surfaces sparked under Jaya's hands.

Jaya could feel the weapon straining against its containment, the obsidian sphere pulsing violently. Each outpour sent electromagnetic surges through her, as alien whispers filled her mind with promises of power.

Power conduits throughout the control hub began to rupture, releasing superheated plasma through emergency relief valves. Through the control hub's viewport, Jaya watched the dying star Moros react to the artifact's instability. The star's surface churned violently, with solar flares painting space in intense radiation and gravitational shifts rippling through space-time. The weapon's influence was spreading, threatening to trigger a premature stellar collapse if not contained.

Warning displays throughout the control hub showed the dire consequences of unchecked artifact activation. A quantum cascade could spread through hyperspace, causing stellar collapses across multiple systems and destroying everything within fifty light-years—including human colonies unaware of the alien threat.

The phantoms' voices grew louder, making it hard for Jaya to think clearly. They argued over choices civilizations had faced for millennia. The voices urging her to unleash the weapon insisted it was necessary to stop the Zynar threat before they fully adapted.

Captain Ward's phantom appeared in front of her, virtually solid now. His hand rested firmly on her shoulder, a reminder of his authority and the guidance he had once provided in their most dangerous missions.

"You know what you have to do," he said, his gray eyes meeting hers with unwavering confidence. But his guidance offered no easy answers, no clear path through the impossible choices that lay before her, choices that would determine not only her fate but the future of civilizations across the galaxy. She saw in his expression the truth—the understanding that some decisions were beyond military training, requiring choices that no preparation could teach.

The artifact presented her with its final ultimatum. Control surfaces appeared around her, responding to her thoughts rather than touch. Two pathways glowed before her, their purposes clear despite the advanced technology that separated human knowledge from these cosmic forces.

One path led to activating the weapon, its violet energy promising unimaginable power to destroy Theron's fleet with precision, leaving no trace. A complete victory, removing the Zynar threat and giving humanity access to technology that could shift the balance of power across known space.

The other path was the self-destruct protocol, glowing red. It would sever the artifact's connection with the dying star Moros, destroying the weapon and the station. Her death would be certain, but it would prevent galactic genocide, stopping these forces from spreading beyond this system.

Jaya's hand hovered over the controls, her fingers trembling under the pressure of billions of lives depending on her choice. The artifact pulsed in time with her heartbeat, its energy vibrating through her. The decision she made would resonate across the galaxy.

Her face reflected the light of the weapon as she finally understood the choice before her.

7

Jaya's finger hovered over the self-destruct button, her decision firm and unwavering. The weight of her choice settled heavily on her, surpassing even the alien pulse of the artifact at her back. She understood what Ward had been trying to convey—some choices transcended tactical considerations, requiring sacrifices that no military doctrine could prepare someone to make.

The control interface reacted to her touch, activating with alien symbols cascading across the screens as ancient systems came to life. Quantum charges throughout Nyx Spire initiated their countdown, their activation accompanied by harmonics that made her feel uneasy. The station's structure vibrated as energy conduits overloaded, briefly illuminating the darkness.

The artifact erupted with energy, sending electromagnetic pulses through every circuit in the control hub. Its obsidian surface writhed with patterns that were difficult to look at directly. The weapon struggled against its containment, aware of the impending destruction that would cut off its connection to cosmic forces. Its pulse became erratic, distorting reality between stable physics and chaos.

Holographic displays flickered with error messages in ancient scripts. Alarms echoed through the station, merging with the sounds of structural stress that the engineering had never been designed to handle. Power conduits ruptured across Nyx Spire, releasing superheated plasma while backup systems struggled to maintain function.

The artifact's link to the dying star Moros started to falter as quantum frequencies destabilized. Through the control hub's viewport, Jaya saw the red giant's surface erupting with increased solar activity, its coronal mass ejections painting space with radiation as the star reacted to the loss of control.

Theron's voice pierced through the turmoil. His transmission crackled with interference as the station's communication arrays faltered. "Lieutenant Moreau, cease this madness now! You're triggering a stellar cascade that will obliterate everything within fifty light-years!"

As realization hit him, his composed demeanor shifted to desperation. "You don't understand the forces you're unleashing! That star will go supernova—your own colonies will be destroyed alongside mine!"

"Some weapons should never exist," Jaya replied, her voice steady despite the surrounding turmoil. Her words cut through the interference with clarity, carrying a conviction that rose above the mechanical upheaval. "I won't give genocide to anyone, Commander. Not to you, not to my own people, not to anyone."

The phantom crew erupted in a wild reaction, their spectral forms fragmenting as the artifact's instability affected their consciousness. Those who wanted unlimited power screamed in rage. Ancient voices cursed her in languages that resonated in the air.

But Ward's phantom stood apart from the chaos, his expression showing the same pride she'd seen numerous times over the years. When their eyes met, he offered a crisp military salute that transcended death itself—recognition from one soldier to another.

"The hardest choices require the strongest wills," his apparition said. Other crew members appeared around him with solemn expressions, understanding the gravity of the moment.

The control hub started to collapse around her, its crystalline structures cracking under stress. Holographic interfaces flickered out, and the station's consciousness—whatever intelligence had governed it—prepared for its own end with mechanical resignation.

Jaya fought her way through the disintegrating chamber toward the viewport, the obsidian sphere crackling with energy that distorted the air around it. The weapon's resistance increased as she moved, electromagnetic discharges making her hair stand on end while she struggled to breathe through the ozone. Her hands grasped the edge of the view portal just as another overload surged through Nyx Spire, throwing her against a wall that alternated between solid and yielding.

Through the viewport, she saw Theron's fleet retreating, their ships illuminated by the violent radiation from Moros. Some vessels were caught in the gravitational distortions, their forms twisted by forces that defied escape. The station convulsed violently as charges reached critical levels, signaling the beginning of its end. Alarms blared, and the emergency lighting flickered in sync with the artifact's erratic energy.

Jaya dislodged the artifact, forgoing the use of the containment unit, then sprinted toward the docking bay where the Astraeus waited, her boots clattering against the unstable deck. Behind her, Nyx Spire continued its destruction—a final farewell to the technologies of ancient empires.

Jaya raced through the corridors; emergency lighting flashed in sync with the artifact's erratic pulse as the station shook violently. Chunks of the alien structure fell around her, their sharp edges threatening to cut through her environmental suit as gravity fluctuated.

She vaulted over a fallen beam, the artifact's weight causing her to stumble against a warm wall. Behind her, sections of the station vanished as the destructive energy reached critical levels, tearing matter apart.

The docking bay came into view, the Astraeus visible amidst the chaos. The ship was battered, hull plating burned and systems venting atmosphere. She dove through the airlock just as decompression swept the bay, the door sealing with finality. Alarms blared as the ship's systems struggled to hold together.

The bridge felt like home despite its damaged displays and the acrid smell of burned electronics that filled the recycled air. She set the artifact down while she focused on startup sequences, emergency protocols racing through her consciousness as the ship's AI attempted to compensate.

The obsidian sphere pulsed once, twice, then erupted with energy that cascaded through the Astraeus's exposed neural pathways. Jaya watched, both fascinated and horrified, as alien patterns began to etch themselves across the displays, showing geometric forms that seemed to shift when she looked at them. The artifact's influence spread through circuits that were never meant for such contact. The integration happened with an unsettling quickness, as alien consciousness flowed through the ship's systems.

Control panels across the bridge lit up with bioluminescent patterns like those in Nyx Spire's corridors. Holographic displays flickered between normal readouts and ancient scripts. Jaya realized with growing unease that her ship was transforming, its systems merging with alien technology in ways that she was not prepared for. The artifact's energy merged with the Astraeus's power grid, creating hybrid systems governed by unfamiliar rules.

Emergency jump preparation began, with systems responding to her thoughts. The artifact created direct connections between her mind and the ship's functions, bypassing the need for manual operation. Her hands moved over the controls as the jump drive charged with unknown energy sources. The Astraeus shuddered under the strain of competing gravitational fields, as Nyx Spire's collapse distorted space-time, making navigation calculations impossible. While the ship's AI struggled to maintain functionality, warnings flashed across surfaces now marked by complex alien language.

As the jump drive powered up, the first shockwave from Nyx Spire's collapse reached them. With nervous hands, she activated the jump just as the station's quantum charges hit their peak. The Astraeus leaped into hyperspace, escaping the impending stellar explosion.

Behind them, Moros began its transformation into something that would be visible from neighboring star systems—a supernova born from the death of weapons that should never have existed.

The Astraeus emerged from hyperspace, battered and unstable. Sparks flew from overhead conduits as the ship's artificial gravity fluctuated. Jaya held onto her command chair, feeling the effects of their rapid escape, both she and the ship altered by forces beyond human understanding.

Unknown stars filled the viewport, configurations her navigation computer couldn't identify. They were in uncharted space, far beyond anything in the Alliance database. The artifact's energy had amplified their jump, taking them farther than the ship was ever destined to go.

Jaya rose from the pilot's seat, every muscle aching. She surveyed the damage, which went beyond typical battle scars. Emergency lights revealed displays now covered in bioluminescent patterns.

The ship's systems were fused with alien technology. Hull plating was etched with shifting patterns, and power conduits glowed with unfamiliar energy signatures. The controls were responsive to her thoughts, creating an intimate link between her and the ship.

The artifact's influence was evident throughout the ship, creating hybrid systems with rules from advanced civilizations. The Astraeus was still fundamentally human-made, but something had changed, making it feel both familiar and alien.

When she tried to determine their location, Jaya discovered that she was at least three months away from the nearest Alliance outpost. The jump drive was damaged, its crystalline matrix cracked and in need of proper repairs. She was stranded with minimal resources and technology that defied human comprehension.

That's when the memory resurfaced with uncanny timing—the final transmission she'd received before everything went wrong at Thanatos Rift. Fleet Command's coordinates and quantum-encrypted instructions had been waiting in her ship's communication buffer while she fought for survival. The numbers imprinted themselves in her mind, a rendezvous point.

"We're going home," she announced to the empty bridge, her voice rough with exhaustion and something that might have been relief. The words echoed through corridors where atmospheric recyclers hummed with alien harmonics, while emergency systems maintained life support through jury-rigged connections that sparked with hybrid energy.

Her reflection in the dark viewport showed damage that went beyond physical injury—stress lines around her eyes that spoke of trauma no amount of rest could heal, while her hands trembled with exhaustion that had settled into her bones like ice forming on metal. Blood caked her forehead from impacts she couldn't remember receiving, while her uniform hung in tatters that testified to violence that had reshaped her understanding of what was possible.

But she was alive, breathing recycled air in a ship that pulsed with an alien consciousness as foreign as the unknown stars she passed by. Survival felt like victory, each heartbeat a defiance against forces that nearly destroyed her.

Phantom whispers began as she set a course for Alliance space, familiar voices now coming from the ship's walls rather than her own traumatized consciousness. The artifact's integration had embedded these spectral echoes throughout the Astraeus's systems.

"What now?" The question came in harmonics that bypassed her ears, resembling Park's technical briefings. The voice came from speakers glowing with patterns too complex to understand, ghost-words formed through alien technology.

"We survive," Jaya said, her hands steady on the navigation controls. "We get home. We warn them about what's coming." The words carried conviction that surprised her exhausted consciousness, professional duty reasserting itself despite the cosmic forces that had reshaped her understanding of reality.

As she moved through corridors that smelled of ozone and recycled fear. Her boots echoed against the deck, while emergency lights pulsed in sync with the artifact's presence deep within the ship.

"What have we become?" she asked herself, the question echoing her transformation alongside the ship's. The console responded, displaying patterns that suggested an intelligence lying just beyond her current grasp.

The artifact's consciousness stirred in response to her words, alien awareness touching the edges of her mind with a contact that felt simultaneously invasive and oddly comforting. Their connection was far from over, she realized with growing certainty—whatever forces had bonded during their escape from Nyx Spire's destruction had created symbiosis that transcended simple technological interface.

As the stars continued their silent course, Jaya thought about the path ahead. She stood at a crossroads of human and alien, aware that her actions would ripple across the galaxy, affecting civilizations yet untouched by the forces she had encountered.

About the author

Paul B Kohler is the International Bestselling author of the highly acclaimed novel Linear Shift. His recent work includes The Silence of the World, along with several short stories. His short story, Rememorations, was included in The Immortality Chronicles - The Best Anthology Of The Year as voted in the 2016 Preditors and Editors Readers Poll. Rememorations was also nominated for Best American Science Fiction.

To learn more about him and his books, visit:
Website: www.PaulKohler.net
Amazon: amazon.com/author/paulkohler
Facebook: facebook.com/Paul.B.Kohler.Author